"I've aske_____ the kids if…if anything happens to me. If I get convicted—"

Lara reached across the table and placed her hand on Michael's. He accepted that this crisis might not come out the way he wanted. He was preparing.

He covered her hand with his. "If I am convicted," he resumed, "I don't want them dislocated again. I think it'll be better if they're already with their grand-parents."

"Your kids are very fortunate to have you for a dad," she said softly. She wished she had more to offer him than a good defense, but for now that would have to be enough.

"Thank you for being here, Lara. You've come to mean a lot to me."

The words should have pleased her, and on some level, they did, but they also frightened her. He wanted her here now, but would he in the future? She shouldn't even be thinking along those lines. They'd renewed their friendship. Nothing more. It had never been more than that to him. She was fooling herself to think it could be anything else.

Dear Reader,

Life is full of surprises, not all of them pleasant. Some events are life altering, in fact. Michael First, the eldest of Adam First's children, is about to undergo one—make that two—of those changes, which will transform his life forever. And they both involve love, the most intimate and emotional of experiences.

This is the fifth and last of THE FIRST FAMILY OF TEXAS series. It's a saga I've thoroughly enjoyed writing. Many of you have told me, and I certainly share this sentiment, that these characters have become like real family. I know these people. I feel close to them. I've come to like them, get annoyed with them, sometimes obsess over them and ultimately smile when they find the happiness they've worked so hard to achieve.

I could say I'll miss them, but I won't. One of the wonderful things about reading and writing is that we never have to say goodbye to the people we meet in books. They are always there. Always available for us to go back to and visit. For me, the members of THE FIRST FAMILY OF TEXAS are like that—good friends I'll always enjoy dropping in to see, if only in my mind.

I enjoy hearing from readers. You can write me at Box 61511, San Angelo, TX 76904, or through my Web site at www.superauthors.com.

Sincerely,

K.N. *Casper*

First Love, Second Chance
K.N. Casper

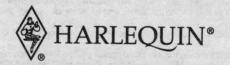

HARLEQUIN®

TORONTO • NEW YORK • LONDON
AMSTERDAM • PARIS • SYDNEY • HAMBURG
STOCKHOLM • ATHENS • TOKYO • MILAN • MADRID
PRAGUE • WARSAW • BUDAPEST • AUCKLAND

ISBN 0-373-71100-X

FIRST LOVE, SECOND CHANCE

My sincere thanks to the people
who gave unstintingly of their time and expertise:
Judge Jerry Jennison
Dr. Gary Hodges, D.V.M.
Dr. Chris Womack, D.V.M.
The mistakes are all mine, guys, in spite of your patience.

To Susan Vaughn and Jackie Floyd,
for their invaluable assistance.

A special thanks to Jan Daugherty
for her insights, patience and inspiration.

And to Lori and Mary, for always coming through.

CHAPTER ONE

MICHAEL FIRST SAT on the cold stone bench and stared at his wife's tombstone. He'd killed her.

A crisp February breeze swirled around him, a milder version of the wind that had buffeted him when they'd last seen each other on Tarnished Mountain.

"Forgive me, Clare," he whispered, though there wasn't a living soul around to hear. He was alone. Unbearably alone.

A few big raindrops splattered the granite markers around him. His mother's grave a few feet away. His brother's beside it. Grandparents and other ancestors, as well as the vaquero families who had helped establish the Number One Ranch. The heritage of nearly two hundred years lined up in neat rows.

The sky was a sea of tumbling gray pearls. "Clouds are so interesting," Clare had always said. She'd never failed to find the silver in them. Maybe these would bring the end of the drought that had plagued this land for the past seven years. She'd looked forward to the green years that would follow. She'd never see them now.

He stood up. Should he leave before the sky opened and drenched him? He'd been here barely a few minutes. Sighing, he sat down again. He could survive a few wet clothes.

It was living without his wife, the mother of his children, that was unbearable. She was gone hardly a month, yet he had so much to tell her. How many times had he turned to speak to her, to seek her advice, and found her not there? How often had he extended his arm across the bed, to feel nothing but cold empty loneliness?

"I miss you, sweetheart," he began. "I don't know how I can go on without you."

Lightning danced along the horizon to the north. The rumble of thunder came later. Like an act performed, its effects delayed.

"The kids miss you, too. Beth Ann cries herself to sleep every night. I hold her, stay with her, but my hard chest can't make up for a mother's warm breast. It's tough when you're only eight. She's old enough to understand what's happened, but she refuses to accept that you're really gone. She asked me the other day why you went away without saying goodbye." His throat tightened. "Sheila's been taking her in for professional grief counseling. I feel so helpless, Clare. Sally and Kristin are coping a little better—they're older. But they still cry a lot."

He folded his hands in his lap. "Elva has been terrific." Yet he'd caught their housekeeper standing over the stove teary eyed more than once.

"I was really worried about Davy. Excuse me. Dave." The fourteen-year-old insisted on the more grown-up name. "He railed at me, Clare. Blamed me. Said it was all my fault."

The lump in Michael's throat burned. He raised his hand to brush away the tears coursing down his face.

"He was right. I am to blame. The accident was my fault. We've taught him not to make excuses, to take responsibility for his actions. What could I possibly tell him? That I didn't understand what could have gone wrong? He scarcely talked to me before the funeral, but then…we cried together. He's being forced to grow up so fast. The others, too.''

The sky above him flashed, a duel of silver sabers, the crackle of their clash adopting an almost constant growl. Michael inhaled through his nose. He should take pleasure in the smell of rain.

''We're falling apart without you, Clare. You're the glue that held us together. I hope you've forgiven me. I never wanted to hurt you.''

A jagged sword of light struck not far away. Thunder shook the ground. The acrid stench of ozone filled the cold damp air. He had no choice now. He was in danger of getting more than drenched. Had there been no one but himself to worry about, he might have stayed, but he still had obligations and a family he loved.

Great gobs of water splattered on the dusty path as he raced to his truck. The sky opened and lashed the earth. By the time he reached his pickup he was soaked to the skin. At least, he consoled himself, when he got home nobody would see the tears on his face.

THE SHERIFF'S CAR was parked beside his father's truck when Michael pulled up in front of his house. Rudy Kraus was an old family friend. He'd been there when the MG was recovered, had personally taken charge at the accident scene. He'd attended Clare's funeral and burial service at the First private cemetery here on the ranch. But Michael had hoped he'd seen the last of the lawman for a while.

He found him at the kitchen table, drinking black coffee with his father, Adam First and Sheila, his stepmother. Kraus was his dad's age, an inch or two shorter, a few pounds heavier, with pink cheeks and a friendly smile. He rose from his chair and offered his hand.

"What brings you out here, Sheriff?" Michael leaned over and gave Sheila a gentle hug, then squeezed his father's shoulder in greeting.

Kraus resumed his seat. "Thought I'd give you the results of our investigation."

"So it's concluded?" That was good news. Every accident had to be investigated. Kraus had been sympathetic when he informed him that an autopsy would also have to be performed. Michael hadn't liked it, but he'd had no choice in the matter.

Rudy nodded, his eyes measuring him. The man had been county sheriff for almost as long as Michael could remember. They'd always been on friendly terms.

"As you can see, I'm sopped. Give me a minute to get into dry clothes, and you can tell me all about it."

As he changed, he reviewed the family schedule in his mind. Dave had soccer practice today after school, so Kyle Ratley would bring him home around six-thirty—unless the rain in town was as heavy as it was here. Then the playing fields would be flooded, and he'd be on the four-thirty bus. The girls had nothing going today, so Michael could expect them in another hour, as well.

He'd never had to keep track of school bus timetables when Clare was alive. She'd been the perfect mother. Always there. Always together. Always keeping him in line.

He made it a point now to be at the house when the kids came home from school. He attended all their regular games, and as many of their extracurricular activities as he could. It meant taking time away from the ranch. Fortunately, his assistant, Brad Lopez, had pitched right in. Being a divorced man with two kids, he understood how difficult it was to be a single parent.

Michael stopped in to see Clare's grandmother in what used to be his den. He'd urged Clare to send Brigitte to a nursing home. Now he didn't have the heart to do it himself. "How is she?"

"Just fell asleep." Elva was sitting in the easy chair at the foot of the hospital bed, knitting. "She rambled on a bit to people who ain't here. Clare might've known who they were."

Michael felt a familiar ache. "Thanks for sitting with her."

Moist-eyed, Elva nodded and resumed her needle clicking.

The three visitors were still in the kitchen when he returned a few minutes later. Sheila was pouring coffee. She glanced at him, her expression solicitous, and motioned for him to take a seat, then filled his favorite mug.

Uneasy, he sat sideways on the hard wooden chair, extended his long legs, one arm on its back, the other on the tabletop. "So what did you find out, Sheriff?"

Michael had already received the autopsy report. The toxicology results had been predictable: no alcohol or drugs in Clare's bloodstream. She'd sustained a broken neck in the crash and probably died instantly. He'd been able to take some comfort in knowing she hadn't suffered.

He'd also learned she hadn't hit a deer or had a blowout, but aside from that, officials had been mighty closemouthed. Sheriff's deputies had come out to the ranch twice. On both occasions Kraus had called beforehand to request permission for them to inspect the garage. Michael had asked why and received the same uninformative answer. "Just routine." What they expected to find was beyond him. But he hadn't objected. After all, he had nothing to hide. At least their snooping would be over now.

Kraus took a cautious sip from his steaming cup. "Tell me about the brake system on an MG-TD."

Michael had taken pride in restoring the classic 1952 English sportster, never dreaming it would become a death car. Clare's death car.

"Not much to tell." He'd been over this before. "They're drum type, small and inadequate by modern standards, intended mostly for the final stop, not for slowing. You're supposed to use the transmission to decelerate."

"What about the emergency brake?"

"Mechanical. Works on a cable."

"Was it operational in your MG?" Kraus asked.

"Sure. But I didn't use it much. Easier to leave the car in gear to keep it from rolling when I parked."

Michael was beginning to feel uncomfortable. He pulled in his legs and swiveled around so he was facing the man across from him. "I assume from your questions, the investigators found a problem with the brakes on the car."

Kraus rubbed the back of his neck as if he couldn't

decide how to answer. He took a fortifying mouthful of Elva's strong black coffee and set the mug down.

"Our forensics people found no hydraulic fluid in the system," he said. "It had all drained out through a hole in the steel tubing leading from the master cylinder."

"Must have happened in the accident," Adam observed. "The car undoubtedly rolled a time or two."

"Six times," Kraus agreed, "as best we can tell."

Michael sucked in his breath and squeezed his eyes shut.

"That has to be when the line snapped," his father said.

Rather than concur, Kraus asked Michael, "When was the last time you examined the brakes?"

Dear God, was he accusing him of negligence in Clare's death? Michael had been blaming himself all along, but the charge, coming now from someone in authority, reinforced his sense of guilt.

"Can't say for sure." He hunched his shoulders and slowly let them droop. "I installed a completely new system just before I dropped in the overhauled engine."

"Could you have inadvertently nicked the line in the process?" Kraus asked.

Could he? "I checked everything out very carefully at the time. I didn't have any reason to inspect the line after that. Besides, I told you, the brakes were working fine when I drove up to Tarnished Mountain to meet Clare."

He'd been in a rotten mood that day. Everything had been going sour of late. He'd run into more problems with Webster Hood, the new general manager the Homestead Bank and Trust had appointed to oversee ranch operations, and Clare's ailing grandmother had started to become more demanding and disruptive. His outlook had improved the moment Clare showed up, but then, she'd always had that effect on him.

"Did you do anything to the car while you were waiting for her?"

"No." He took a deep breath. "There was no reason to. I'd been driving the car for several weeks and never had a lick of trouble. Sheriff—" the word came out as a plea for understanding "—if I'd had the slightest inkling there was anything wrong with the brakes—" Sheila reached over and covered his hand with hers "—I would never have let Clare drive it, especially down the side of a mountain."

Kraus pursed his lips. "Here's the situation. Our inspection of the wreckage revealed two problems. First, the hydraulic line was cut."

Michael rubbed his temples. "Cut?" His voice rose. What the man was suggesting was insane. "Do you mean on purpose?"

Sweat broke out on the back of his neck. If someone intentionally cut the brake line, it could only mean one thing—that person was trying to mess with him. No one knew Clare was going to drive the MG. He didn't know it himself until he tossed her the keys.

"That's the way it appears." Kraus looked at Adam. "We started off with the same assumption you did—that the hole resulted from the accident itself. But no matter how we played it, we couldn't make the facts mesh. The line has saw marks on it."

"Who would do such a thing?" Adam asked in astonishment.

"That's the big question. Another is when."

The chair screeched as Michael shoved it back and rose to his feet. He was finding it difficult to digest what he was hearing. His chest pounding, he paced the open area near the door. Surely Kraus wasn't suggesting murder. There must be a logical explanation for this, a fact somebody was missing.

"It doesn't make sense," he insisted, stopped. "The cut, as you call it, had to have been made by a rock or other debris striking the line, or the chassis twisting while it tumbled."

"We might have bought that, except a few other details don't fit."

Michael's stomach tied itself in a painful knot. "What details?"

Kraus worked his lips in and out before answering. "The emergency brake was also disabled. The cable was cleanly severed."

An image burst into Michael's mind of Clare frantically pulling on the emergency brake handle as the car caromed down the rugged mountain road and the moment of terror she must have experienced when she realized there was no stopping.

Michael's stomach heaved. He bolted to the sink, sure he was about to be sick. He closed his eyes and took long, slow breaths through his nose as he leaned over the stainless-steel bowl.

Sheila sprang up, removed a glass from an overhead cabinet, filled it with water from a bottle in the refrigerator and handed it to him. Gratefully, he drank.

Behind him, he heard his father. "You said a few other details. What else?"

"When we searched the garage—with your son's permission," he was careful to point out, "we found a hacksaw. Microscopic examination of its teeth revealed it contained particles of steel consistent with the hydraulic line material, as well as brake fluid. Michael confirmed to my deputy that it was his saw.''

Getting his sour stomach under a semblance of control, Michael turned around to face the sheriff. Kraus wasn't a vindictive man. He'd served the county well for many years. His office walls were crowded with awards for excellence, community service, leadership. He had no animus against the Firsts. In fact, he'd been very supportive on the few occasions when they'd run into problems with the law. Michael trusted him, which made his statements all the more frightening.

"There's another thing," Kraus said. "We also found wire cutters we believe snipped the brake cable. On the workbench. They belonged to Michael, as well."

"So my tools were used," Michael observed angrily, nearly shouting. Had utilizing his tools been a matter of convenience for the perpetrator? If Michael had himself been killed and this evidence uncovered, would it simply have been dismissed as carelessness on his part?

"Who could have done this?" Sheila's eyes were glassy, her voice unnaturally weak.

Kraus peered at Michael. "I was hoping you could tell me."

Michael moved on rubbery legs to the table and sat down. His hands were shaking as he reached for his cup. He pulled them back. "This can't be true." He scrutinized the lawman. "You must have this wrong."

"I wish I did," Rudy Kraus said sympathetically.

"But I made sure they double-checked everything. The evidence has all been confirmed."

Michael gazed at the scrubbed oak tabletop and shook his head. There had to be a logical explanation, but he was too confused at the moment to figure it out. The room was silent for several minutes.

"What now?" Adam asked.

Kraus pushed his empty mug toward the middle of the table and heaved himself to his feet. After removing his buff-colored Stetson from a hook by the door, he paused, then turned to face his hosts. "I was duty bound to turn the things I just told y'all about over to the DA. This is no longer an accident investigation. He's reclassified it as a criminal matter." He studied Michael for a long interval. "I suggest you get a good lawyer."

THE CHILDREN were in bed. Sheila and Elva had settled Brigitte for the night and were in the living room, probably dozing in front of a Saturday-night movie on TV. Michael and his father had retired to the front porch of the ranch house. There had been dustings of snow twice since the New Year, but this evening was unseasonably warm for mid February. Wearing only windbreakers, they sat in oversize rockers next to each other.

"I'm scared, Dad," Michael said, his eyes staring levelly into the blackness beyond the porch rail. "I don't like admitting it, but I am."

Adam pursed his lips, his expression somber. "Rudy Kraus knows you would never do anything to hurt Clare."

"He's a friend. I don't think he would have come out here today and suggested I get a lawyer if he didn't believe I was in real trouble." As well, the lawman was probably opening himself up to serious criticism in tipping him off.

His father didn't dispute the point. "That's what we're going to do—get you a good lawyer."

Michael could always count on his father. "I'll talk to Spooner Monday morning."

The two men quietly sipped their beers as their chairs rocked.

"Dad, I don't know what I would have done this past month without you and Sheila," Michael said. "The whole family has been great, but the two of you have been here every day, helping the girls with their homework, helping Dave with his Boy Scout projects. That means a lot to the kids—to know they're not alone. It means a lot to me." He closed his eyes and lowered his head. "God, I miss her."

"We all loved Clare," Adam replied, his voice gruff with emotion.

Silence lingered between them for several minutes. Michael washed a slug of beer past the lump in his throat.

"If anything happens to me," he finally said, "if I get arrested, put in jail—" he couldn't believe he was saying this, that it was even possible "—I'd like you and Sheila to take care of the kids. I know it's not fair of me to ask you. You've done your child-rearing. You shouldn't have to do it again. But they're closer to you than they are to anyone."

Adam reached over and covered his son's hand with his, a rare gesture of affection between the two men. "You never had to ask, Michael. Those kids are as precious to Sheila and me—"

"If—" Michael's voice thickened "—if I get sent

to prison…or worse…I want them brought up on the Home Place, on the land. I want them to know their heritage. It's what Clare would have wanted.''

Adam cleared his throat. ''You have my promise.''

THE LAW OFFICE OF Nelson Spooner, the First family's attorney, was located downtown on a side street off Coyote Boulevard. The single-story cream-colored brick building was well-maintained, unembellished, yet projected a staid, prosperous dependability. Spooner and Stovall was engraved on the polished brass plate beside the door. The civil attorney had taken on a new criminal-law partner a few months ago, following the retirement of Jim Donnelley. A woman this time, as Michael recalled, but he hadn't met her.

Carol, the receptionist, who was in her early thirties, glanced up from her paneled desk and greeted him with a reticent smile. He'd met a lot of these lately. People wanted to be friendly but were uncomfortable with a man in mourning. Since he'd called ahead, Spooner was expecting him and emerged from his office as soon as he heard Michael's name mentioned.

Nelson Spooner was a nondescript bachelor in his midforties, who liked to wear expensive clothes. He was heavily involved in community affairs and sat on the boards of several charities, as well as the local symphony. An accomplished actor, he regularly played prominent roles in the town's civic theater. He offered Michael a warm handshake and a cold drink, and ushered him into his office.

''Probate will take a couple of months, as I told

you," Spooner reminded him. "Did you remember something else for the inventory?"

"This isn't about probate."

Michael had given scant attention to the subject since furnishing the lawyer the information he'd requested. Having come from a modest background, Clare had brought little private property into their marriage and, other than her grandmother, had no direct heirs outside the First family. "I have another matter I need to discuss with you."

He told the attorney about the sheriff's visit, about the accident results being referred to the D.A. for criminal investigation and the possibility that he could be charged in his wife's death.

Spooner rubbed his chin and eyed Michael with concern. "You need to talk to my partner, one of the best criminal lawyers in the state. If anything develops from this, she'll be the person to handle it." He picked up his phone, spoke into it and rose to his feet. "She's available now. Let's go see her."

They left their soft drinks and crossed the reception area to a pair of double doors. Spooner tapped, twisted the knob and pushed it open, then extended his arm for his client to precede him.

The room was large, light and comfortable. Michael got halfway across the wide expanse of plush beige carpet and stopped short.

Lara.

CHAPTER TWO

MICHAEL WAS THUNDERSTRUCK. What had Spooner called her? Stovall? She'd been Gorley when they hung out together in high school, running in the same pack. Before he'd met Clare.

"Lara?" He wasn't sure why it came out as a question. "I… It's been a long—"

"Michael." She circled the end of the desk, her hand extended. "I'm sorry we're meeting under such sad circumstances." The smile on her face faded. "My condolences on the loss of your wife."

He accepted her hand. "It's good to see you again. I had no idea you were back—"

"You know each other?" Spooner spread his arms in obvious delight.

She let out a soft chuckle, her gaze never leaving Michael. "We graduated from high school together."

"A long time ago." He smiled back.

Those had been fun-filled days—hiking and horseback riding, talking and enjoying each other's company. Mostly as part of their crowd, at movies, parties, sporting events. But in the three years hanging out, there had been private moments, too.

Then they'd gone off to college together—at least, for their freshman year. That was where he'd met Clare Levine and his world had taken a different course. He'd always scoffed at the idea of love at first sight, but that was the way it had been for him with Clare. In a matter of hours, if not minutes, it was as if they'd known each other all their lives. She was the woman he wanted to marry, to make babies with, the woman to whom he wanted to devote the rest of his life.

"Michael has a legal concern that's in your bailiwick," Spooner explained. "So I'll leave him to you. As I said," he reminded Michael, "Lara's the best. I'll keep you posted on probate and phone if we need any more information."

Michael was more aware of Lara standing a few feet away than of the man shaking his hand. "Thanks. I'll be in touch if I remember anything else."

Spooner waved as he closed the door behind him. Lara resumed her place behind the desk. Her eyes collided with Michael's. After a dozen heartbeats, she waved him to the client chair. They both sat. "Now, what's the problem?"

For a silly moment, he was tempted to swing his arm in an arc and say, "Doctor, it hurts whenever I do this."

She'd reply, "Well then, don't do it."

They'd both laugh, and the tension would be broken. But his being here wasn't a joke. He planted his feet squarely on the floor. Where to begin?

"The sheriff paid a call yesterday. I think I'm about to be accused of murdering my wife."

She didn't even blink. "If he or anyone from his or the D.A.'s office comes to see you again, don't make any statements to them. Nothing. Tell them unequivocally that you refuse to discuss the matter without your lawyer being present."

"Doesn't that make me look like I have something to hide?"

"No," she declared emphatically. "It makes you look smart."

There was steel in the assertion, a kind of ruthlessness he didn't recollect from years past. He wasn't sure he particularly liked the savvy woman who'd evolved from the studious girl he used to know. But then, strength was exactly what he needed in a lawyer.

Her flaming-red hair was just as brilliant as he remembered, though it was shorter now, no longer pulled back in the nearly waist-length ponytail of twenty years ago. The gray suit and pale-lavender blouse she was wearing were too old for her, stodgy in his opinion, but he supposed the outfit was appropriate to her professional status. Jeans had been her trademark when they were teenagers.

He shook his head. Lara, a married woman, a lawyer. True to her craft, she got out a yellow tablet and picked up a pencil.

"Let's go over the case against you," she said. No small talk. No catching up on old times. Well, that was all right. He wasn't here to reminisce. He was in danger of being accused of killing his wife, of murdering the woman he'd loved deeply and devotedly for more than half his life. Maybe another time he and Lara could wax nostalgic about their teenage years. For now he needed to get this ape off his back.

He had to admit, though, that he was both impressed and intrigued by his old girlfriend. Had he not met Clare, there was a good chance he and Lara would have continued their relationship, maybe even gotten married. She'd changed, though. The sparkle he remembered had gone from her eyes. He used to find their ocean-green depths fascinating. Now he saw a jade hardness, a barrier that seemed to forbid familiarity, friendliness. He wondered what events in her life had brought her to this detached state?

"Why does the sheriff suspect you of killing your wife?"

He drew in a breath and let it out. "You may have seen the story in the papers—"

She raised her hand. "I've learned not to put much credence in the media. Assume I know nothing about what's happened."

He eased deeper into the chair and crossed one leg over the other. "On Saturday, January 19, my wife, Clare, and I arranged to meet on Tarnished Mountain to get away for a little while."

She glanced up from the notes she was taking. "Why did you choose that location?"

"It was our special place, where I proposed to her. Whenever we wanted to be alone, we went there, sort of a renewal—"

She nodded vaguely, her gaze lowered. "Sorry for the interruption. Go on."

"Anyway, I took my restored 1952 MG-TD," he said. "Clare used the family Suburban. On the spur of the moment, when we were ready to come down from the mountain, I offered to switch cars with her. I left in the Suburban, expecting her to join me at the house. An hour later, I received a phone call from Brad Lopez, my ranch assistant. He'd just found Clare." Michael looked down at his hands. "She'd driven off the road and been killed."

"Obviously," Lara said, after a discreet pause,

"the authorities have decided it was more than an accident. Why?"

He told her about the cut hydraulic line, the severed brake cable, the metal particles and brake fluid on the hacksaw in his garage and the timing that seemed to preclude anyone but him from sabotaging the sportster.

She studied him. "Why do they think you would want to kill your wife?" She spoke calmly, but her words had an accusatory edge.

"I had absolutely no reason to murder her." He matched Lara's calculating composure, his eyes never leaving hers. "I loved Clare." He paused. "As a matter of fact, I don't believe she was the intended victim. I think I was."

Her pencil fiddling ceased. Her brows went up, and she stared at him. "What makes you say that?"

"Because no one knew we were going up to Tarnished Mountain or had any reason to think I might let Clare drive the MG. As I said, it was a spur-of-the-moment decision."

"And it was your idea to trade cars?"

"Yes. I'd only had the sports car on the road a month or so and hadn't let anyone else behind the wheel. Whoever monkeyed with the brakes must have been trying to kill me."

"Who would want to do that and why?"

He shook his head disconsolately. "I don't know. There are people who don't like me, but not this much."

"Who doesn't like you?"

Michael heaved a breath. "Webster Hood, the ranch manager, and I disagree on a lot of issues, but so what? He really has nothing to gain by bumping me off. I fired a ranch hand a couple of months ago, but he left town. We've laid off a few other workers, but that wasn't my call.'' He shrugged. ''I just don't know.''

She pursed her mouth, green eyes steady on his. ''Were you and your wife having marital problems?''

His impulse was to say it was none of her business.

''Her name was Clare,'' he stated a little too forcefully. ''And no, we were not having marital problems.''

She regarded him a moment. ''If murder charges are brought against you, Michael,'' she said patiently, with a note of sympathy, ''there will be a lot of questions about you, about Clare, your children and your parents. I'll need to know things you probably won't want to tell me, but if I'm to defend you effectively, you'll have to trust me.''

Michael dragged his fingers through his hair. ''We'd had a difficult few months and needed to regroup. That's why we went up to Tarnished Mountain. To discuss what we could do to get back on track.''

''Back on track,'' she repeated. ''Then you *were* having marital problems.''

He paused. ''That's putting it too strongly. We hit a few bumps in the road, that's all. We needed to get away, spend time by ourselves, so we decided to drive into town and book a Caribbean cruise.''

Lara scribbled on her pad. ''What kind of bumps?'' she asked without looking up.

He rose to his feet and paced toward a wall of bookcases filled with intimidating, leather-bound tomes. ''Clare's grandmother, for one.''

"Her grandmother lives with you?" Lara sounded appalled.

He understood why. Lara's paternal grandmother had resided with them when she was growing up. The senior Mrs. Gorley had been an unpleasant woman who seemed to take perpetual delight in criticizing people, including her only grandchild. She apparently got away with it because she had the money in the family.

"I like Brigitte," he went on. "We've always gotten along. When she fell and broke her hip six months ago, I had no qualms about her coming to stay with us during her recuperation. It didn't take long, though, to realize she wouldn't be returning to her house in Spokane or living by herself anymore. She's eighty-five, physically feeble and has Alzheimer's. Most of the time she doesn't know where she is or recognize the people around her."

"So you wanted to put her into a nursing home," Lara concluded.

"It wasn't really what I would have preferred, but she was becoming very disruptive."

"In what way?"

Michael wasn't about to mention that the old woman had interrupted their lovemaking more than once. Even when she hadn't, Clare had often been too exhausted by the time she got to bed to be interested in the kind of intimacy he wanted. None of that was Lara's business.

"Very demanding," he said. "She'd go into hysterics for no apparent reason, insist Clare stay with her. Occasionally, she'd throw things. Brigitte had been such a gentle person. The drastic change in her personality was tearing Clare apart."

"But she still refused to put her in a nursing home."

He nodded. "She kept hoping against hope Brigitte would get better." He resumed his seat. "You have to understand, Clare's parents were killed in a car accident when she was twelve. Brigitte and her husband, Gus, took her in and raised her. When Gus died a few years ago, we invited Brigitte to come and live with us, even offered to build her a mother-in-law house behind ours, where she'd have her privacy and still be part of the family. But she wasn't interested."

"Why, if she and Clare were close and you got along with her?"

He glanced across the desk. Lara was sitting back in her executive chair, observing him as if from afar.

"Independence," Michael offered. "Familiar ground, I guess. She'd lived in the same house over fifty years. All her friends were nearby. She was active in the community. Her world was in the green hills of Washington State. Our lifestyle didn't match it." He shifted in the seat, uncomfortable with Lara's veneer of calmness. "As you know, our spread is thirty miles from town. Brigitte felt isolated there. She preferred four seasons and tall trees. We don't have much of either."

Lara tapped a fingernail to her lips. "So that was the bump in the road you and Clare had to smooth out. You wanted to put the old woman in a nursing home and she refused?"

The statement probably wasn't intended to be accusatory, but that was how Michael heard it, maybe because he felt so guilty in even suggesting it.

"That was part of it." He raised an eyebrow. "Is that so bad?"

Lara's expression softened. "From my perspective, no." She straightened. "Did you resolve the matter while you were up on the mountain?"

Blinking slowly, he shook his head. "Not completely, but Clare could see the person living in our house wasn't the grandmother who'd raised her."

"You say Brigitte was part of the problem between you." Lara suspended her pencil over the yellow pad. "What else was there?"

He hesitated a moment. "The ranch. She felt I was obsessed with it." His voice was low, self-conscious. "Maybe she was right."

Lara angled her head. "In what way?"

He rearranged his legs, seeking comfort, not finding it. "Several years ago, my sister Kerry had a serious drinking problem." He hated talking about this, recounting the pain she had brought to their father and the rest of the family, hated reliving the guilt he himself felt for not preventing it.

Fidgety, he rose once more to his feet. This time he strode to the tinted window that looked out on a perfectly manicured lawn under a perfectly trimmed shade tree. He crossed his arms over his chest.

"She's sober now," he said, his voice bouncing off the plate glass. "Before she dried out, though, she sold her share of the family ranch to the Homestead Bank and Trust, giving them controlling interest. Dad found the situation intolerable and opted out. With the help of Sheila, my stepmother, he gave up his interest in the Number One in exchange for independent title to the original homestead. I still live and work on the Number One, however. As you might imagine, my goal has been to someday reunite the entire ranch."

"Did Clare oppose you?"

"Not at all. She loved the place as much as I do."

"I'm confused, Michael. What's the problem here?"

He turned around, positioned his hands beside him on the pink-marble windowsill, closed his eyes and took a deep breath. "Several months ago, the bank appointed a new general manager. I'm the livestock manager and work for him. Like I said, Webster Hood, the new guy, and I have very different philosophies about how the place should be run. He's also not a hands-on sort of supervisor. I've had to pick up a lot of the details his predecessor normally attended to. It's consumed a good deal of my energy and kept me away from the family a lot."

"At a time when Clare was struggling to take care of her grandmother," Lara observed.

He nodded.

"So to work all this out, the two of you decided to take a Caribbean cruise?"

"The prospect of ten days or two weeks on the Love Boat put us both in a happy mood."

"Was anyone else aware of these plans of yours?"

"I told you—" he fought to control his growing impatience with this inquisition, with Lara's stony detachment...as if she were examining a bug caught in a web, which was precisely how he felt "—we only made them when we were up on the mountain."

"Which means there's just your word that you and she had reconciled."

She was taunting him. *Get used to it,* he chided himself. *It's what lawyers do.* Michael ran his tongue between his lips, refusing to rise to the bait. "You make it sound as if we were at each other's throats or on the brink of divorce. We weren't. Because we had our disagreements doesn't mean we didn't love each other. We did.''

Ignoring the reply, Lara went on to her next question. "How long were you alone on the mountain before she arrived?''

"About ten minutes.''

"What did you do during that period?''

"Nothing.'' He faced the window again. The pristine world out there was so inviting. "I stood at the edge of the mesa, noticed how dry everything was, worried about grass fires. We'd had a few. Fortunately, we were able to contain them.''

"What did the two of you do after she arrived?''

"We sat on a rock outcropping. Talked, held hands.'' Kissed, but he didn't mention that. Their last kiss.

"Where were the cars?''

"Less than fifty feet away. I'd nosed the MG close to a boulder. She'd parked the Suburban right behind it. That's why I left ahead of her. If you're asking whether anyone could have gotten access to them while we were up there, the answer is no. We were absolutely alone.''

Was that a fatal admission?

"You were up there by yourself ten minutes before she arrived. Adequate opportunity to tamper with the brakes.''

"I didn't kill her.''

"Can you explain how you were able to drive up the mountain in a perfectly good car and your wife was killed in it coming down, without anyone else being there?''

He'd been over it repeatedly in his mind. Clare starting the car and putting it into gear. Tapping the brakes. Because she'd never driven the MG before, the feel of it was unfamiliar. She wouldn't have been able to tell if the sponginess she detected was normal. She began her descent, probably in second gear. They'd been joking only minutes earlier. In her enthusiasm, she was probably going a bit fast. After all, she knew the road and where it went. And then...

He clenched his jaw. "As a matter of fact, I think I can. The sheriff said the brake line was sawed partway through. He didn't specify how much, but I suspect we're only talking millimeters. I did an experiment this weekend. I filled a tube with hydraulic fluid, cut a tiny hole in it and applied various amounts of pressure."

She looked at him curiously. "Go on."

"I may have patted the brakes backing out of the driveway—I certainly didn't stomp on them. Actually, I doubt I touched them at all on the drive up the mountain."

"You're saying the tampering didn't have to be done up there? It could have been done while the car was still in your garage?"

He didn't miss the note of hope in the question or the doubt lurking behind it. Her distrust irritated him. She irritated him. "I didn't kill her, Lara. You've got to believe me."

She waved her hand and slouched against the back of her chair. "It doesn't make any difference what I believe, Michael." Her tone was neutral, almost condescending. "My job will be to defend you, to convince a jury that the district attorney hasn't proved beyond the shadow of a doubt that you murdered your wife."

Michael winced. This definitely wasn't the answer

he'd anticipated. He'd expected her to give him her unqualified support, to say she didn't believe for a moment that he could possibly murder anyone, much less the woman he loved. But she said none of these things. If she was trying to make him feel lower than a snake's belly, she was succeeding. "Do you have any more questions?"

"Who profited from your wife's death?"

"Profited? Nobody profited." He narrowed his eyes. "My God, Lara, are you suggesting I killed the mother of my children for her insurance?"

"I'm not suggesting anything, Michael."

"Really." He kept his voice mild, contained. "How would you phrase the question if you were?"

She stared at him for a long moment. "Calm down, Michael. If you think I'm being accusatory, wait till the D.A. gets around to grilling you."

He strode to the door, angry, bitter—and scared, then turned to face her. "I'll have to tolerate his hostility, Lara, because it's his job, because he believes I'm guilty."

"Don't be naive, Michael," she retorted, showing the first sign of her own emotions. "District attorneys prosecute cases because they think they can win them. Defense lawyers defend people because even the guilty have a right to counsel and a fair trial."

So much for his simplicity. "Are we done?"

She shoved back from her chair and stood up. "I think we've covered enough ground for today. Go home and mull over what we've discussed. Unless something happens sooner, I'll call you in a few days, and we can go over this again."

She walked to the door and opened it for him.

His heart raced. She was dismissing him without a word of encouragement.

LARA DROPPED into her chair, her mind in turmoil. She'd forgotten the effect Michael First could have on her. She'd accepted from the moment she decided to return to Coyote Springs that at some point she was bound to run into him—at a restaurant, the rodeo, a fundraiser or a party. She'd convinced herself she was prepared, that she could handle their meeting again. They hadn't seen each other in close to twenty years. Then Spooner buzzed her on the phone to say Michael was in the office and he was bringing him over to see her, and her mind instantly conjured up an image of the tall strapping teenager who'd held her in his hard-muscled arms and kissed her. If only Michael had understood how much she'd wanted him to continue touching her, how much willpower it had taken to let him go, how devastated she'd been when he'd said goodbye.

Of course he'd changed since she'd last seen him. His big-boned frame had filled out, become more powerful, more mature. What had startled her, though, was his entrancing blue eyes. Once so carefree and confident, they were deeper now, mysterious and…weary. She glimpsed in the instant of their meeting a careworn fatigue that hadn't existed in the younger man.

Maybe she should turn down this case. But on what grounds? That she was acquainted with Michael First? That she'd attended school with him two decades ago? Half of Coyote Springs knew the other half, and since when was a lawyer obliged to be a stranger to her client? There wasn't any conflict of interest here. Except in her own head—and maybe in her heart. She and Michael First had long since gone their own ways. Now he needed legal representation, and she was a damn good lawyer.

What it came down to was that she didn't trust herself as far as Michael First was concerned. There was something disquieting about him, something that made her feel vulnerable. The notion was ridiculous, of course. She had nothing to fear from him. He was a family man mourning the loss of his wife and in danger of being arrested for her death. Concentrate on the legal business at hand, she admonished herself. Not the man.

Did she seriously think Michael First had sabotaged his own car in order to kill his wife? It didn't seem likely, but the truth was, she didn't know. There would undoubtedly be plenty of character witnesses to say he hadn't, that he was a good man. But good men made mistakes. Good men committed crimes. Good men had flaws. The people we loved let us down, hurt us. And sometimes they didn't even realize they were doing it.

Ever since she'd heard of Clare First's tragic death, her mind had been crowded with memories, images, recollections of Michael, of the time they'd shared together. The way he laughed. The way being with him made her feel. When he'd kissed her, she'd thought their relationship was going somewhere. Naive. She hadn't realized their friendship hadn't meant as much to him as it had to her. Afterward, she'd asked herself what she should have done to advance it, to make him see how much she cared for him. Should she have gone to bed with him? She would have if she'd thought it might have kept him. Instead she'd ended up giving herself to… She wasn't going to dwell on Clay. Not now. Maybe not ever.

What she had to concentrate on was how to defend Michael First against the charge of murder. He had the kind of emotional appeal she could draw on in the courtroom. A wealthy but modest-living rancher with four exemplary young children, orphaned by the loss of their attractive and socially conscientious mother. Michael's father, Adam, was a pillar of the community, a man who had himself suffered the tragic loss of his first wife and his youngest son, then seen his family's empire destroyed by his alcoholic daughter. Lara could milk those tragedies with a jury.

The dilemma still remained, however. Was Michael First capable of killing his wife?

As a teenager, he'd had a reputation for being imperturbable, laid-back, easygoing, but he'd had a subtle but wicked anger, too. Like when Rocky Danners put a burr under his saddle at a junior rodeo. Instead of bulldogging a steer, Michael had been thrown in its path and nearly trampled. He'd gotten up, brushed himself off, then laughed, as if it were all so much fun. She'd seen the expression in his eyes, though. He hadn't been as sanguine as he'd pretended, just well disciplined. At the following event, the practical joker's saddle girth broke. Rocky tumbled off, was stepped on by his horse and ended up with a broken foot, which put him out of competition for the rest of the season. Michael had denied cutting the cinch, naturally, but everyone knew he'd done it—and nobody really blamed him. The joker had it coming.

People's habits and lifestyles might change, she reminded herself, but their essential natures didn't. She wouldn't have dreamed him capable of murder twenty years ago, but then, she'd never really known him—otherwise his leaving her wouldn't have come as such a shock.

NELSON SPOONER was standing at the receptionist's desk, removing a piece of lint from his sharply creased gray pants, when Michael stepped out of Lara's office. The senior partner greeted him with a smile. "How did it go?"

"You have a minute? I'd like to talk to you."

Spooner looked at him curiously. "Sure thing. Come on into my office."

Unlike Lara's workspace, Spooner's hadn't been recently renovated. Although it was impressive at first glance, closer inspection revealed worn upholstery and fading wallpaper, traffic patterns in the carpet and nicks and scratches on the expensive wooden furniture.

"Sit down," Spooner invited with a wave of his hand. "Remember something else?"

"I need a different lawyer." At Spooner's crooked eyebrow, he went on. "Lara doesn't seem to have much confidence in my case. I think I'd be better off with someone who feels more positive about my prospects. I was hoping you could recommend—"

The attorney's forehead furrowed with worry. "Did she say she wouldn't represent you?"

"No, but she wasn't very encouraging."

Spooner relaxed, chuckled. "She's shown you the prosecutor's hand, eh?" He rested his forearms on the edge of the desk. "Don't let her fool you. She's on your side. She would have turned you down flat if she didn't think she could win your case."

Michael needed to win, not just for himself but for

his family. But he wanted her to believe him, too. His silence prompted Spooner to go on.

"In the past five years she's defended three capital murder cases and won all of them. I'm honored she agreed to join me."

Lara Stovall. A criminal lawyer. It wasn't what he'd imagined she'd become, though he wasn't sure what he'd expected. That she was among the best didn't astonish him. Lara Gorley had been smart enough to do anything she set her mind to. She'd always had an eager, logical mind. While other girls rhapsodized over the latest male teenage heartthrob in *People* magazine, Lara read classics and bestsellers.

He remembered when he told her he wouldn't be seeing her anymore. She'd been philosophical, which had been a great relief. He'd been afraid she might make a scene, though he should have known that wasn't her style. She'd wished him well. Her family had moved at the end of the semester. She'd transferred to another school and vanished from his life. His attention after that had been riveted on Clare and Clare alone. He'd all but forgotten Lara.

He hadn't seen her wearing a wedding ring. Before he even realized he was posing the question, he asked, "Is she married?"

"Widowed."

CHAPTER THREE

"HURRY UP, DAVE," Michael called out from the kitchen, "if you want breakfast. Your ride will be here any minute."

The fourteen-year-old thundered down the stairs three at a time, whipped around the newel post and flew into the kitchen. "Soccer practice today. You coming?" He threw a leg over his chair at the table.

"Count on it." Michael dished out the oatmeal Elva had prepared before going off to feed Brigitte her breakfast.

The boy slapped a generous pat of butter on the grayish goo, dusted it with too much brown sugar and splashed milk into the bowl, then stirred it vigorously. Incredibly, none of it spilled over.

"You eat like a pig," Sally sneered as her brother gulped down the hot cereal. She daintily wiped her mouth with a cloth napkin. "Boys. Yech."

Michael grinned to himself. At twelve, her attitude was about to undergo a transformation. He wasn't particularly looking forward to it—especially without Clare to help guide the way.

"Put your dish in the sink and finish your juice. Grandma Sheila said she'd pick you up at school this afternoon. She wants to get you some new shoes."

"Can I get platforms? Everybody's wearing them."

"They're really cool," Kristin, two years younger, contributed. "But I want stacked mules."

"Me, too," Beth Ann, the youngest, announced. The other girls rolled their eyes. Michael didn't really know what his daughters were talking about, and he had a pretty good idea the eight-year-old didn't, either.

"It's up to your grandmother." He probably ought to go with them. Maybe he could pick up a few pointers about handling three girls. He smiled to himself. Not. He'd just come away scratching his head. He'd never understood the female fetish for footwear. As far as he was concerned, shoes were things you put on your feet to protect them. He had to admit, though, he had liked it when Clare wore high heels. They did something for a woman's legs.

"Those clunky things look dumb," Dave mumbled between mouthfuls.

"Do not," Sally retorted.

"Do, too."

Michael sighed. "Knock it off, both of you." He barely suppressed a grin.

A horn sounded outside. It might as well have been a fire alarm the way the four kids scrambled.

"Come back here and put your bowls in the sink," he ordered, as they bolted to the door to the hallway. "Dave, comb your hair. Sally, don't forget your hat. Kristin, I think I saw your spelling book on the floor in the living room."

He laced Beth Ann's tennies and zipped up her coat. "See you all this afternoon. Have a good day," he called out as they charged out to Kyle Ratley's van.

A minute later the kitchen was deathly silent. He

took a deep breath, poured himself a cup of coffee and dished up a bowl of oatmeal.

Had Clare taken this time every morning to marshal her resources for the coming day? He felt close to her at this moment. In this kitchen they had designed themselves. At the table she'd found in a secondhand furniture store in town and he'd refinished. So much of their life together had been spent in this room— early mornings, drinking coffee and sometimes late at night sharing a beer. If he closed his eyes, he could feel her in this room, at the stove, at the refrigerator, smiling at him across the table. He could almost reach out and touch her.

But he had to keep his eyes open. He had to face reality, cope with it. Ten days had passed since the sheriff's visit. Maybe the crisis was over, and the authorities had decided Clare's death was an accident after all, or Kraus had convinced the D.A. that he couldn't possibly have murdered his wife. Later he'd call Lara and ask if she had any news.

He still wasn't sure what to make of her, still wasn't completely comfortable in her presence. Their second meeting had gone a little better than the first. He accepted that the adversarial approach was necessary, that she had to test and challenge him under pressure. But sometimes he had the feeling the hostility was genuine, and that bothered him. Maybe, he thought, hostility was too strong a word. Doubt? Suspicion? They'd been good friends once. Michael found it hard to believe she actually considered him capable of this hideous crime. Yet how else could he explain her attitude?

He was loading the dishwasher when Webster Hood telephoned to announce a meeting in half an hour in his office. This was Wednesday. The general manager's regular weekly get-togethers were on Friday afternoons, so Michael immediately prepared himself for something unpleasant.

The drive to the new headquarters, located in a shallow draw amidst live oak trees, took less than ten minutes. The previous general manager, E. J. Hoffman, an old cowboy who spent more time outdoors than in, had adapted an unused cabin as his home and office. Hood hadn't been satisfied with it and immediately moved in a double-wide trailer to serve as his residence and operations center. Michael didn't object to the overseer having better accommodations, but the plush leather furniture and Jacuzzi did rub him the wrong way.

Instead of the normal assembly of crew chiefs crowding around the spacious living room, only two people besides Hood were there: Brad Lopez, Michael's assistant livestock manager, and Chase Norman, who was now handling the agricultural side of the multifaceted ranch operation. The three men helped themselves to mugs of hot black coffee from the machine tucked into the corner of the fully stocked wet bar. The loose-capped bottle of Jack Daniel's beside the carafe suggested their host had spiked his.

"We've cut back our herds these past few months," Hood said, when the others were comfortably seated in the upholstered chairs across from his desk.

The sales had been a mistake in Michael's opinion. The First family policy had been to maintain a stable core of livestock. Hood's approach was to go for the fast buck and maximize current profits. Michael had fought hard against reducing the breeding stock, arguing that it diminished the ranch's ability to ramp up to meet future market demands, but he'd been overruled.

"As a result," the general manager continued, "we have excess grazing capacity, which affords us other opportunities."

Michael's head shot up. "What opportunities?" He was almost afraid of what the answer would be.

"I've received bids to lease our pastureland," Hood explained, "from several of the ranches south of here that have been adversely affected by the drought."

"We're in a drought, too," Michael reminded him. Which was the excuse Hood had used for scaling back to begin with, that to keep rotating pastures and supplementing feed was too expensive.

"We have better water resources than they do," Hood countered.

"If we have the means to support other people's livestock, why have we been selling off our own?" Michael sipped coffee.

Hood slouched in his chair, an expression of impatience on his face. "Because it was profitable. And we'll lease land now because people will pay us for the privilege. Making money is what this enterprise is all about."

Michael bristled. He could have responded that the Number One wasn't about money, but that argument would hardly gain sympathy from a minion of the bank. Dollars and cents were all Hood was interested in. Pushing out of his seat, Michael took a step away before turning back to face his boss square on. "Don't do this."

Hood glanced up, apparently more amused than concerned about his livestock chief's reservations. "Why not?"

"All it'll bring is trouble. We've established our own breed of cattle. For generations, they've been isolated from other animals, effectively quarantined from outside sources of contamination. Bring in foreign stock and you change their habitat and leave our bloodline prey to diseases they've never built up a resistance to."

Hood displayed no concern as he rose from his desk and sauntered to the bar. "Lease agreements will stipulate that all stock brought on Number One land must have the full range of shots."

Michael shook his head. "That'll protect *them* from getting sick. It won't protect *our* stock from what these outsiders might carry."

"Haven't our animals been fully immunized?" Hood asked over his shoulder.

"Only against diseases they're prone to in this environment," Michael responded. "Additional inoculations could cost us a lot more than we're likely to gain from the leases."

Brad Lopez nodded in agreement. "He's right."

The room fell silent.

"There might be an alternative, though," Lopez observed cheerfully. The others zeroed in on him. "Keep the herds completely separated."

"On a spread that covers three-hundred-and-fifty-thousand acres, that shouldn't be difficult," Norman declared, speaking up for the first time.

Michael stared at his friends, displeased by the suggestion, disappointed in their unwillingness to support him. "We'll still have to rotate pastures. Contamination can reside in the soil, be windblown and carried by insects. We're making ourselves extremely vulnerable with very little return on investment. We'll have to inoculate our livestock, install additional fencing and possibly hire more people to control separate herds. All of that will take time and money.''

Hood waved his objections away. ''As far as wind and bugs are concerned, we're susceptible whether the cattle are grazing on our turf or somebody else's. Soil contamination? We can safeguard against that by having temporary holding areas where outside animals are quarantined before they're put out to pasture.''

''You're buying trouble,'' Michael warned again. ''I strongly advise against it.''

''Well, the decision isn't yours.''

Michael contemplated the contents of his coffee cup and fought to restrain his building anger. ''So this meeting wasn't to confer with us or seek our recommendations.'' He looked up. ''You've already made up your mind.''

''This isn't a democracy,'' Hood said disdainfully. ''I'm the boss. I say what goes.''

Michael glanced at his companions, but they refused to make eye contact. Partly, no doubt, because they were embarrassed for him, but he suspected they were also ashamed of their own silent complicity in what everyone recognized as the gradual demise of the Number One. Michael would have loved to vent, to fly into a rage, to fight the feeling of humiliation and impotence welling inside him. But nothing would be accomplished by a display of temper. He refused to compromise his dignity.

They spent the next hour determining which pastures could be used exclusively for outside livestock and setting up timetables for rotating them. Chase Norman promised to develop a field cultivation and overseeding schedule to mesh with theirs. After adding too much brackish coffee to his already acidic stomach, Michael left with the others. Norman waved goodbye and drove off.

"I was afraid we'd never get out of there." Lopez checked his watch. "I'm supposed to meet Gretchen for lunch. She's bringing stuff from town. Wouldn't want to keep the lady waiting."

At the moment, Michael couldn't have cared less about his assistant's love life. Selma Lopez had divorced Brad last year because he was playing around. About six months ago, he'd started going with Gretchen Tanner, a pert twenty-something blonde who ran her own investigative service.

"Damn it, Brad, why the hell didn't you support me in there?" Michael leaned against Lopez's diesel pickup, his arms folded.

Brad's eyes widened. "What do you mean? I did agree with you. I just came up with what I figured was a reasonable compromise. Especially since Web was fixing to do what he wanted anyway."

"You didn't know that," Michael objected, then realized Lopez had referred to the general manager by his first name. "Or did you? Had he already briefed you on his plans before I got there?"

Lopez pulled back, his face darkening. "N-no," he stammered. "I didn't know nothing about it until he told all of us. Ask Chase if you don't believe me." He paused to exhale loudly. "Come on, Michael. This ain't so bad. It's better than mixing stock."

"But not as good as not having them here to begin with."

Brad wasn't well educated or particularly sophisticated, but they'd always gotten along, and Michael was grateful for his taking up so much of the slack since Clare's death.

"You heard what he said," Lopez pleaded for understanding. "It was obvious he'd already made up his mind. That's why I suggested keeping them separate. Hey, you know I would never do anything to hurt the Number One."

That much was true. "In the future," he said curtly, "I'd appreciate it if you'd talk to me before making suggestions that undermine my position."

"I didn't realize—" He broke off. "I was just trying to help."

"Maybe it'll work," Michael reluctantly conceded, after a pause. "I sure hope so, because the alternative could be disaster."

HIS FATHER AND SHEILA WERE at the house when Michael got there. The previous evening at dinner, Sheila had broached the subject of disposing of some of Clare's personal effects. Six weeks had passed since her death, but Michael hadn't had the heart or desire to remove her things from closets or chests.

"Elva and I can go through her clothes, if you like."

He'd jumped at the offer. Now, as he watched them neatly folding underwear, shirts, pants, blouses and jeans and tucking them into cardboard boxes, he wished he hadn't come home so soon. Memories. Too many memories. Reliving them in his mind only brought pain, yet he didn't want to forget them, either.

It was time to move on, he told himself. For his children's sake, he couldn't afford to become a recluse, a madman living in the past. They needed him, and he needed them more than ever before.

He was carrying a carton filled with nightgowns downstairs when he heard a vehicle crunch to a halt in the gravel driveway. Friends and neighbors came around to the rear. Only strangers stopped in front. He sensed who it was before he ever got to the door. A leaden weight lodged itself in the pit of his stomach.

He stood on the porch and watched a man in a khaki uniform emerge from the driver's side of the white-and-blue county vehicle. In his early forties, big-framed and a bit rumpled, he took a fortifying breath after adjusting the wide leather belt that supported gun, bullets, radio and handcuffs. Another deputy, younger, more trim, exited the other side of the sedan.

"Mr. First—" the senior man approached "—my name's Wesley Janick. I'm a deputy with the sheriff's department."

Michael wondered how the man had gotten on the property, since all the gates were kept locked. Before he could inquire, Janick held up a piece of paper.

"Mr. Michael First, I have a warrant for your arrest."

Adam and the two women had come up behind him.

"On what charge?" his father demanded authoritatively, though Michael detected anxiety.

"The charge is murder in the first degree for the death of Clare First."

Sheila gasped and clutched her husband's arm. Michael's heart sank. He'd been afraid this was coming, but deep inside he'd hoped to be rescued at the last minute. Now, like the inevitable climax in a suspense movie, it came as a shock, sending a frisson of fear streaking through him.

"Call Lara Gorley...er...Stovall," he told his father. His voice sounded dry and cracked, even to himself. He couldn't believe he was saying the words he'd rehearsed only in his darkest nightmare.

IT WAS AFTER TWO O'CLOCK when Lara received the alert from Adam First that his son had been arrested for murder. She was no closer to deciding if he was innocent or guilty than she had been when he'd come into her office ten days earlier. Now that he was officially charged, she'd have access to the evidence the police had gathered against him, and she could get a clearer fix on what approach the prosecution might take. Even without that access, however, she knew they had a strong case.

"Be prepared for big bail," she advised Adam.

"If necessary, I'll call my son-in-law Craig Robeson. He can raise any amount of money the court demands."

"You're lucky to have that kind of backing."

"We're family," Adam replied simply.

The statement, intended to reassure, was a painful reminder that she'd had no such family support in her life. Her mother had been remote and venal; her father, weak, yet driven. Then there had been dear Grandmother Gorley—cold, judgmental, faultfinding and vindictive.

"I'll be in touch," Lara told Adam, and hung up. She dialed the D.A.'s office. Malvery was in. Fifteen minutes later she was walking down the hall of the county building across from the courthouse.

Burk Malvery was a handsome man, tall and lean, with a chiseled jaw, dark hair and chocolate-brown eyes. The bronze glow of his smooth skin suggested he spent a lot of time either on the golf course or the tennis court. Or maybe in a tanning salon.

He greeted her almost gleefully. "Hi, Lara. Come on in. Get you something to drink?"

"No, thanks." She followed him into his office.

The room was long and richly paneled in dark wood. A conference table butted up against his wide desk, T-fashion. He took his accustomed place, inviting her to sit at the table.

"Now, what can I do for you?" The corners of his mouth curved upward.

"Michael First. You're holding him for murder."

"Yep. Got him dead to rights, so to speak." He shot her a reptilian grin.

"He didn't do it. You've got the wrong man."

He quirked an eyebrow in amusement. "That's your opinion. It's not mine."

"Come on, Burk," she implored. "He's from one of the most prominent families in Texas. His record is spotless, his reputation impeccable. Not the profile of a man who calculatingly murders his wife."

Malvery curled his hands around the ends of his armrests and gently rocked the swivel chair. "That's not the way I see it. Because he's from a prominent family, he's got friends in high places, friends like Sheriff Kraus and Judge Mayhew. So his name not appearing on the blotter doesn't impress me."

"Are you suggesting Kraus and Mayhew are corrupt?"

He snorted. "Of course not. They're honest public servants. But I'm not naive, Lara. Friends help friends, protect one another."

"It didn't keep his sister Kerry's son from being arrested for underage drinking and driving." Nelson Spooner had been a font of information on the First family's legal history—within the limits of confidentiality, of course.

"No, but Kerry Durgan—" she'd married the high-school bad boy "—routinely got escorted home instead of charged with DWI, as she deserved. Maybe if she'd been thrown in the tank a time or two her son wouldn't have followed in her footsteps."

Malvery was right, but Lara wasn't about to concede the point. Besides, Michael's sister and nephew weren't the issue. Michael was. She pictured the lost look in his eyes when he talked about his last time together with Clare. A person would have to be a totally insensitive fool not to see the man loved his wife. For a fleeting moment, Lara wondered what it would be like to have a man love her like that. She shoved the sentiment aside.

"So because Michael First doesn't have a record of misdemeanors," she continued, "he must be guilty of felony homicide. Brilliant logic, Burk."

Malvery pouted. "Now you're insulting me."

"What about motive?" Lara asked, since that would be the key sticking point.

"He was having problems in his marriage."

The statement was so bland and nonspecific she wondered what he wasn't telling her. "What couple doesn't run into rough spots from time to time? You're going to have to come up with something better than that, Burk. We're not talking about a guy who's prone to murderous rages."

He shrugged, unconcerned. "It only takes one. Besides, this homicide was well thought out."

"You'll lose," she warned.

He didn't appear in the least discouraged. "Actually, I see this as a win-win situation." He grinned.

She didn't need to ask what he meant. If he managed to get the First family's eldest son convicted, maybe even executed, Burk Malvery would go on record as tough on crime, as a prosecutor who didn't stop until the ends of justice were met. If he failed, he could still point his willingness to take on the establishment, the wealthy, powerful vested interests.

She folded her arms, aware of the way his gaze swept her breasts. "You're only looking at the sunny side. You also run the risk of coming across as vindictive and incompetent." His narrowed glare told her he didn't like her choice of words or the implication that she would use that tactic. "And, as you say, the Firsts have friends, people with a lot of money and influence."

He took umbrage and let it show with a downturn of his mouth. She suspected he practiced the expression in the mirror.

"I'm offended, Lara, that you would imply I'm doing this for political reasons." His rocking motion ceased. Now he had his hands laced officiously in front of his flat belly. "Your client killed his wife. I can prove it to a jury, and I intend to."

"Has it occurred to you that, instead of his wife, Michael First may have been the intended victim?"

Malvery laughed, then grew serious. He peered at her before answering. "Please don't underestimate me, Lara. Of course I've considered the possibility. Is that the defense you're planning to use? Interesting. But all the evidence points clearly and emphatically to Michael setting his wife up, viciously and with malice aforethought. That's first-degree murder.''

"It's all circumstantial, Burk, not direct proof.''

He waved the comment aside. "We both know most cases hinge on circumstantial evidence, unless there's a confession. Now, if you're interested in a plea bargain, we might be able to work out a deal.''

"Thanks for seeing me.'' She rose, straightened her skirt and picked up her briefcase. "I'm sorry you're doing this, not just on behalf of my client but for your own sake. Nevertheless, this is a free country. See you in court, Counselor.''

His demeanor instantly reverted to the pleasant, accommodating public official. "You find a better candidate for the dock, Lara, and I'll put him there.''

CHAPTER FOUR

SITTING IN THE BACK of the sheriff's car, Michael vowed to follow Lara's admonition to remain silent and not answer any questions until she showed up, but being passive went against his every instinct to meet a crisis head-on.

His mind kept conjuring up images of his children being taunted at school about their father being a jailbird, a killer. Kids could be so cruel. How would he be able to face his four, assure them he wasn't going to be sent to prison, snatched away from them permanently like their mother? They were so young.

More than anything, he had to protect his children. But how? Should he have his father and Sheila relocate them somewhere else until this all blew over? His sister Kerry and her husband lived in Dallas. Michael knew they would help them without a moment's hesitation. It was some consolation that his children would always have family around to love and support them, but their mother's death had disrupted their lives so much already. Would they feel more secure staying with him during this crisis, or was he a liability to their sense of well-being? At least they hadn't seen him taken away in handcuffs.

His mood slammed between a desire to weep with frustration and an impulse to strike out with violence. But at what, at whom? He wanted to go on the offensive, not depend on somebody else to fight his battles for him. Could he count on Lara, especially when she wasn't convinced of his innocence? She'd been a good friend once, a confidante. Why didn't she trust him now?

He'd spent most of his life outdoors. On foot. On horseback. At home they didn't even lock the doors and windows. A major attraction of the MG had been the sense of freedom it gave him, its easy response, the way the wind blew in his face. Now he was sitting in the back of a police car. The door and window handles had been removed, and a wire screen separated him from the two men in the front seat. He was caged. If they locked him up for good, he'd go mad.

The county jail was co-located with the sheriff's department. He'd driven by the building thousands of times, but he'd never been inside. His mental image of a jail came from old cowboy movies. This three-story windowless yellow-brick-and-mortar edifice in no way resembled any hoosegow he'd seen in *Gunsmoke* or *High Noon*.

The two deputies escorted him through the gray-steel rear door into a drab, fluorescent-lit reception area. Rudy Kraus was standing behind the counter, his thumbs tucked into his broad, black leather belt, his usual easy manner replaced now with a somber scowl. Janick said something that sounded like "lawyered up," but it was too low for Michael to hear distinctly. Kraus nodded.

"You've retained counsel?" Kraus's tone hinted at approval.

"Lara Stovall should be here soon." At least, he hoped she would. This place made him feel dirty. "Until then, I have nothing to say."

Kraus nodded. "We'll go ahead and get you booked, then wait for her."

Janick led him to an inner cubicle, where he was ordered to empty his pockets and remove his belt and jewelry. Another uniformed deputy fingerprinted and mug-shot him. The cold, impersonal way the young woman ordered him around, avoiding eye contact, added to his sense of unreality, of being abandoned.

From there, he was led down a narrow corridor to a small, fetid interrogation room. It contained a scarred vinyl-topped metal table and four badly stained stiff wooden chairs. He wasn't offered coffee or any amenities. He was left alone, though a large mirrored glass in one wall made it obvious he was under constant surveillance. The room was probably bugged, too. He paced for several minutes before finally sitting down.

Michael propped his elbows on the table and clamped his head between his hands. What had brought him to this? Six weeks ago he was a happily married father of four. Now his wife was dead, and his children looked at him with hurt, frightened eyes.

A full hour passed before the door opened and Lara appeared. She was wearing a lavender skirt suit with a pale-green silk blouse. He didn't normally notice what people were wearing. Clare used to tease him that if she went missing, he'd never be able to describe her clothing, except to say she was wearing some. But Lara, with her brilliant red hair and spring-fresh attire reminded him of the first scene in the *Wizard of Oz* when Dorothy finds herself no longer in Kansas. Lara was the only color—and hope—in this drab world of black and white.

"Michael," she intoned with concern, "are you all right?"

He managed a mirthless grin. "They haven't used any rubber hoses on me yet."

She squeezed out a smile. "Have you told them anything?"

"Mum's been the word." He resisted the childish urge to press a finger to puckered lips. Maybe he was going stir-crazy.

"In a minute, a judge will come in to arraign you," she said. "Since arraignment has to take place within twenty-four hours of arrest, it's normally done here in the jail. This is just a legal formality to officially advise you of the charges against you, of your right to counsel, to accept your plea—not guilty, of course—and to set bail. It's not a trial. It won't take more than a few minutes, and then we'll get you out of here."

The prospect of being released made his emotions soar, so much so that he grinned at her. "Okay."

She walked over to the reflective glass window and tapped. A second later, the door on the right opened and the sheriff came in, followed by a man wearing a blue pin-striped suit and gray tie. Michael needed a moment to recognize Burk Malvery, the district attorney. A large middle-aged woman in a baggy brown dress entered behind them.

"Mr. First, I'm Judge Ellen Diego, here for your arraignment."

Not sure a response was necessary, he nodded.

"You have been charged with first-degree murder. Do you understand that?"

"Yes."

Judge Diego proceeded to enumerate his rights. To

have an attorney present during any interview or interrogation. To have an attorney appointed if he didn't have one. To remain silent and to stop an interview at any time. That if he chose to speak, anything he did say could be used against him in a court of law. After each statement, she asked him if he understood. To each question, he responded yes.

"How do you plead?"

His pulse was racing. He couldn't believe he was standing in jail, being asked if he had murdered his wife. "Not guilty, Your Honor." He was totally amazed when his voice sounded normal.

She addressed Malvery. "What is the state seeking in the way of bail?"

"Due to the particular heinousness of the crime, Your Honor, we request the defendant be remanded without bail."

Michael glared at Lara, his entire body going rigid. Sweat pooled under his arms and the small of his back. They couldn't lock him up. Lara said he'd be able to leave. Had she lied? Miscalculated?

"Your Honor," she interceded calmly, "Mr. First is a prominent member of this community without any criminal record, who has close family ties in the area. I ask that he be released on his own recognizance."

"That's ridiculous," the prosecutor responded. "The man has significant financial resources and therefore constitutes a major flight risk."

"He also has four orphaned children who desperately need him at home," Lara pointed out. "He's not about to bolt."

Malvery relented, as though he were making a tremendous concession. "One million dollars, Your Honor."

Diego screwed up her mouth and shook her head. "I wish you two would save it for the courtroom. Fifty thousand dollars, cash or surety." She signed off on a piece of paper and departed.

Michael released the breath he hadn't realized he'd been holding.

Lara opened her attaché case and removed a blue folder, which she presented to the prosecutor. "Motion to dismiss."

"I'm not surprised." He gave the impression of a man who enjoyed the chase. "See you in court, Counselor." Curling the legal document in his hand, Malvery followed the judge out the door.

Within minutes, Lara's telephone call resulted in a courier delivering a cashier's check for the full amount of the bail.

"You're free to go," Sheriff Kraus told him somberly. "You can collect your things at the front desk."

Michael stuffed his wallet and keys in his pockets and self-consciously put his wedding ring back on his left hand. He threaded his belt through his pants' loops, then secured the large silver buckle with the Number One brand on it.

Silently he and Lara exited the building through the front door. Michael was flabbergasted to find his brother Gideon leaning on the fender of his van at curbside.

"What are you doing here?"

"I always hang around the jailhouse," Gideon replied with a mischievous grin. "Never know what interesting people you'll run into."

A grossly obese man in a filthy undershirt, smelling ripely of stale beer and body odor, hurried by, escorted by a scarecrow of a woman in equally slovenly slacks and shirt.

"Fascinating lot, jailbirds," Gideon continued. "A real study of the human condition."

"Lara, I don't know if you remember my kid brother, Gideon. This is Lara Gorley…Stovall, my attorney."

Gideon put out his hand. "You may not remember me, but I sure remember you. I had a crush on you, or rather on your red hair, when I was about ten." He continued to hold her fingers while he brazenly surveyed her face and body. "I still could, except I'm a happily married man now—and I plan to stay that way."

Michael watched her laugh for the first time. Her face lit up, changing her demeanor completely. The glow reminded him of when they'd gone on a hayride with a group of their friends. She'd laughed as they rode through the star-filled night. He'd loved that smile, loved being with her. Until he'd met Clare.

"And I remember you as the towhead who was always tagging along after your big brother," she rejoined. "Still doing it, I see."

"Old home week," Michael interjected, unaccountably annoyed that the two had hit it off so easily, so fast. "Maybe we should all go have a few beers and talk about old times."

Lara cast him a curious glance. She'd been a lawyer long enough to know people just released from jail often reacted unexpectedly. "Not now. Go home to your family. I'm sure they're worried. Preliminary hearing before Judge Wilcox is set for tomorrow morning at ten-thirty. I'll meet you at the courthouse at ten-fifteen. Don't be late.''

"Do you want to get together before that at your office? I can be there whenever you say.''

"That won't be necessary. The burden of proof will be on the district attorney to show probable cause why you should be bound over for a grand jury. I'll object, bring up counterarguments and move for a dismissal, but it won't do any good. The D.A. has enough to indict. Besides, I have other commitments," she concluded in businesslike fashion. "Ten-fifteen. We'll have plenty of time to talk before the grand jury meets.''

She was holding out about as much hope as a West Texas March without wind. "I'll be there.''

Michael observed her step around the front of the van, her attaché case in hand. A determined woman. A widow. He still didn't know if she had any kids. She looked both ways, then strode purposefully to a BMW parked on the other side of the street.

"I like the way your old girlfriend's grown up," Gideon commented a minute later as they pulled away from the curb in his van. "I had no idea she was back in town. Did you?''

Michael shook his head. Life was getting too complicated, spinning him in circles. "Not until I went to see Spooner and found out she was his new criminal law partner.''

"Yep, very attractive woman. Bet she's good at her job, too.'' He maneuvered around a slow-moving city bus. "How do you feel about being defended by your old lover?''

"We weren't lovers," Michael snapped. "It is possible for a guy to like a girl without going to bed with her, you know.''

Gideon didn't say a word. Michael wanted to kick himself. His younger brother had fathered a child out of wedlock, a little girl he'd since taken full and unqualified responsibility for. This certainly wasn't the time to be judgmental.

"Sorry," he said contritely, "I didn't mean that the way it sounded."

"Forget it," Gideon said easily. He flipped on his directional signal and turned onto the road that would take them to the Number One.

"Besides," Michael said, "it was a long time ago."

He wondered if his brother noticed he hadn't answered his question.

As LARA HAD PREDICTED, the preliminary hearing before Judge Wilcox the next morning didn't take long. This wasn't a trial, simply a judicial review to verify that the prosecution had sufficient cause to charge a person with a crime. Lara's motion to dismiss, based on the paucity of motive, was denied. Michael's bail was continued and he was again released, pending appearance before the grand jury, which was due to meet April 16.

Michael had hardly stepped beyond the double doors of the courtroom when reporters and flashing cameras surrounded him. A woman of perhaps twenty-five blocked his way, a microphone in her hand. "Do you think the district attorney has a vendetta against you?"

Someone else yelled, "What did you and your wife fight about?"

"Was she having an affair with someone?" another male voice called out.

Michael's head buzzed with the loaded questions. As he worked his jaw, not sure how to respond, Lara insinuated herself between him and the woman reporter, effectively pushing her back.

"Mr. First has no comment, nor will he in the future." She barged ahead and he followed in her path.

"Thanks for rescuing me," he whispered in her ear a minute later after the press finally left.

"Don't ever give them anything. They're not your friends, no matter how sympathetic they may sound. They'll twist and distort what you say to suit their own agenda—namely, a sensational story. Your only statement is 'no comment.' Understood?"

"Yes, ma'am," he said with the beginnings of a smile.

Others now gathered around them. He introduced members of his family. She'd already met Gideon. His wife, Lupe, was petite and dark, a lovely woman with intelligent black eyes. Michael's sister Kerry and her husband, Craig, had flown to Coyote Springs in their private jet from Dallas. Lara remembered Kerry from high school as a wild but essentially unhappy teenager. They'd traveled in different circles back then. Now Lara had the feeling they could actually be friends. Craig Robeson was tall and handsome and clearly loved her. For the first time, Lara found herself envying Kerry.

Michael's other sister, Julie, and her husband, Rolf, were also there. Lara had only a vague recollection of Julie, who was almost seven years younger than Michael. She'd been a cute, spirited little girl. The woman gave the impression of having the same qualities, though she was serious and supportive at the moment. Her husband, who was also quite good-looking, appeared to be some years older.

Finally, Lara met Adam and his wife, Sheila. She remembered Michael's father very well. In twenty years he'd changed little. The crow's-feet and the lines bracketing his mouth were deeper. The hair that had been jet-black was streaked now with gray at the temples. But the essential handsomeness and dignity of the man hadn't diminished.

When she and Michael had been pals, Adam had seemed the ideal dad—a strong, compassionate man who was comfortable in his own skin and demonstrated his confidence with unconscious generosity and personal warmth. She'd seen those qualities in Michael, too. Maybe that had been part of the reason she'd started to fall in love with him.

Lara liked Sheila from the moment their eyes met. She radiated a strength that matched her husband's.

"What happens now?" the older woman asked, clearly voicing everyone's concern. "What's the next step?"

Attention was riveted on Lara. "In about two months, Michael will appear before the grand jury to answer questions. They'll decide if there's sufficient evidence against him to bring him to trial."

"What's your gut feeling?" Adam asked, his apprehension undisguised.

"Based on the information we have now, they'll indict."

Kerry bit her lip, reached for Michael's hand and clasped it greedily. "How long before he's brought to trial?"

"Another six to eight months after that."

Michael squeezed his eyes shut and shook his head. "I don't want to wait almost a year to prove I'm innocent. It isn't fair to my kids or the rest of the family for me to be under this cloud of suspicion for months on end."

Lara understood his impatience. For the innocent, the process was too slow; for the guilty, it was too fast. "Actually, a lengthy discovery period gives both sides time to sort through the evidence for exculpatory information. Of course we'll be conducting our own investigation."

Michael nodded. "Maybe you can hire Gretchen Tanner." Without thinking, he took Lara's elbow as they descended the steps toward the splashing fountain. At the bottom, suddenly aware of their closeness, he released her and subtly increased the distance between them. "She's a friend of Brad Lopez, my assistant. Runs an investigative agency. Sharp gal. She's spent time on the ranch with him, so she knows people and what's going on."

Craig Robeson, Kerry's husband, patted Michael on the shoulder. "You seem to be in good hands. We have to get back to Dallas," he said. "I have a few irons in the fire—"

"I understand," Michael agreed. "Thanks for coming."

"If you need anything, you know you have only to ask." Kerry rose on tiptoe and kissed him on the cheek. "I love you, Brother. Hang in there. We'll get through this."

He kissed her forehead. "You bet."

As they started to walk away, the others came up to say their goodbyes and give promises to come out to the ranch on the weekend.

"Tell Dave I'll see him at soccer practice tomorrow night," Gideon called back, as he held the car door for his wife.

Michael watched them leave, his face set, strained.

"I hope you can join us at the ranch for lunch," Sheila said. "I understand you used to come out there when you and Michael were in school together. I'm sure you'd like to see how it's changed."

Lara was ambivalent. It had meant a lot to her once—the sense of freedom and independence it represented, its association with the man—boy, really—she'd developed an infatuation for. But she'd long ago put that interval of her life behind her. Revisiting old haunts rarely gladdened the heart. Either they recalled unhappy events, or they turned out to be disappointments.

"I imagine you'll want to look around, see things for yourself," Michael added. The lines around his mouth tightened. "I can take you up to Tarnished Mountain."

Which was the last place she wanted to go. To him, it represented the site of his betrothal to Clare. For her, it was the place where he'd first kissed her, not in a playful, teasing way, but the way a man kisses a woman. She didn't want to be reminded of how foolishly she'd misinterpreted that moment of intimacy. As his lawyer, though, she'd have to inspect the site, determine if there might be alternative explanations for the tragedy that had taken place there. Perhaps she could come up with a line of defense based on the lay of the land.

"Plan on spending the afternoon," Adam said, adding his endorsement. "That way you can meet the kids when they get home from school."

His children. Another reminder of what might have been, what couldn't be. She'd have to meet them eventually, of course. She didn't like putting children on the stand, but she couldn't close her mind to the possibility that it might be necessary.

"I'd like that," Lara told him, pasting on a smile. "Let me check in with my office and make sure I can reschedule the rest of today's appointments."

She moved a few paces off and extracted a cell phone from her purse. Carol assured her she could rearrange her afternoon appointments.

"I ought to stop off at my house and change clothes," she told him after hanging up. The combed-linen burgundy suit and silver-gray silk blouse she was wearing were hardly appropriate for the ranch, especially if they were going to Tarnished Mountain. "Can I just meet you out there?"

Michael had come into town with his folks. Lara wondered if he would volunteer to accompany her. It would give them a chance to discuss the case and begin the painstaking process of identifying potential witnesses and outlining strategies. But it was Sheila who offered to ride with her. Michael and his father wanted to make a quick detour to a cabinet shop where Adam was having bookcases custom built for his den.

Lara de-alarmed her BMW parked at curbside and unlocked the vehicle electronically. They climbed in.

"I live in the Woodhill Terrace section," Lara explained. "It's practically on the way."

The Tudor-style house, with its steep gables and leaden windows, was too big for one person. She didn't need four bedrooms and a formal dining room in addition to a spacious den. The swimming pool was a foolish extravagance she rarely used. It was a far cry from the clapboard bungalow she'd grown up in the Oakdale section of town. Maybe that was the point.

"I'll just be a minute," she told her guest when they were inside the spacious, marble-floored entryway. "Make yourself at home."

"What a lovely place you have." Sheila stepped into the living room, which Lara had had professionally decorated in shades of maroon and taupe.

The dining room was off the entryway to the right. Sheila was immediately drawn to the large porcelain plate in the middle of the shiny mahogany table. "Imari?"

"Yes." Lara smiled. "It belonged to my grandmother. She inherited it from her father, who claimed it was presented to his grandfather by the emperor when he accompanied Commodore Perry to Japan in 1854 in his campaign to open it to the West. I don't know if the story's true, but an appraiser did date the plate to around that period." Lara pointed to the china and crystal in the glass case. "Some of those pieces are quite old, too."

While Sheila admired delicately designed sake cups, Lara went to her bedroom and changed into jeans and a cotton shirt. She rejected donning her old riding boots in favor of running shoes with thick rubber soles. Her grandmother would have been pleased at Sheila's appreciation of the heirlooms, Lara mused, the only things of her family she'd retained. Actually, she'd been tempted to sell them a few times, especially when she moved and had to have them specially crated. It wasn't as if they provoked fond memories, after all. Still, they were valuable reminders of where she had come from.

They left the house a few minutes later.

"Do you think Michael will really be put on trial?" Sheila questioned after they buckled up and were under way.

Lara recognized the plea. Sheila wanted desperately to be told the case was weak and would never see the inside of a courtroom. But Lara also sensed the woman wouldn't tolerate being patronized. This was a person who prayed for the best but could handle the worst.

"As it stands right now, the case against him appears to be open and shut. But things can change," she added.

"Turn right. We'll take the loop. He loved Clare, you know. Deeply and unconditionally. He would have died himself rather than see any harm come to her or see his children go through this nightmare."

Lara had no doubt the woman beside her believed what she was saying. But having dealt with so many people accused of serious crimes, Lara knew some of the vilest acts were committed by people who exuded charm, intelligence and selfless devotion. Their neighbors and their closest intimates were often genuinely shocked by the revelations of their treachery.

Lara waited until they were on the highway to the ranch. "I understand Michael's aim is to reunite the Number One. How realistic is that?"

Sheila sighed. "Not very at the moment, I'm afraid. The Homestead Bank and Trust has majority interest and absolutely no incentive for giving it up. It's a cash cow." Sheila snorted. "No pun intended."

Lara was impressed by her companion's objectivity. "Losing it must have been difficult for your husband."

Sheila interlaced her fingers in her lap. "A lot harder than people realize. Adam's good at hiding his negative emotions, but they're there. Michael takes after him in that regard. Calm and serene on the surface, but you know the old saying about still waters running deep."

The unimproved public road to gate number five hadn't changed, though the gate was now electronically controlled. Since the keypad was on the driver's side, Sheila gave Lara the code. In the rearview mirror, she watched the plume of chalky caliche dust her car was kicking up as they crossed the wide valley. She searched the top of the mesa on the right—the spot where the ranch headquarters had loomed so proudly.

"Blown away in a tornado," Sheila explained.

Lara remembered the butler's pantry between the kitchen and dining room. Michael had stolen a playful kiss there. They'd been interrupted by the housekeeper, who gave them the eye but said nothing.

Michael's home was situated in a copse of huge green live oak and pecan trees. The two-story house was big but not a mansion, more like a gentrified farmhouse. At Sheila's direction, Lara followed the circular gravel driveway past the open garage on the right to the rear of the building. Dogs were barking, but it was an enthusiastic greeting rather than a ferocious warning.

"You've never been here?" Sheila inquired, as Lara turned off the engine and surveyed the area.

She shook her head. "Only the headquarters, and I remember the burned-out place by the springs."

Sheila's face softened. "The Home Place. Adam restored it. That's where we live now."

They exited the BMW, walked toward the back porch and were instantly greeted by two large dogs—a black lab and a golden retriever. Sheila introduced them as Knight and Day. They were beauties. But being a stranger, Lara decided to exercise caution.

"Don't worry—" Sheila chuckled "—the biggest danger they pose is that they might lick you to death."

Lara was massaging them both behind the ears when the kitchen door opened and a woman stepped out.

CHAPTER FIVE

"AS SKINNY AS EVER." Elva extended her arms for a hug.

The Firsts' housekeeper hadn't changed much, either. Maybe a bit chubbier, but it filled out the wrinkles and gave her an ageless appearance. A little more salt in her salt-and-pepper hair seemed the sole concession to the passage of time. Just as Lara remembered, she smelled of cinnamon and spices.

The country kitchen they entered was large and light. The stainless-steel appliances were commercial grade, but potted plants, colorful wallpaper and the rich tones of ceramic tile lent the room a coziness that was friendly and inviting.

"Dinner will be ready as soon as the men get here," Elva announced. "I hope you still like chicken mole."

Lara smiled, remembering the noon meal was the big one for ranchers and farmers. Before she could answer, a bell rang.

"I'll go," Sheila told Elva, who had opened the wall oven and was poking a pair of roasted chickens that smelled piquant and delicious. "Clare's grandmother," Sheila explained. "We haven't told her about Clare. Not much point. Excuse me."

On impulse, Lara asked, "May I go with you?"

Sheila brightened. "Of course."

A tiny, wizened woman lay in a hospital bed in a room that resembled a library.

"Brigitte, this is Lara Stovall. She's Michael's friend."

"There's a wasp nest out there." The old woman huffed with annoyance. "I told Gus he had to get rid of it. I need to plant the petunias."

Lara remembered Michael mentioning that Brigitte's husband, Gus, had died several years ago.

"What can I get for you, dear?" Sheila asked.

Brigitte spread purple-veined, wrinkled hands over her comforter to smooth it out. "Tell Clare to open a can of tuna for Fluffy."

"I'll do that," Sheila replied patiently. "Would you like a cup of tea?"

Brigitte stared at Lara with curious eyes. "Who are you?"

"My name is Lara. I'm a friend of Michael's."

"Oh, but he's already married."

The non sequitur felt like an elbow jab to the chest. Sheila caught her wince and, no doubt interpreting it as sympathy for the old woman, gave Lara a sad smile.

"I'll get you some chamomile," Sheila said gently. "She used to be such an interesting person," she added after they left the room. "Alzheimer's, you know."

Michael and his father arrived before Lara could pursue the conversation. Within a few minutes, they were seated in the dining room, though Lara suspected their usual place was at the kitchen table.

Adam folded a flour tortilla around a piece of marinated chicken. "How will you proceed with Michael's defense?"

Lara stole a glance across the table at her client. He was concentrating on his food but eating little.

"I'll be working at three levels," she explained. "Prove someone else did it. If that's not possible, show there's reasonable doubt that he committed the crime, and of course be alert to misconduct or mistakes on the part of the investigators that could be compelling. If none of those succeeds, develop a plea for mercy in the sentencing phase."

"Great." Michael rolled his eyes. "Pass the salad dressing."

Lara scooped up black beans. "Your premise that you didn't have to use the brakes going up the mountain, but Clare did coming down, makes sense. Granted that she may not have realized the brakes were low when she started out, why didn't she use the transmission, like you did, to control her speed? You said she was an experienced driver."

"She was." He dipped a piece of tortilla in the rich chocolate mole sauce. "I hadn't replaced the gearbox. It was well used but serviceable, a project I figured I could put off till later. A common characteristic of a worn transmission is a tendency to pop out of gear. Under normal conditions, it's no big deal. You simply slip it back in, but in the panic of a downhill ride…"

The others, he noted, had ceased eating and were looking at him with concern.

"Clare was a good driver." He leaned back in his chair. "If the transmission popped out of gear, she would have slammed on the brakes. Which would have forced out the hydraulic fluid in a matter of seconds. By then she'd be working the clutch and shift lever. But the car would have built up too much momentum." He was nearly breathless as the scene flashed before his eyes. "The next thing she would have done was grab the emergency brake."

"Except that had been cut, too," Lara finished quietly.

He heaved a grumbling sigh, once again imagining the terror that must have consumed Clare's last moments as the car accelerated out of control, as she fought desperately to stay on the road, only to have gravity and centrifugal force defeat her.

The tension around the lace-draped table thickened, broken only when Elva bustled in with a pitcher of iced tea to refill their glasses.

"We need to find out who had access to the car between Friday night and Saturday morning." Lara raised her eyes to Michael. "Was anyone here that morning?"

He willed his heartbeat to slow its painful pounding and forced himself to concentrate on the question. "Brad Lopez came by around eight, had a cup of coffee with us, then he and I went in his pickup to the cattle barn to get ready for the inoculations we had scheduled for the following week. He dropped me off again a little after ten."

"He left immediately?"

"I watched him go. The muffler on his truck was shot. I remember the racket he made as he drove away."

"Anyone else?"

"Not that I'm aware of."

"You said a person with a rudimentary knowledge of cars could have found the master cylinder and the brake line."

"It wouldn't take any special skill," he agreed.

"Since you didn't drive the car that morning," Sheila ventured, "maybe it was done in the middle of the night."

"Wouldn't the dogs have barked?" Lara asked.

"They bark periodically during the night at anything and everything," Michael replied. "Coons, rabbits, coyotes, rattlers. We don't pay too much attention to them. They're pussycats when it comes to people, especially if they know you. Talk nice to them or pat them on the head and they'll lick your hand." Michael took a swallow of his tea. "They're utter failures as watchdogs, I'm afraid. Just good companions."

"Webster Hood came by right after you took the girls to the lake," Elva announced. She'd been hovering throughout the meal, checking dishes, filling tea glasses. Listening.

Michael swiveled to face her. "What was he doing here?"

Elva shrugged. "Didn't say. Asked for you, but you'd already left."

"When was this?"

"You'd been gone only a few minutes. Must have been around eleven."

"How long was he here?" he persisted.

"Don't rightly know." Elva poured tea into his glass. "I'd just finished sweeping the front porch when he drove up. I called Clare, then went to pack for my shopping trip in San Antonio. Clare talked to him. He was gone when I took my bag out to the car a little while later."

"What time was that?" Lara inquired.

"I left at eleven-thirty."

"Any idea what he might have wanted?" Adam asked his son.

Michael shook his head, bewildered. "Clare didn't say anything to me about him showing up."

"You really suspect Hood might have something to do with this?" Sheila scanned the people at the table, settling on Michael.

A shrug served as his reply. But he was going to find out.

"YOU KNOW ALL ABOUT ME," Michael announced when they were in Lara's car a little while later. He'd let her drive up to Tarnished Mountain, figuring it was important for her to get the feel of the land.

Sitting across from her at dinner had given him a chance to observe her at close hand. Her aloofness and reserve had initially bothered him, made him question her skill, her dedication. Now he realized she was simply being professionally detached, trying to see things objectively. He couldn't fault her for that. Still, he liked her better away from the office and the trappings of the law. Here on the ranch, she seemed more...natural, more at ease and approachable. He smiled to himself. They hadn't seen or heard from each other in nearly twenty years, yet some things hadn't changed. The freckles on her nose still darkened when she was upset or excited.

"Tell me about yourself, about your folks."

"Not much to tell. They're all dead now." She was trying to make the comment sound offhand, a fact to be stated, a chain of events with no emotional impact. He puzzled over why she was so reluctant to acknowledge the pain of their deaths.

"I'm sorry." He wasn't particularly surprised that

her grandmother had passed away, though the woman had struck him as ornery enough to last forever. But her parents were no older than his father, who wouldn't turn sixty until next year.

"Grandmother went first—" Mrs. Gorley had insisted Lara formally address her as Grandmother, never Grandma or Granny "—a few years after we left Coyote Springs." Lara stared straight ahead at the empty road. The sun streaming in from the side window made a fiery halo of her hair. She smiled sardonically. "I used to fantasize about the day I'd tell the old miser off."

"But you never got a chance." He would have liked to have been there to witness it. "Take the right fork."

Lara chuckled with a kind of self-deprecating mirth. "I was planning to do it right after graduation, but then, in the last semester of my senior year, Beatrice Gorley had the good grace to go to bed one night and not wake up in the morning." Lara downshifted as the road coarsened and began its ascent.

"Doesn't seem fair," Michael muttered. After a minute, he added, "Your grandmother always struck me as a very bitter woman."

He'd witnessed the straight-backed old tyrant nearly reduce her granddaughter to tears for things that in Michael's opinion were trivial and silly. The belt she was wearing, the way she had her hair arranged, the shade of her lipstick.

"You have to realize," Lara explained, "she was born with a silver spoon in her mouth."

"Painful," he quipped. "How did your dad take his mother's passing?"

Lara's father had reminded Michael of an aging,

vaguely inept prince, waiting for the dowager queen to finally kick the bucket so he could inherit the throne and his dignity.

"Fine," she declared, "until he found out the wealth she'd boasted of receiving from her father had long ago been exhausted by inflation and bad investments. She'd been tightfisted because she was broke."

Even in profile, Michael could see a sadness come over Lara's face.

"He drank more heavily after that. Six months later he put an end to his humiliation with a single bullet to the head."

Again, she recounted it calmly, white knuckles on the steering wheel alone indicating how much his death had affected her. In Michael's estimation, Herbert Gorley hadn't been a bad person, just a weak one. He'd failed to protect his daughter from his mother's venomous tongue, yet Lara had loved him. Perhaps she'd seen the man he wanted to be instead of the man he was.

"Lara, I'm so sorry," he intoned. "I had no idea."

She was trying to remain stoic, pretending she'd already gotten past the grief brought by death, but her glassy-eyed concentration on the rough road gave her away.

"Mom hung on for another six years, drank too much, but then she always had."

Michael realized his life had been placid compared with Lara's. The death of his mother had been hard, but supportive family had always surrounded him. He'd had a father to look up to and a way of life he loved. Lara, on the other hand, had constant turmoil at home and no role models to emulate or inspire.

She'd clearly overcome those obstacles and made a success of her life. He had to admire her for that. What might their lives have been like if he hadn't met Clare, he mused, and Lara's family hadn't moved away from Coyote Springs?

He had no right to prod unhappy memories, but he felt compelled to learn more. "Spooner says you're a widow."

For a brief moment, her breathing slackened. Then with a shrug that resembled surrender, she relaxed. "Yes."

Clearly, she wasn't eager to pursue the subject. He would have liked to learn more, but he vowed to respect her privacy. She was fascinating, though, this woman who'd matured from the quiet, unassuming girl to the successful criminal attorney.

"After we moved to Alpine," she blurted out, as if compelled to speak, "I attended Sul Ross University. That's where I met Clay."

Michael listened, aware of the strain in her voice, the shyness that came close to pain. "He was an engineering student, in ROTC. We were married right after graduation. He got a commission in the army and earned his wings as a chopper pilot." Her fingers flexed on the steering wheel. "We moved around for a while. Then the Gulf War started, and his unit deployed to Saudi Arabia. Two months later he was killed in a helicopter crash."

Michael again offered his condolences. The loss of a spouse by violence was something they had in common. "Do you have any children?"

The corner of her mouth sagged, as if from a buried ache. She inhaled deeply. "I was pregnant when Clay went overseas. A few days after I was notified of his death, I suffered a miscarriage. The doctors told me I would never be able to have children after that.''

"I'm very sorry, Lara." The words were, as always, inadequate. He wished he could find some way to comfort her, some way to ease the anguish of loss. He had a family to lean on. She'd had no one as far as he could tell.

Silence lingered between them.

Michael knew people who'd enjoyed successful marriages were likely to remarry after the death of a spouse. She hadn't. He wondered why. Did he want to? He couldn't imagine plodding on without Clare. He'd never loved another woman, never wanted another woman to love.

"What was Clay like?" He wouldn't have blamed her if she'd told him it was none of his business. "Did you love him?"

Her lips smiled, but even in profile, Michael could see her eyes didn't.

"Handsome. Intelligent. Had a wonderful sense of humor. And yes, I loved him."

"Sounds like a nice guy."

"The women in his life thought so," she said dryly.

He nearly gaped at her. This might explain the wounded look he sometimes caught in her green eyes, her aloof reserve, her somberness. He couldn't imagine being unfaithful to a woman like Lara. She, too, was attractive, intelligent and possessed a wonderful sense of humor—at least, she had. He hadn't seen much evidence of it this time around.

Michael guessed the kind of betrayal she'd experienced could sour a person on matrimony, but more than a decade had passed since her husband died. That ought to be enough of an interval to get over it. Maybe not. Would he forget his love for Clare in ten years? No. Even if by some chance he found another woman to share his life with, he'd never stop loving her.

Observing Lara against the backdrop of distant mesas, Michael suddenly realized, as if for the first time, just how beautiful she was. The sweeping waves of hair that changed so dramatically with the light, from gold to copper to rich russet. The way they framed her oval face with its creamy soft complexion. The way she moved, with fluid grace and elegance, a woman of strength and dignity.

A change of subject was in order for both of them. "I'm a little surprised you went into law. I don't recall your being particularly interested in it when we were in school."

Her hands loosened on the wheel; her face muscles relaxed. "I majored in business when I transferred to Sul Ross and had to take a basic course in business law. It hooked me. The following year I changed my major."

"Why criminal law?"

She shrugged. "The challenge, I suppose." She shot him a smile. "And I do get to meet interesting people."

For someone who'd been so damaged, that astonished him, too. He would never have imagined her enjoying the rough-and-tumble of violent crimes and their perpetrators. "Civil cases don't have the element of danger that criminal law holds, is that it?"

She glanced over at him, a sly grin curving her lips. "How did you guess?"

Like a flickering image, he remembered that twinkle when he kissed her. The image disturbed him, and he instantly banished it. "You used to go for the action adventure movies most of all, the ones where people were in mortal danger."

"Vicarious bravery," she conceded. "I could share other people's terror, but I would never put myself in a position to be afraid. Maybe it's the same now. Other people's lives are at stake, but whether I win or lose, I get to go home and sleep in my own bed."

Maybe that was why she'd never remarried. She must have had opportunities. He'd always considered Lara Gorley to be strong and brave. He was shocked to realize Lara Stovall didn't see herself that way. Because she'd never stood up to her domineering grandmother? Or was it that, in failing to shield her from the old woman, her parents never let her feel worthy of love. Even her late husband, it seemed, hadn't respected her enough to be faithful to her.

Michael wondered if he, too, might have contributed to her feelings of inadequacy when he'd broken off their relationship. She hadn't fought him, hadn't begged him to stay with her, hadn't shown real disappointment at their splitting up. Had her passivity, her apathy been nothing more than a front, a defensive facade?

MICHAEL RADIATED discomfort as Lara maneuvered the narrow road onto the peak of Tarnished Mountain. He'd told her he'd come up here just once since Clare's death—to show a sheriff's deputy where they'd parked. Lara heard the ache in his voice when he identified the spot where Clare had plunged to her death. Lara slowed, peered over the sheer drop-off, acknowledged it with a silent nod, but she didn't stop.

They reached the summit. She turned off the engine.

"Shall we get out?" she asked, when he made no move to do so.

"It's windy. Your hair will get messed up."

She recognized the delaying tactic and gazed at him with concern. "I can comb it."

After another second's delay, he opened his door against a blast of early March winds, circled the front of the dusty vehicle and came around to Lara's side. She already had her door open. He offered his hand. She glanced up at him. His features were set. He didn't want to be here. But then, neither did she. After a moment, she accepted his hand—it seemed to swallow her in warmth—and got out.

He released his grip, and they walked together in silence to the edge of the mesa, to the spot where he said he and Clare had stood on their last meeting. She felt dwarfed by him. Looking up, she noted his eyes were shiny, unfocused, his mind far away.

"Are you all right?" she asked, just loud enough to be heard against the brash assault of the chill wind.

He glanced over at her, as though startled to find her there. "I'm fine."

But she could see he wasn't. This man had loved and been loved. For that she envied him. He'd lost that love. For that she grieved for him. His suffering ate at her. She surveyed the broad sweep of land stretching below them. Delicate pastel tints of yellow, pink, brown, parchment and green. He was right. This place was beautiful. She needed to confirm a few things before they left, for she knew they'd never come here again. Too bad, she mused sadly. Reluctantly but with determination, she withdrew from the precipice.

He followed a moment later.

"Where did you park that day?"

He showed her.

She bent, swept her tangled hair out of her face and examined the gravelly surface. There was nothing specific or obvious to indicate this spot was special.

"The sheriff's people—" she stood up "—found fresh hydraulic fluid." She dusted her hands against each other. "Using your scenario, it might indicate the brakes were already leaking when you got here."

"It doesn't prove anything." He followed her to the car.

"I can argue that the cut wasn't intentional, that you might have slipped with a saw at some point but didn't realize you'd actually punctured the line."

"I didn't cut the line, Lara. Intentionally or otherwise."

He wanted black and white, but the world was composed of shades of gray.

"I didn't kill her. I loved her." The wind tore at his words, leaving them ragged, but there was power in them, a strength that compelled her to reach out and touch him.

She placed her hand on his forearm and felt the throbbing heat of his pulse. "I'll do everything I can to get you acquitted."

"Because you believe me?" he appealed quietly, "or because you want to win the case?"

She refused to flinch. "My job is to represent you whether you're innocent or guilty. It's much easier, of course, if you're innocent," she said, trying to lighten the moment with a smile. When that didn't succeed, she added more seriously, "I've told you before, what I believe isn't important."

He curled his fingers over hers. "It is to me."

Should she tell him what he'd meant to her so long ago? It seemed so unimportant in the present. "We were friends once," she said, giving in to a rare urge for candor but still unwilling to be totally honest. "I truly valued that friendship. It was important to me then. I still treasure the memory."

She shivered, perhaps because of the raw, spring wind, except that the source of the chill seemed to come from inside. She wished she could retract her statement. No good would come of this conversation. Whether she called it friendship, a teenage crush or infatuation didn't make any difference. They'd been kids, immature, experiencing the first rush of independence, exploring new sensations, new emotions. At the time, she'd thought she was falling in love. Obviously, he hadn't felt the same way. Even if he had, it was irrelevant in the present.

Michael raised a brow, confused. He watched the freckles on her nose darken at the same time melancholy swept across her features, darkening her eyes. He remembered that expression, the tightly held-in sadness from years past. At the time, he'd attributed it to her unhappy home life. Now he detected another aspect of it.

"We better go." She checked her watch. "Didn't you say the kids would be home around five?"

Releasing her hand, he saw embarrassment, which was akin to shame. But what did she have to be ashamed of? Then it registered. She'd said friendship when she'd meant something else, something much more intense.

The flash of epiphany stunned him and added further to his confusion. Could he really have been that blind?

He'd been like most guys when he was a teenager, clueless about what girls were really thinking and feeling. He'd recognized that she liked him. He certainly enjoyed her company and at some level entertained notions of exploring it further. But he hadn't been in love. That hadn't come until he met Clare. Then Lara receded into a distant memory.

With a wordless nod, he moved toward the BMW, but his attention never left her. He handed her into the car, felt her tremble as their fingers slipped together, then apart. He continued to study her after he dropped into the passenger seat. They buckled up in silence. Her movements were self-conscious, clumsy as she twisted the key in the ignition. They began the long, bumpy descent.

Michael waited till they were safely at the bottom before speaking. "Lara, I never meant to hurt you."

"It was a long time ago." She didn't look over at him. Didn't dare. It was hard enough to keep her tone neutral. "I'm sorry I brought it up. I shouldn't have."

A tense minute passed.

"Forgive me," he begged her softly.

"There's nothing to forgive." She smiled over at him this time, then redirected her attention to the road ahead. "What we have to concentrate on now is getting you exonerated."

He nodded. "And finding the real killer."

CHAPTER SIX

"THIS IS SALLY." Michael placed his hand on the shoulder of his twelve-year-old daughter. They were standing on the back porch of the house. Sheila had picked the girls up at gate five, where the school bus dropped them off.

Sally closely resembled the pictures of her mother that Lara had seen in the house. She was at an awkward age, her features in transition, her poise uncertain.

"I'm pleased to meet you, Sally." They shook hands. The girl mumbled a greeting while avoiding eye contact.

"Are you the lady who got my daddy out of jail?" Kristin, Sally's younger sister, had her father's strong jaw with a slight dimple in the chin. If Lara's guess was right, she would be a stunning beauty in a few years.

"Yes, I am."

"I don't want my daddy to go to jail anymore," announced Beth Ann, the eight-year-old standing beside her.

"I'll do my best to make sure he doesn't," Lara pledged.

All three girls had their parents' dark hair and blue eyes, yet each was unique. Lara sensed a trio of distinct personalities. They were fortunate to have one another. Lara's mother had had a second daughter about a year after Lara was born, but the baby died a few months later. Lara often wondered what it would have been like to have a sister, someone to talk to, a companion who understood her world.

Only once had she heard her father stand up to his mother. Grandmother Gorley had made a cutting remark that Lara had not understood about Dorothy losing the baby. Herbert had become red-faced and told his mother never to mention the subject again. As far as Lara was aware, the old woman never had. He should have learned from the experience that he could stand up to the tyrant and win. On the other hand, Lara had no idea what that bit of defiance might have cost him.

A diesel truck rumbled to a halt behind the Suburban Sheila had used to pick up the girls. A teenage boy jumped out of the passenger side and slammed the door behind him. The driver waved to Michael, backed up and left. Lara recognized without being told, that the dark-haired adolescent was Michael's son. He had the same rangy build and loose-limbed carriage Michael had had years earlier. He also shared his father's strong features and good looks, though they hadn't yet taken on the ruggedness of maturity.

"Dave," Michael called out, his pitch hopeful but guarded. "I want you to meet Mrs. Stovall. She's my lawyer."

Dave showed no great interest in meeting her. "Hi," he murmured.

Taking the initiative, Lara stepped forward and extended her hand. When the boy accepted it, she tightened her grip. Involuntarily, he did the same. "I'm glad to meet you," she said. "Your dad tells me you're quite a soccer player."

He scrunched up his mouth in an attempt at nonchalant indifference, but Lara could see he was pleased with the recognition. "Yeah."

"I'd like to see you play sometime."

"Sure. I've got homework to do." He started past her, then whipped around, his face dark with anger. "He didn't kill my mother."

"I'm going to do my best to prove it," Lara countered gently.

"It's crazy to think he would hurt my mom." The boy seemed suddenly on the point of tears.

"I'm sorry I never met your mother. She must have been a wonderful person."

Beth Ann clung to her grandmother and began to sniffle. Sally and Kristin held each other's hands and were glassy-eyed.

Michael reached out and grasped the boy's shoulder. Dave seemed to draw strength from the touch. For a second, he lowered his gaze, then he ran into the house. His father followed him with his eyes, his own expression one of bereavement.

"Come on, girls," Sheila said quietly. "Let's see what we can find." At Michael's arched brow she explained, "I told the girls they could go through their mother's costume jewelry and pick out what they want to keep."

"Oh, that ought to be fun." Lara tried to lighten the moment, to be positive. The task of disposing of the belongings of her grandmother, parents and husband had fallen to her exclusively; it had been far from fun.

Elva appeared in the kitchen doorway. "We eat in an hour."

"I'd better be on my way," Lara announced.

"You stay for supper," the housekeeper declared. It came across as a command, rather than a gracious invitation.

"Thanks, but I've spent too much time away from the office already. There'll be a stack of things waiting for me—"

"You have to eat."

"Do stay, please," Sheila seconded.

Lara gazed at Michael. While he didn't specifically ask her to hang around, the request was clearly expressed in his eyes. She should leave, she told herself. Getting close to Michael once had been a mistake. Getting close to him again, especially now, under these circumstances, would be a bigger one.

"An hour?" Which meant she wouldn't get home for another three hours.

Elva smiled. "You can help me fix the salad."

"I FIGURED YEARS AGO you and Michael were serious about each other." Elva took a head of iceberg lettuce out of the refrigerator and set it on the wood-block island counter, then returned to retrieve carrots, tomatoes, celery and a red onion.

"We were very young," Lara replied casually.

"And he didn't see the look in your eyes."

The comment stunned Lara. This woman had noticed what nobody else seemed to have. Or had Lara been more transparent than she realized?

"It was many years ago."

"And he met Clare."

Lara felt strangely uncomfortable. This woman was

uncannily insightful and clearly had a long memory. "Were they happy?"

Elva nodded solemnly. "Yes, they really cared about each other and their children. It isn't the same around here without her."

Lara peeled off the crinkly outer skin of the onion. "Tell me what you remember about the day it happened."

Elva scraped a carrot. "It was an ordinary Saturday." She removed a large wooden bowl from an overhead cabinet. "Michael did his chores. The kids slept in. Clare took care of her grandmother, then went to her studio."

"Studio? What studio?"

Elva looked up. "Didn't Michael tell you? Clare used to be a graphic artist. She quit when the kids came along, but last year, with all of them in school, she took it up again. Everyone was after her to do designs for T-shirts or posters for their clubs and organizations."

"Sounds like she was good. I'd like to see some of her work."

Pride blossomed on the woman's face. She led Lara through the laundry room to a small sunlit area that had probably been intended as a sewing room. Art supplies were neatly aligned on shelves. An easel stood empty near the windows. Posters of various subjects and sizes were tacked on the walls amid several framed and unframed paintings.

Lara didn't consider herself an expert in art or even very discriminating in her tastes, but she knew what she liked, and she liked what she saw. The style was straightforward, uncluttered, yet there was a richness and warmth about it that was very appealing. She stared at a watercolor. The edge of a mountain wood-land. Sun-sparkled green, brown, golden tan. Violet, pink and yellow forest wildflowers bloomed in counterpoint to the blue sky. Lara found herself drawn into the picture. She could feel the cool damp air, smell the pungent scent of moldy earth and wild mint.

Was this where Clare had grown up with her grandparents in Washington State, a world of ever-changing beauty? The world she'd given up for the harsh semidesert of West Texas in order to be with the man she loved?

Suddenly, Lara felt she understood and liked this woman. They could have been friends. Sadness welled up in her at the loss. This woman who had so much to give was gone, dead, murdered.

They returned to the kitchen. Elva removed blue-checkered place mats from a sideboard. They wouldn't be eating this meal in the dining room but here at the table near the bay window.

"Michael said Clare was changing her mind," Lara commented, "about putting Brigitte in a nursing home."

"The incident with Dave made her realize things couldn't go on the way they were."

Lara wrinkled her brow. "What incident?"

With a snap, Elva slammed the stem end of the lettuce head on the counter and silently removed the core.

"Elva," Lara implored sympathetically, "I'll find out. I'd rather hear it from you than depend exclusively on other people's versions. You'll be helping Michael by telling me."

The older woman pursed her lips and seemed to weigh Lara's words. Taking a breath, she handed Lara a sharp knife to use on the onion. "Dave was picked up at school—" she snagged a jar of black olives from the pantry "—for smoking marijuana."

Lara was disappointed but not shocked. This was a serious crack in the image of the perfect family, but not fatal.

"When was this?"

"Last semester, just before Thanksgiving."

Two months before his mother died, Lara calculated. "What exactly happened?"

"Davy claimed it was the first time he'd ever tried it. Said it was just an experiment."

"Was it?"

Elva tore lettuce leaves into bite-size pieces and dropped them into the bowl. "He doesn't lie."

Lara could have told her people lied all the time, intentionally, defensively, occasionally because they were fooling themselves about the truth, sometimes by simply omitting things.

"'Actions have consequences,' Michael told the boy, then he grounded him for a month."

Lara's mind raced back in time. How often had she been put on restriction at the insistence of her grandmother for infractions that were far less serious than smoking pot? She'd never fought back; she'd been brought up to be a dutiful daughter. But she remembered her resentment. Had Dave gone further? Had he actually done something to get back at his father? Like mess with his car? The notion sent a lick of dread down Lara's spine.

Dave was fourteen, an age when kids began to assert themselves, when they searched for identities and begged for recognition. Lara had defended enough delinquent boys to appreciate adolescent urges to prove their manhood. The drive for independence often led them astray, sometimes with tragic results.

As horrible as the idea was, Lara had to consider the possibility that Dave might have sabotaged his father's car. Not necessarily with the intent of doing serious harm. He might have had enough confidence in his dad's driving skill to expect him to recover from the situation as soon as he realized the brakes weren't functioning properly. On the other hand, wouldn't the kid more likely have done it when he was on restriction, than wait until a month after he'd served his sentence?

Elva twisted off the jar lid and scooped the shiny black pitted olives onto the chopping block. ''Michael and Clare were upset with him and with each other.''

Lara cut the sweet red onion into thin slices, saying nothing, sensing the other woman would elaborate on her own.

Elva clicked her tongue. ''He accused Clare of spending so much time with her grandma that she wasn't paying enough attention to what the kids were doing.''

''Was it true?''

''She was doing her best. It wasn't all her fault. Michael wasn't around a whole lot, either, and Clare didn't hesitate to remind him that a boy needs a father, too.''

Elva lifted the lid from a cauldron simmering on the back of the stove. The spicy aroma of Mexican vegetable soup filled the room. She picked up a wooden spoon and stirred it gently.

''Mommy and Daddy had a big fight,'' Beth Ann blurted out. She'd entered the kitchen without either woman hearing her.

Startled, Elva spun around, nearly dropping the pot lid. "I thought you were upstairs with Grandma Sheila."

"She sent me to get the utility scissors."

Clearly shaken by the interruption, Elva covered the simmering soup, went to a drawer at the end of the counter near the wall telephone and rummaged inside.

"Your mommy and daddy had a big fight, huh?" Lara asked the child casually, as she continued to slice the onion. "What was it about?"

"They're here somewheres," Elva said too loudly, angrily.

"My brother." Beth Ann screwed up her face. "'Cause he smoked pot, and they didn't like it, and he got grounded for a whole month." She was breathless. "Boy, was he mad."

Elva shoved the drawer shut with a bang, brought over a large pair of shears and offered them to the child. "Be sure to carry them with the point forward and take them directly to your grandma."

The girl accepted them carefully. "Can I have a root beer?"

Elva picked up a celery stalk and took it to the sink to wash. "It's too close to supper."

"Oh, poo," the girl replied, but she didn't debate the decision.

"Did your mommy and daddy argue very often?" Lara asked, ignoring the sharp look from Elva.

"Not like that," Beth Ann told her. "They were yelling at each other. I stayed in the other room 'cause it made me scared, but my friend Kim, she said her parents yell at each other all the time. Then Daddy left. He slammed the door and made the windows rattle. When Kim and me came out into the kitchen to get a drink, Mr. Hood was holding Mama in his arms, like Daddy does.''

''Take the scissors to your grandma,'' Elva insisted as she ushered the girl to the door leading to the hallway. ''And don't run on the stairs.'' She waited until the child was gone before whirling on Lara. ''Those children have gone through enough without you prying like that, setting them against their parents. It isn't right. You ought to be ashamed.''

Lara wasn't surprised by the woman's protectiveness or offended by her tone. Still, the accusation stung. Elva Hernandez was obviously more to this family than a housekeeper.

''I don't like having to ask those questions, but I'm not ashamed of doing it. My intent is not to hurt,'' Lara assured her. ''Other people will be asking the same things. I have to know what they know.''

Elva huffed, only slightly mollified. Lara also glimpsed uncertainty. ''It wasn't important.'' She checked the pot of soup once again, giving it a quick stir. ''It didn't mean nothing.''

''So it did happen,'' Lara prodded gently, as she crosscut the onion slices.

''Clare was just upset. Michael never yells, but he did that day. I could hear them from the laundry room. He was mad as a hornet because of what Dave did, and he was taking it out on her.'' Giving in to building emotion, Elva sank onto the upholstered bench under the bay window, turned away from Lara and gazed out at the wooded hillside.

''I never seen him make her cry,'' she went on in a low quaver. ''She was being run ragged by her grandma. Then Dave gets himself in trouble. It wasn't fair of him to say it was her fault, that she was failing as a mother, not minding the kids like she ought.'' Her round shoulders slumped even more. "He knew he was wrong, too. Apologized later for it. Even had flowers delivered to her. Never seen him do that before, either.''

Definitely the actions of a man with a guilty conscience, Lara mused. "But Webster Hood did hold her in his arms," she reiterated. "Beth Ann and her friend witnessed it.''

"Hood just happened to be there. A second later, Clare pulled away. It didn't mean nothing, I tell you.'' Anger and a note of fear peppered the housekeeper's words.

"I'm sure it didn't," Lara agreed in conciliation. She also wished it had never happened. Another complication to contend with. "But now that I'm aware of it, I'll be prepared in case the subject comes up. We lawyers don't like to be surprised.''

Elva snorted.

Lara continued preparing the salad, her mind preoccupied. Men and women generally reacted differently to infidelity, the suspicion or the appearance of it. Women tended toward self-reproach when their husbands strayed, castigating themselves for real or imagined flaws and inadequacies. Isn't that how she'd reacted when she discovered Clay's philandering? Men, on the other hand, projected their hurt and humiliation, blaming their wives or the other man. Women retreated; men became aggressive.

Lara had to ask herself if Michael knew about this incident, and if he did, what face he put on it. Did he agree with Elva that it meant nothing? Or was his male pride wounded to the point where he'd become capable of violence? The only way to find out was to question him about it. That was precisely what she planned to do.

DINNER WAS UPBEAT. Sheila had allowed the girls to wear some of the pieces of jewelry they'd elected to keep. The incongruous combinations of brooches, necklaces and bracelets hit Michael squarely between the eyes, reminding him of Clare as they did. He caught Lara's appraising glance, then quickly put on an approving smile for his daughters. The girls glowed, especially since their grandmother had also let them put on lipstick and a touch of blush. Dave started to make a disparaging remark, but Michael interrupted him to tell his sisters how pretty they looked. The boy got the message and added his own endorsement. "Cool."

"How did school go today?" Michael asked his son. So far he hadn't heard of any ugly incidents, but that didn't mean there hadn't been any. It wasn't human nature to share humiliation or ostracism by peers.

"Drum is a jerk," Sally commented.

"In general or particular?" her father inquired, hiding his anxiety behind a spoonful of soup.

"Drummond Whittaker is in Dave's eighth-grade class," Sheila explained to Lara. "Sally's in six. They're in the same middle school."

"Don't keep me in suspense," Michael prompted his daughter. "What happened today?"

"It was no big deal," Dave interjected carelessly.

Sally screwed up her mouth. "For you, maybe." She looked at Lara, sitting across from her. "He followed me to the soda machine at lunchtime and tried to take the change when I got my drink. Davy stopped him.''

"My name is Dave," he reminded her.

"What did you do?" Michael was concerned he might have gotten into a fight.

Dave shrugged. "Just told him to buzz off, and if I ever caught him bothering my sister again I'd beat the crap out of him."

Michael was caught on the horns of a dilemma. He wanted his son to defend his sisters, but he couldn't approve of initiating violence.

Lara caught his eye and sucked in her cheeks. "Did it work?"

Dave said with a disparaging lift of one shoulder, "He's a bully. All you have to do is stand up to him and he backs down. I told Sally that's what she has to do."

The girl lowered her head. "Easy for you to say," she muttered.

"Dave is right. Bullies count on other people not opposing them," Lara agreed. "Still, you're very lucky, Sally, to have a big brother to stand up for you. I always wished I had a big brother when I was growing up."

"Do you have any brothers or sisters?" Kristin asked.

"Nope. Just me."

"And friends." Michael watched her. She put on a neutral front, but after their conversation on the mountain, he knew she wasn't nearly as calm inside. He'd been her friend, and he'd disappointed her. "Mrs. Stovall is right. We have to stand up for ourselves, but sometimes we need other people to help us."

"Like her defending you in court?" Sally queried, more enthusiastically.

He smiled at Lara. "Exactly."

"Drum says you're hiding behind a woman's skirts," Sally observed, eyes again averted, but clearly waiting to see what the reaction would be.

Lara's eyes twinkled as she raised one brow in curiosity.

"You're right, Sally," Michael replied with a chuckle. "Drum is a jerk."

"How did you feel when Dave defended you, Sally?" Lara asked.

After a glance at her brother sitting beside her, she concentrated again on her food. "Pretty good, I guess," she admitted reluctantly.

Dave stuffed a piece of buttered corn bread in his mouth, pretending he was ignoring her, but his chest expanded just a little.

Lara grinned. "I'm glad you were there to help your sister, Dave. That was a nice thing to do."

His face darkened with embarrassment. "I didn't do anything," he said modestly, but it was easy to see he was pleased by the compliment.

"I think you made some friends over supper," Michael told Lara later when they were outside, standing by her car. He clasped her forearms and leaned forward, gently kissed her on the cheek. The lingering scent of perfume on her skin caught his breath, and he quickly retreated. "Thanks for hanging around. The kids enjoyed meeting you."

"You have a wonderful family, Michael," she said. "You can be very proud of them."

His pulse accelerating, he held the car door for her, watched her slip her long legs beneath the wheel and closed the door. Then he stepped back. "Drive carefully," he said, and lingered as the car pulled away and receded into the twilight.

A FAMILIAR ACHE SETTLED in Lara's stomach as she began her trip back to town. She hadn't had many close friends since leaving Coyote Springs. Her dearest confidante had been her roommate in college. She and Lindsey still talked on the phone every few months, but Lin was married now with three kids, a dog and two cats. She seemed to spend most of her waking hours running between her sons' soccer games and her daughter's dance classes, when she wasn't doing freelance interior decorating. The comfort level they'd shared with each other in school was still there, but they were worlds apart now in points of reference and interests.

She'd met a few men since Clay's death, men who seemed sincerely interested in her and who probably would have made decent husbands, but she hadn't let them get close enough to find out. She'd misjudged once. All it had brought her was pain.

Reaching the paved road into town, she shifted her thoughts. News of a nearly violent argument between Michael and Clare bothered her. From the sound of it, their marriage had indeed hit a rough spot. The D.A. would capitalize on it as a motive for Michael to get rid of his wife.

Elva had been adamant that Webster Hood's embrace hadn't meant anything. Since everything Lara had heard indicated Clare was a good wife and mother, she was inclined to believe it. That didn't mean, however, that Hood had seen it the same way. What kind of a reputation did he have? She didn't even know if he was married. She'd check him out. What she was sure of was that wedding bands and marriage vows weren't enough to keep a man faithful.

Michael claimed to have been the real target of the sabotage of the MG. Who had a motive to kill him? Who gained by his death?

What about Webster Hood? If he calculated he had a chance with Clare, that might give him a reason to get rid of her husband. He'd been to the First house that morning. Had he had enough time by himself to sabotage the car? As far as Lara could tell, there had been no witnesses to the actual meeting between Hood and Clare on the day of her death, and there didn't seem to be any way to find out if he'd remained in her sight during the entire visit.

Lara swiped a loose strand of hair from her face as another question presented itself. Had the aftermath of the argument between Michael and Clare been the first time there'd been physical contact between her and Hood? Had Clare's separating herself from him been completely spontaneous and voluntary, or had it been a guilty, knee-jerk reaction to her daughter's catching her in the general manager's arms?

CHAPTER SEVEN

THE MEETING Lara had scheduled with Michael for the next morning was predictable. She had one like it with virtually every client at some point in their association. Michael's was coming relatively early in the process, which was good. Fewer past mistakes to correct. Still, she wasn't looking forward to it.

He arrived at nine o'clock sharp. A good sign. She liked punctuality. Carol showed him in and closed the door.

Lara remained seated at her desk. She didn't greet him as he stood before her, holding his Stetson at his waist like a nervous suitor. "Sit down, Michael."

Her businesslike manner set the tone and had his attention. He looked at her warily. "What's up? Has something happened?"

She waited until he was perched across from her. Using a mildly accusatory tone, she said, "You didn't tell me your son was picked up for smoking pot at school."

Michael stared at her, then crossed one leg over the other and balanced his hat on his knee. "I didn't think it was important."

"You didn't tell me you had a violent argument with your wife over it, either."

The vein in his neck pulsed. "It wasn't a violent

argument. It was a heated discussion. And it was none of your business.''

''Wrong.''

Their eyes locked. Silence boiled for a full minute.

''Let me explain something to you, Michael. You are accused of murdering your wife by coldly, callously and calculatingly sabotaging your car so that she would meet a brutal death. Your enemies have very convincing circumstantial evidence to prove it. What they don't have is a clear and compelling motive. They're going to work damn hard to find one.''

His face had gone from dark with anger to almost pale with fear as she reiterated the situation against him. She noted that his hands shook when he moved them to keep his cowboy hat from falling to the floor, and his breathing had slowed and deepened.

''If you want me to represent you effectively you're going to have to tell me everything that could even remotely impinge on your defense.''

''I—''

''No excuses,'' she continued, not giving him a chance to justify himself. ''For the record, let me make something perfectly clear. I have absolutely no personal interest in your private life. I don't give a damn about what kind of scrapes your children get into, or what you and your wife argued about. But as your attorney, I need to know everything, the good, bad and embarrassing. If you're willing to be completely honest with me and let me decide what's relevant and what's not, I promise you my total and unstinting support. If you're not…you better find yourself another lawyer.''

He glared at her, stunned, for what seemed an eternity, his eyes measuring her. Suddenly, his gaze seemed to turn inward. He expanded his chest, held it and slowed deflated it.

"Dave only did it once, as an experiment," he said defensively.

She admired his wanting to protect his children. Not all parents did. "It doesn't make any difference. It happened," she stated. "And as a result, you and Clare had a bitter fight."

He worked his jaw. "How do you know all this?"

"Because Elva and Beth Ann overheard the two of you." She ignored his scowl of disapproval. "Did you know that after you left, Webster Hood appeared at your back door and gave Clare his shoulder to cry on?"

This time the hat did fall to the floor. He made no attempt to retrieve it. Shaken badly, he only stared across the desk at her. "What the hell are you talking about?"

She had to sympathize with him. The fear, the outrage, the pain were clearly readable in his blue eyes.

"Elva overheard your argument from the laundry room. Beth Ann and her playmate, Kim, from the dining room. They all went into the kitchen a minute after you left and found Clare in Hood's arms."

He jumped to his feet. "I don't believe it." He shook his head. "She would never—"

"There are three witnesses. None of them had any reason to lie. And before you get upset with them for tattling, remember my job is to get information out of people. I'm pretty good at it, too."

He finally bent down, picked up his hat and resumed his seat.

"So is the D.A.," she added. "If this had been witnessed only by Elva and your youngest daughter, we could probably keep it under wraps, but Kim saw it, and we have to assume she told others. Which means the prosecutor's office will find out, as well. Now do you understand why you have to tell me everything?''

He nodded, his jaw set. He didn't say a word.

"What else happened that I need to know?"

"Nothing." But the word lacked conviction. "I can't think of anything."

"What florist did you have send Clare the flowers?"

He raised his eyebrows, again surprised by the completeness of her knowledge. "Springtime, on Travis Boulevard."

"I'll check it out."

"You don't believe me?"

"I believe you, Michael, but my word isn't going to convince anyone any more than yours will. I'll need the florist's record of purchase and date of delivery to substantiate it."

He twirled his hat, straightened the band. She waited. "You asked the other day who might have hated me enough to try to kill me." He took a deep breath. "I don't like to think that anyone does."

"But," she said, sensing this was a preamble.

"I told you I fired a ranch hand. There was an incident about a week or ten days before Clare was killed."

Lara rested back in her chair. "What kind of an incident?"

"His name was Wayne Fischer. I hired him as a day worker, a drover, last October for our fall roundup. He seemed like a good man at the time. He rode well and knew his way around livestock. Turned out to be a loser. Drank a lot, and he was careless. He left a gate open. Several cattle got out and delayed things. I almost fired him on the spot. Should have, but we were shorthanded, and like I say, he knew livestock, so I gave him a second chance. A couple of weeks later, he left another gate open. This time some of our prize young horses got out. Took us hours to round them up. One of them had broken a leg." He shook his head in disgust. "The colt had to be put down. I confronted Fischer that evening at the bunkhouse. He took a swing at me, and I coldcocked the SOB." Michael stroked his chin. "Turned out I'd broken his jaw. He had to have it wired. I heard later he swore he was going to get even with me."

"Did you believe it?" Lara asked, buoyed by the possibility that this could be their man.

"I looked over my shoulder a few times, but then I heard he left town."

"Was he capable of this sort of violence?"

"I think if you check his rap sheet, you'll find he spent a fair amount of time as a guest of the county for drunk and disorderly."

"Would he know how to sabotage the MG?"

"I'm sure he would."

"Could he have gotten onto the ranch without anyone noticing him?" Lara asked.

"We change access codes whenever anyone leaves, but it would have been easy enough for him to obtain the new numbers from one of the other hands. All he had to say was he left some things in the bunkhouse and wanted to go back for them."

"Why didn't you mention this earlier?"

"Frankly, I forgot about him. He was a hothead.

When he didn't retaliate right away, I figured the crisis had passed. Then I heard he left town, so—''

"Okay," Lara conceded with a nod. "That's a lead with promise." She rose from her chair and came around the side of the desk.

He got up, clutching his hat and walked with her to the door.

"Keep searching your memory for any other episode or fact that might even remotely impact on your defense," she said, as she let him out.

LATER THAT MORNING, Lara was sitting at the conference table in her office, drinking coffee with her partner.

"You just missed the grand jury." Spooner bit into a raised chocolate donut, holding a paper napkin carefully under his chin to prevent crumbs from spilling onto his gray pin-striped trousers.

In some heavily populated counties, like Dallas, grand juries met every day. In others, Spring County among them, monthly or bimonthly sessions were adequate.

"That's not completely bad." She'd had a bear claw earlier, and one was definitely her limit. "It gives us almost two months to come up with exculpatory information." She sipped her black coffee. "I need to hire a private investigator. Michael and his father recommended Gretchen Tanner. I have an appointment with her in a few minutes. Carol said you've used her."

Spooner nodded assent. "Yep, she's good. Great at tracking down deadbeat dads and other people who don't want to be found. She's aggressive, thorough and professional." He chuckled. "With lots of contacts in high and low places."

"What can you tell me about her background?"

He swallowed the last bite of his pastry, carefully checking his shirt and tie before wiping his fingers on the paper napkin.

"Comes from Southern California, just north of L.A. Arrived in Coyote Springs about two years ago and set up her agency. No criminal record. I checked."

That didn't mean a complaint or two hadn't been lodged against her. P.I.s tended to step on toes and about the only recourse a "victim" had in retaliation was to swear out a complaint for trespassing, breaking and entering and occasionally theft. A lot depended in such cases on the jurisdiction and the attitude of the local prosecutor.

The telephone rang. Carol announced that Gretchen had arrived.

Spooner rose. "Let me know if there's anything I can do." He walked to the door. "Michael First deserves the best."

For a private investigator, Gretchen Tanner was younger than Lara had expected. In her late twenties, blond-haired and athletically built, she impressed Lara as a woman who could take care of herself.

"How big a staff do you have?" Lara asked, after they were seated at the conference table, each holding a diet soft drink.

Gretchen crossed her legs, exposing a small rosebud tattoo above her right ankle. "Officially, I'm a one-woman show, but I have several people who work for me on an as-needed basis, mostly running computer checks. I do the legwork myself."

Not an unusual arrangement. An unbelievable amount of information could be gleaned from the Internet.

"How large a caseload do you have right now?"

"Nothing that would take priority over this." Gretchen paused, a determination coming into her doe-brown eyes. "Clare First and I were volunteers together on several charity drives. We weren't real close, but I spent time with her and saw her interact with people often enough to respect her. From everything I've seen and heard, she was a good wife, a super mom and a generous friend. I want to do whatever I can to find the guy who did this to her."

Lara tilted her soda can toward her mouth but kept her eyes on the younger woman. "You don't think Michael did it, then?" She drank.

Gretchen stuck out her lower lip. "Men are capable of lots of things. I know. I've caught too many of them in the act. But not Michael. He's a sweet guy. You'd only have had to see him and Clare together once to realize they really loved each other."

A sweet guy.

"Oh, there was strain between them from time to time," Gretchen added, "but every marriage has that."

Lara's ears perked up. If Gretchen Tanner, who wasn't a close family friend, was aware of their troubles, how many other people were? "What kind of strain?"

"The problem with their son a few months ago, for one. If the worst thing the kid ever does is smoke a little pot, he'll be all right, but from what I hear, Michael got pretty upset about it. Then there was the issue of Clare's grandmother. The old lady's bats and was driving them crazy.''

''Where'd you hear all this?'' Lara had tried to make her questions sound casual, but the smile in the other woman's eyes said she'd failed.

''It's no secret. I'm keeping company with Brad Lopez, Michael's assistant. Brad's been a sounding board for him a few times.'' She chugged her cola, placed the can on the tabletop and continued to finger it. ''Brad got divorced last year—I don't play around with married men—and Michael was there for him. As far as Brad's concerned, the guy walks on water.''

Except he's got a big mouth, Lara noted. She'd have to tell Michael to be careful who he confided in. ''What would you do if you uncovered evidence that proved or strongly suggested Michael really had killed his wife?''

''I'd pass it on to you and hope I was wrong,'' Gretchen said without hesitation. ''I realize he's ultimately paying my bill, but when it comes to murder, especially of a woman who didn't deserve to die, my allegiance is to justice. I don't believe he did it, but I can go into this with an open mind. As far as I'm concerned, you're hiring me to help find Clare's murderer, not to protect her husband.''

''And if your friend Brad turned out to be the bad guy?''

Gretchen laughed. ''Brad and I make a good team. Someday, well...we might make it official, but believe me, I'm not interested in sleeping with a murderer or a murder accomplice. There are too many other members of the male species out there to choose from.''

Lara chuckled. She liked Gretchen, liked her levelheaded attitudes and commitment. She gave her a list of discharged ranch workers to locate. "There's one in particular. Wayne Fischer."

Gretchen made a face. "I remember him. A class-A loser."

"That's what Michael said."

"If he's still breathing, I'll find him," she vowed.

"Also, here's a list of family members and local people I'd like you to check for alibis. If you need more help, say so. I can get you whatever additional resources you require." For a change, money was no object, not when the accused had a billionaire brother-in-law.

MICHAEL WISHED it hadn't taken so long for him to find out Webster Hood had been to his house the day Clare had been killed. But now that he did know, he was determined to pursue it.

Hood had come to the funeral and cemetery and then stopped by the house later for the traditional postinterment get-together. He hadn't stayed long, just grabbed a sandwich and a beer, offered his condolences to various family members and departed. It had been enough of an opportunity for him to mention his visit with Clare that morning, if he'd wanted to. Michael wondered why he hadn't.

He drove to Hood's Hideaway, as everyone was beginning to call it. The shiny maroon pickup parked by the front door indicated the "boss" was in. Michael mounted the steps, tapped on the door frame, opened the screen and walked in. Hood sat at his desk, reading papers. Probably another lease agreement, Michael speculated unhappily.

Hood dropped the sheet he was holding and leaned

back in his well-padded chair. "Hello, Michael. What can I do for you?"

Michael sat across from him. "I'm trying to reconstruct Clare's last day, her final hours. I understand you came by the house that morning. You never mentioned it."

Hood picked up his glass of amber liquid and twirled it, making the ice tinkle. "I figured you knew."

Michael shook his head. "What for?"

"To see you."

The guy was obviously intent on making him dig out every morsel of information. Michael wondered if it was just an automatic game for him or if he had something to hide. "What about?"

"I guess Clare didn't get a chance to tell you. I stopped by to let you know I was taking a steer to slaughter and contributing the meat to the food bank."

Michael removed his cowboy hat and set it on his knee. "We gave a head of beef to the food bank just before Thanksgiving, like we do every year. What was the occasion for this out-of-cycle donation?"

"They had a drive going on. Reckoned it was good public relations."

The food bank was always having drives. There was more to this than charity.

"Does that mean we'll be giving a head every quarter? I'm sure they'll appreciate it."

"Haven't decided." Hood sipped the liquor in his glass.

"We had a staff meeting the afternoon before," Michael reminded him. "Why didn't you tell me then?"

He shrugged. "Slipped my mind."

More likely a game of one-upmanship, Michael conjectured. As the livestock manager, he should have selected the steer and taken it in to market. This was another of Hood's ways of reminding him who was in charge.

"How long were you there?"

Hood regarded him with a guarded expression. "About as long as it takes to say 'Howdy, I wanted to let Michael know I'm taking a steer into slaughter for the food bank.'"

"Was Clare with you the whole time you were there?"

Hood's lips twitched, as if he was aware of the suspicions lurking in Michael's mind. "No, your housekeeper was the one who greeted me, then she went inside to find the lady of the house. Clare was real nice about me interrupting her work, but I could tell she was in a hurry. She said something about getting a poster finished. So I didn't keep her with a bunch of small talk."

"Did she tell you we were meeting up on Tarnished Mountain?"

"Like I said, she didn't have time for chitchat."

Michael had only Hood's word he hadn't been there more than a minute or two. Not that it would have taken more than that to sabotage the MG. If Hood did it, the question was still why.

"Was that the only reason you stopped by?"

Hood rocked out his chair and ambled to the wet bar across the room. "What are you getting at, First?"

"I understand you were over at the house once before and overheard an argument between Clare and me.'' In spite of his best intentions, anger took over. ''What the hell were you doing around my house, besides eavesdropping?''

Michael had the impression the other man was barely holding back a smirk. ''Actually, I stopped by to talk to you about leasing out our pastures. Wanted your input. But when I heard your raised voice, I decided to hold off. You stormed out the back door in such a huff you didn't see me. She was pretty upset. I let her cry on my shoulder for a minute, then left. Never did give her the message. Decided there was no hurry. It could wait.''

Cry on his shoulder. The bastard had held his wife in his arms. Rage had Michael about to blurt out that if he ever touched his wife again— But he stopped, jolted. Clare was dead. His wife was gone. He pressed his eyes shut.

''Where were you parked? I don't remember seeing your truck.'' His voice was gravelly.

''In front. I walked around the side.''

Michael realized he could easily have walked to the garage and taken off in his truck without seeing anyone parked in front.

He got up and strode out of Hood's Hideaway without saying goodbye.

THREE DAYS WENT BY. As important as Michael's case was, other legal matters also had a claim on Lara's time. Most of them were fairly routine. Cases of theft, use and sale of drugs, DWI and assault. Three-quarters of her clients were guilty, either by admission or by overwhelming evidence. Her obligation toward them involved plea bargaining, including gaining various levels of immunity for further information and minimizing sentences.

She was in the process of drawing up a motion to suppress evidence obtained in an unwarranted police search of a private residence, when her secretary announced Gretchen Tanner's arrival. She'd been calling or dropping by every few days in the week since Lara had hired her.

"Sorry I didn't get here when I said I would." She blew a hank of blond hair out of her face. Her appointment had been for half an hour earlier. "But I had to turn in a rental car. This jerk in front of me—"

"What's wrong with yours?"

"Nothing. I use different rentals when I'm on a case. That way people don't see me coming. It can make for interesting discoveries."

Lara chuckled. "I bet."

Gretchen flung herself into the leather armchair in front of Lara's desk. "Okay, here goes. Wayne Fischer. No luck so far, but my daddy used to say scum always comes to the surface. We'll find him. We have managed to locate a few of the other former employees, though." She handed over the folder she'd carried in. "One's terminally ill in San Antonio. Another's been in Alaska for the past six months. Well—" she pointed to the file "—it's all in there. You also wanted a detailed report on where people were on Friday and Saturday of the weekend Clare was killed. I've been able to account for all the members of the First family."

Lara backed out of the computer file she was working on and swiveled around to face her guest. By force of habit, she picked up a pencil but twirled it between her fingers.

"Essentially, Adam and Sheila First, Michael's father and stepmother, were at the Home Place." Gretchen read from the small notebook she took from her jeans pocket. "Several ranch workers vouch for them. His brother Gideon and his family were in Coyote Springs. His wife's former mother-in-law, Elena Amorado, lives with them and verifies it. So do several neighbors."

Lara flipped through the sheets of meticulously documented details. Names, dates, places, corroborating witnesses all neatly lined up.

"Michael's sister Kerry and her husband were at home in Dallas," Gretchen continued. "Julie Murdock, Michael's other sister, her husband, Rolf, and his four kids were visiting his mother, who lives in a retirement village in Mesquite, on the east side of Dallas. In fact, when Adam called Kerry to pass on the news of Clare's death, they all flew here together in Robeson's Learjet, stopping off on the way to pick up Kerry's son, Brian, at Texas Tech in Lubbock."

One big happy family, Lara mused before she realized how cynical she was becoming. "We can eliminate all of them from the suspect list."

It didn't bring her any closer to finding the killer, but at least she wouldn't have to pit relatives against one another. When that happened, the innocent often suffered more than the guilty.

Lara weighed the information she was given. "What about friends and business associates?"

"Plenty of those," Gretchen commented, and nodded to the folder on the desk. "My staff have already done general background checks on most of them.

Next week I'll start interviewing the ones I haven't caught up with so far. I have to tell you, no one believes he did this. To a person, they swear he's innocent.''

"There are two rules that apply to murder," Lara noted. "Check the people closest to the victim, and follow the money."

"That doesn't seem to be a factor in this case."

"He had a million-dollar insurance policy on his wife, with double indemnity for accidental death," Lara pointed out. "Two million bucks ain't exactly peanuts."

Gretchen chortled. "It could be in this case. When Michael's father gave up the whole enchilada in exchange for the Home Place a few years ago, he reportedly received fifty million in cash."

Lara whistled softly. "A tidy sum."

"The family's loaded. Michael's brother-in-law Craig Robeson is reputed to be a billionaire."

"No black sheep?" Lara asked.

"Not of the murderous sort. Family members get in trouble from time to time, like Kerry getting drunk and selling her share of the ranch, her son getting picked up for DWI and underage drinking. Gideon discovered last year he was a daddy after his former girlfriend was killed in a car accident. And you know about Dave getting picked up for smoking pot. They're not perfect, but they're not bad people." Gretchen's brown eyes sparkled. "You're forgetting the third rule."

Lara angled her head. *"Cherchez la femme?"*

"Look for the woman," Gretchen confirmed. "Webster Hood claims he walked in on Michael a week before Clare was killed and found him in an embrace with Felicity Sanchez. Says they seemed real fond of each other.''

An image flashed before her eyes. Clay in their bed with another woman. Something had drained out of her at that moment. She'd quietly closed the door on him, literally and figuratively. As far as she knew, he never realized she'd found out. She'd kept up the act, the dutiful wife. But the heat of loving had turned to cold ash. She'd kissed him goodbye, sent him off to war and never seen him again.

In the years since, dealing with felons, she'd come to see the dark side of people. She wasn't usually affected by accounts of their flaws, infidelity being among the most common. But hearing this report, she now realized she'd hoped for more from Michael First.

Learning that Clare had cried on the shoulder of the general manager had been bad enough but hardly devastating. At most it besmirched the victim. It didn't give Michael a motive to kill her. If he was really upset about it—assuming, of course, there was more to it than Elva had described—it gave Michael a motive for killing Hood rather than Clare.

To discover Michael himself might have been involved with another woman... Lara closed her eyes, trying to shut out the sense of humiliation and shame she'd felt when she first learned Clay had been cheating on her. To this day she wasn't sure what she would have done if he'd lived, if their baby had lived. Stayed with him for the sake of the child, ignoring his infidelity? Prayed he reform when he became a father?

''Who's Felicity Sanchez?'' In her own ears, Lara's voice sounded as unsteady as her heartbeat.

"The daughter of a vaquero family and one of the best mechanics on the place. I've met her. She's in her early twenties and definitely doesn't look like your typical grease monkey."

Lara's mind was in a scramble. Michael not only involved with a woman, but a young woman who was an expert in mechanics. A person for whom sabotaging a vehicle might be a natural choice. It didn't bode well.

"Has Hood told anyone else about this?" Not that it would make any difference. In high-profile cases, the D.A. was doubly thorough. He'd find out.

"He says he hasn't. Not even Michael," Gretchen told her. "Claims he saw what was happening and left. Didn't want to get involved. As far as he's concerned, what Michael does in his private life is his own business."

"How credible is this guy?"

Gretchen extended her right hand, palm down, and rocked it from side to side. "He's got a reputation with the ladies. Hell, he even came on to me one day when I was waiting for Brad. He's harmless enough, though. Pulled in his horns as soon as Brad showed up. He hasn't hit on me since." She laughed. "The fact that Brad has about four inches in height and fifty pounds in muscle on him might have influenced his decision, of course."

"Did Hood offer any corroboration for what he says he witnessed?" Given the strained relations between the two men, he didn't exactly make a disinterested witness.

"Nope. Says he was by himself and didn't mention it to anyone."

Lara hadn't told Gretchen about his consoling

Clare. "Did you ask Hood how he got along with Clare?"

She nodded. "Says she was a real lady."

"Nothing else?"

Gretchen shook her head. "Should he have?"

Lara shrugged lethargically in response. "How about this Felicity Sanchez? Have you talked to her?"

"Not yet. Was planning to—"

"Leave her to me," Lara said. "I need to go out to the ranch and nose around anyway, talk to people myself, evaluate them firsthand."

CHAPTER EIGHT

"WHAT ARE you suggesting?" Michael's shoulders seemed to broaden as they stiffened.

Lara was sitting behind her desk. It was late the following afternoon. She was tired. She hadn't been sleeping well since this case began.

"You think I was fooling around with Felicity Sanchez?"

"Were you?" Her gaze didn't flinch from his.

"Lara," he drawled, as if praying for patience, "I was not having an affair with Felicity Sanchez or anyone else."

She gripped the pencil between her hands almost to the breaking point. "Why would Webster Hood lie?"

"There isn't much I'd put past that guy." Michael shook his head. "He's been a thorn in my side ever since he got here."

"Why?"

His eyes hardened at her rapid-fire interrogation. "It's no secret that the two of us don't get along," he answered dryly, rose to his feet and paced toward the wall of books. "He was appointed by Nedra Cummings, the bank vice president, as the general manager—"

"And you think you should have been," Lara concluded.

He stopped, spun around, his quizzical expression asking why she was being so hostile again. "I was born and raised on the Number One. It's in my blood. No one, except Dad, knows that ranch more intimately than I do. I got along fine with the last general manager, E. J. Hoffman."

"Because he listened to your advice and took it, right?"

Michael propped himself against the side of the conference table, his large hands resting on its edge, feet crossed at the ankles. "Why are you making this sound like a conspiracy?" His brow furrowed. "If anything, it was a pact between us to do the best thing for the ranch, for everybody concerned."

"What's the problem between you and Hood?" she persisted, trying to ignore the way his jeans and black T-shirt molded themselves to his work-hardened frame. Trying not to acknowledge the treacherous way her body reacted to his presence.

He huffed and moved back to the visitor's chair and plopped into it. "He's shortsighted."

"Give me an example."

Michael worked his jaw. "Last fall, he sold breeding stock. Dad spent thirty years working with Texas A and M, developing our bloodline."

"Was that a bad business decision or merely one you didn't like?"

He shook his head at her apparent obtuseness. "Short-term it's profitable enough, but long-term it hurts us. It's also illegal." At her raised brows, he explained further. "The First family registered our breed. It's also trademarked. When Hood sold the initial lot—without my knowledge, I might add—I got together with Spooner, and he obtained a restraining order prohibiting any further sales.''

"What was Hood's reaction?"

Michael snorted. "What do you think it was? He wasn't a happy camper. Claimed the bank bought the trademark with the ranch. Now the court will have to decide.''

He rested back, balanced one boot on the other knee. "There's another reason he doesn't like me. Right after he got here, he told Brad he wouldn't mind buying a chunk of the Number One if he could talk the bank into selling to him. When Brad mentioned it to me, I went to Hood and explained that in the agreement the bank made with my father, the family has the right of first refusal on any land sale. I let him know we'd outbid him at any price.''

"So Hood has a double reason to think of you as his enemy. You stand in the way of his buying Number One land, and you fight him in matters of ranch management. Is he lying when he says he found Felicity in your arms?"

Michael lowered his head. "No. It's true." He resumed eye contact. "Felicity got engaged to Johnny Alvarez three months ago. They're planning a June wedding. Johnny's an infantryman in the reserves. His unit had just been called up for deployment to central Asia. She's terrified he'll be killed. We were talking about the MG when she broke down and started crying. All I did was try to comfort her."

It sounded weak, clichéd. So weak and so clichéd, in fact, that Lara believed him.

"One more thing," she said. "You're going to have to be more discreet about what you say to whom. You've already seen how the press picks up on things. We don't want this situation tried in the court of public opinion.''

"What are you talking about?"

She could see his nerves were raw, but there wasn't much she could do about that. "I wouldn't impart any confidences to Brad Lopez in the future."

"Brad? What's he done?"

"Gretchen Tanner knows all about your fight with Clare over Dave's pot smoking and that you and Clare were experiencing differences concerning Brigitte. Maybe it was only pillow talk with her, but there's no telling who else he might have mentioned it to. Rumors like this start," she concluded, "and can quickly get out of control."

MICHAEL SPENT the rest of the hot day personally inspecting over sixty miles of fencing that had to be repaired or replaced and submitted the requisitions for the materials and extra hands needed to get the work done. After eating supper with his kids, he climbed once more into his pickup, the vehicle he'd reverted to since Clare's death, and drove to Brad Lopez's place.

Brad lived in one of the newer houses on the sprawling ranch. Built in the early seventies, it was contemporary rather than Spanish in design, ordinary to the point of boring. Brad had stayed there alone after his divorce last year. His ex-wife and kids now lived in Coyote Springs. He brought his son out to the place every other weekend, but the thirteen-year-old seemed more interested these days in football and his friends than horses or cattle.

Michael parked in the rear. The sun was just going down.

Brad leaned against the open kitchen doorway.
"Want a beer?"

"I can be persuaded." Michael sat in one of the
lawn chairs on the patio while his friend ducked inside and retrieved a frosty bottle. "Did the inoculations go all right this morning?" he asked after the
first cool taste. "Sorry to leave you in the lurch like
that."

"All taken care of." Brad parked himself in a
neighboring chair and stretched out his long legs.

Michael shook his head. "Thanks. I really appreciate it."

"How's the investigation going? Any leads? I hear
your lawyer hired Gretchen."

"She tell you that?" Did everybody in this town
have a big mouth? On the other hand, she couldn't
very well go around asking questions without stirring
up speculation.

"Nah. She called me a couple of days ago, wondered if I knew where Wayne Fischer might be.
Wouldn't tell me why, but I figured it was to help
you."

"Do you know?"

Brad rotated the beer bottle. "Nope. Last I heard,
he left town. So are you making any progress?"

Michael paused. "I've got a bone to pick with
you."

"If it's about pasturing other livestock on the Number One, I already told you I'm sorry."

"It's not about that." Though it still stuck in the
craw.

Brad scrunched up his mouth, like a teenager being
faced with another lecture. "What did I do now?"

"You've got a big mouth, Brad. You told Gretchen

about me and Clare and her grandmother. That was man to man. I didn't expect you to blab it all over the place."

Brad bit his lip. "It was only Gretchen. I didn't think I was doing any harm. She wouldn't say anything to anybody else."

"You violated a trust."

"I...I'm sorry. I didn't mean to," he said contritely.

"I expected better of you," Michael went on, feeling a little like he was reprimanding a delinquent kid.

"I said I'm sorry," Brad retorted more harshly. "Anyway, it won't be a problem anymore." He paused, then grinned boyishly. "Selma and me are getting back together again. She's willing to give me another chance."

"Hey, that's great. Congratulations." Michael crooked an eyebrow. "Don't blow it this time."

"We'll try harder. I will. She wants me to go into counseling with her. I'm not exactly excited about it, but Sel thinks it'll help."

"I'm glad for you, Brad." Michael held up his beer in a toast. They clinked bottles and drank. "Have you told Gretchen yet?"

Brad shook his head. "That's going to be the hard part. I hope she don't think I've been leading her on. Damn, that gal's a wildcat in bed." Sheepishly, he averted his gaze and lowered his voice. "I mean I like her...she's even hinted at getting married, but after that expensive divorce and my child support payments, who can afford another wife?" He grinned.

"I'm sure she'll understand." Michael was very much aware he was in no position to give advice to the lovelorn after how he'd treated Lara so many years ago.

He still found it hard to believe he'd been so dense. They'd been going together, more or less steady, for three years. He'd enjoyed her company and should have realized it had become more than just a casual friendship. They'd started kissing in a way that promised more, and he had to admit he'd been entertaining notions of "going all the way." Until he'd met Clare and simply lost his mind. It embarrassed him now to realize how insensitive he'd been toward Lara. He'd patted himself on the back for doing the honorable thing and formally breaking off with her rather than just dumping her without an explanation. When she'd taken it so calmly—or appeared to—he'd jumped to the convenient conclusion that she'd understood.

"Yeah. She's a good kid." Brad got up, went inside and retrieved two more bottles of beer. It took Michael a moment to realize Brad was talking about Gretchen. All he could picture was Lara's face when she told him on the top of Tarnished Mountain that he'd nearly broken her heart. Twenty years ago, and it was still on her mind. No, it hadn't been just a friendship to her. God, he felt like a louse.

Michael put his second beer on the concrete slab next to his chair. He wasn't finished with the first one yet. "Did you see anyone around my place when you came by to get me that Saturday morning?"

Brad didn't have any trouble keeping up with the quick change of subject. "Not a soul."

"What about Hood?"

"At that hour? Are you kidding?" He scoffed. "He doesn't even get up with the chickens in the winter when they sleep late." He looked over at Michael, his face skeptical. "You don't reckon he monkeyed with the MG, do you?"

Michael shook his head laconically, unwilling to admit it was exactly what he suspected. "Doesn't seem like his style."

Brad snickered. "You mean he'd have to get his hands dirty?"

Hood's predecessor had spent his days in the saddle or his pickup, checking things out for himself, pitching in when it was needed to get things done. He was at heart an old cowboy, a man who loved the land and all it stood for. Hood passed most of his time in his plush double-wide, wearing pressed jeans and pearl snap button shirts, sipping whiskey, reading reports and making decisions based on market values, not ranch values.

"Did you know he took a steer to town for the food bank that day?"

Brad indulged in a long slow quaff of beer. "Uh-huh. He gave me the paperwork."

"When was that? He never said anything to me."

"The day before the funeral. He said he didn't want to bother you with it," Brad said uncomfortably. "Drink up. You're behind."

ON WEDNESDAY, April 17, almost four months to the day since Clare First's tragic death, the grand jury of Spring County, Texas, convened at 8:00 a.m. to consider whether there was sufficient credible evidence to indict Michael First for her death. The charge was first-degree murder with special circumstances, which meant the district attorney would be asking for the death penalty.

To Michael's surprise and secret discomfort, life

had begun to settle into a predictable pattern. His shame wasn't that he didn't miss Clare. He did. Terribly. What troubled him was that he was beginning to get used to her absence. He still caught himself turning to tell her things, only to find she wasn't there. He still asked himself how she would handle particular situations, especially about the girls. But he also realized that in his dreams, in his restless, nightly fantasies, her image was getting confused with Lara's. He needed someone to talk to, and Lara was increasingly the woman who came to mind. He looked forward to spending time with her, all the while feeling guilty for wanting to be with her.

"The prosecutor runs the show," she explained, as they sat on the hard wooden bench outside the jury room, waiting for him to be called. Adam and Sheila were there, as well as Gideon and Julie, who'd taken time off from their jobs to lend him moral support.

"The D.A.'s not limited to the same rules of evidence that apply in the trial itself," Lara continued. "His job isn't to prove that you committed the crime, but to show the jurors that the preponderance of the evidence points in that direction. There won't be any cross-examination. You'll be on your own. I won't even be present."

The last statement unsettled him. Her being in his corner had come to mean a lot to him. A minute later, he was called. Hands reached out to reassure him as he moved toward the door.

The courtroom was closed. The judge on the bench said nothing. The twelve jurors listened intently as the prosecutor quizzed him, though they too were allowed to ask questions through the prosecutor.

"On January 19 of this year, you met your wife on

Tarnished Mountain. Is that correct?'' Malvery's voice was intense and commanding.

''Yes,'' Michael responded.

''Who got there first?''

''I did.''

''In your vintage 1952 MG-TD?''

''Yes.''

''How long were you there before your wife arrived?''

''Ten or fifteen minutes.''

''Was anyone else up there at any time besides your wife?''

''No.''

''Did you have any car trouble on the way up the mountain?''

''No.''

''But when your wife drove down the mountain, the brakes failed.''

''That's what I've been told,'' Michael responded.

''Who worked on your car besides you?''

''No one.''

''Whose idea was it to switch cars?''

''Mine.''

''Had your wife ever driven the MG before?''

''No.''

''You'd gone up to Tarnished Mountain to resolve some marital problems, didn't you?''

''We went up there,'' Michael replied, ''to discuss some problems in our family.''

''Two months earlier, you'd had a violent argument with your wife, hadn't you?''

''We had a heated discussion. There was nothing violent about it.''

''You blamed her for your son's delinquency.''

''I blamed myself, as well.''

A few minutes later, Michael was dismissed. Other witnesses were called.

At noon, the clerk of the court came out into the courthouse hallway and handed Lara a piece of paper. Michael and the members of his family gathered around. She opened it, read, and slammed her eyes shut.

Directly behind the clerk two uniformed sheriff's deputies stepped forward. One recited from a card. "'Mr. Michael First, you are under arrest for the murder of Clare First. You have the right to remain silent...'"

The bright lights of cameramen suddenly flooded the area and a cacophony of voices echoed off the marble walls.

"Mr. First," a reporter shouted above several others, "is it true you filed a two-million-dollar insurance claim after your wife's death?"

Lara raised her arms to try to stanch the onslaught. "Mr. First has no comment."

"Is it true your wife was getting ready to divorce you and take half the ranch?" a female demanded, even as Lara was speaking.

"Were you having an affair with another woman?"

"Did you find her with another man? Is that why you killed her?"

Stunned by the vitriol, Michael was grateful when the two deputies flanked him and escorted him through the mob scene. Behind him he could hear Lara still insisting there would be no interviews and no statements.

An hour later, his bail was continued, and he was released.

LARA HAD NO TROUBLE remembering the code Sheila had given her to open gate five or Gretchen's directions to the maintenance barn where Felicity Sanchez worked. Half a dozen tractors of different sizes and vintages were lined up on its far side. A huge combine and several cotton trailers were neatly parked next to them. After halting the Beemer next to a pair of pickups, she entered the cool dimness of the cavernous building and heard the clang of metal striking metal.

A man stood over to her right drinking coffee. In his late thirties or early forties, wearing greasy jeans and an equally smudged blue cotton shirt with the cuffs rolled up at the wrists, he stepped forward. His eyes asked who she was and what was she doing here, but his manner when he spoke was polite. ''Can I help you, ma'am?''

''I'm looking for Felicity Sanchez.''

''And you are?''

''Lara Stovall. I'm Mr. First's attorney.''

He nodded. ''She's over there.'' He pointed to a pair of tan work boots sticking out from under a small pickup. ''Hey, Fel, you have a visitor.''

The legs flexed and a female torso emerged on a castered pallet. The woman glanced up, dropped her hammer and chisel and rose easily to her feet. She was a couple inches shorter than Lara's five-seven, but even in a shapeless jumpsuit, her feminine contours were easily discernible. She had ebony hair tucked under a baseball cap and eyes that were virtually black. Her skin was olive-toned and flawless.

Lara stepped forward, extended her hand and introduced herself. Felicity rubbed her right palm on a coarse red rag she pulled from a hip pocket. Her grip when they shook was firm.

"The coffee isn't great," she said, "but it's hot. Care for a cup?"

"If you're having some."

The woman, almost a girl, pulled off her cap and laughed. "I wouldn't touch it without a taster sampling it first, either. Come on." She ran her fingers through the ponytail she'd set free, the thick shiny hair bobbing above the slender column of her neck.

The two women moved off to a small office in the back of the building, where a large coffee urn sat on a table outside the door. Felicity filled a heavy china mug and handed it to Lara, then poured another for herself.

"Let's go inside," she offered. "We'll have privacy there."

Lara wondered if Michael had called her to coordinate their stories. "When was the last time you spoke to Mr. First?"

"About two weeks ago. Why?"

"He hasn't called you since then?"

Felicity shook her head. "What's this about?"

Lara didn't detect apprehension in the woman's question or manner. Just curiosity. Was she as innocent as she seemed or a very accomplished actress? Would Michael be interested in this young woman? Would he cheat on his wife with her? More significantly, Lara told herself, would a jury of his peers believe that he had?

"What's your relationship with Michael?" she asked bluntly.

The smooth brow wrinkled; the eyes grew wary.

"Relationship? We get along fine, if that's what you mean?"

"As friends?"

"Sure we're friends. I've known him all my life."

"Are you lovers?"

Felicity choked on her coffee, spewing it out. She wiped her chin. "You're kidding, right?" She put her mug on the desk. Her hand was shaking. "You can't be serious. He's almost old enough to be my father. Besides, he's a married man...." She bit her lip for a moment. "Or was." She glanced up again. "And I'm engaged to be married." She stared at her visitor. "I'd laugh, if the suggestion wasn't so insulting to both of us."

Lara touched the other woman's arm reassuringly. "Sorry, but I had to ask."

"Why?" Felicity stared straight into her eyes, no flinching, no hesitation. Just affronted anger.

"Webster Hood claims he saw Michael holding you in his arms."

Confusion drew Felicity's dark brows together. Lara could see her mind working, sorting through memories. The light dawned.

"It wasn't like that," she objected.

"Tell me what happened."

Felicity leaned against the desk. The story she recounted was the same as Michael's. Lara paid close attention to her body language. If the girl was lying, she was damn good at it. Gretchen would have to check to see if she had a history of deception.

Her explanation was plausible, but ever the skeptical lawyer, Lara considered other possibilities. Even if Michael was being honest, Felicity could be more smitten with him than she admitted. Father figure maybe, but he was also a very attractive, very appealing man, and some girls were infatuated by father figures. With her fiancé away, Felicity might be drawn to the rugged security of an older man. Having been a service wife, Lara knew firsthand that spouses and lovers weren't always faithful.

Whether she believed them wasn't important, Lara reminded herself. If he was perceived as having an affair, it furnished the prosecution a motive for him to get rid of his wife. It also gave Felicity a reason for wanting Clare out of the picture. This comely young woman certainly had the expertise to tamper with the sports car's brakes. Could he and Felicity have schemed together to kill Clare?

The notion was ludicrous.

The man she remembered from twenty years earlier was capable of total blindness. He never recognized how much she cared for him. And he might well not have realized Felicity Sanchez was hung up on him, too. In his relations with women Michael had been remarkably straight-arrow, hardly the devious, calculating Casanova. His splitting with her when he met Clare was precisely a case in point. He found somebody else, so he immediately broke off with Lara. He didn't play with both of them, as some of his friends would have.

If Michael had decided he no longer loved Clare, or if he'd wanted someone else, he would have asked for a divorce, not killed her.

Or was that what they'd talked about on Tarnished Mountain? Lara had only his word they were making up, planning a Caribbean cruise to rediscover the magic in their marriage. Had Michael demanded a divorce and Clare refused?

CHAPTER NINE

IT WAS FIVE-THIRTY in the afternoon. Nelson Spooner and Carol had left for the day. Lara was filling in a template for a motion to suppress evidence obtained in a flawed search of a private residence, when she heard someone knocking on the front door of the building. She chose to ignore it. Anyone with an emergency could telephone, and the answering service would contact her. If it wasn't an emergency, whoever it was had no right bothering her after business hours. The knocking stopped.

A minute later, she jumped when she heard tapping on her window. The reflective film prevented anyone from seeing in, but it was still unnerving. Her pulse tripping, she swiveled toward the window, and was stunned to see Michael standing on the other side of the glass. Her heart rate accelerated.

She bolted from her chair and ran out to the reception area. Her fingers fumbled with the dead-bolt lock. Finally, after managing to release it, she swung the door wide. He was standing there, a broad grin lighting up his face below the black Stetson. ''Michael, is…is something wrong?'' But of course he wouldn't be grinning like a satisfied cat if something was wrong.

''We saw your car still in the side parking lot.''

''We?''

"Sally and I. We're on our way to Skoops for a hot fudge sundae and thought you might like to join us."

Lara relaxed—enough, at least, to return his smile. "Skoops, huh?"

Sally came up beside her father. "Will you come?" she asked eagerly. "I signed up for cheer tryouts. Daddy said you used to be a cheerleader and maybe you could give me some pointers." She looked both expectant and anxious.

"Eighty girls have signed up for the preliminary round," Michael said, "for twenty openings. So the competition's strong."

Lara felt an old excitement ripple through her. She'd only been on the cheer squad a year. Her grandmother had made her quit because she didn't consider it dignified. "As long as you don't want me to do any of the jumps," Lara said with a playful grin. "Advice, hmm? Skoops is a pretty hard bribe to turn down." The legendary soda fountain was a landmark. It served the best ice cream in town, the old-fashioned, hand-packed kind. "I think I can squeeze in a few minutes. Let me close up shop, and we'll be on our way."

"Leave your car here," Michael suggested, "and come with us. I'll bring you back later."

"Sounds like a plan."

Within five minutes, she'd set the building security alarm and the three of them were sitting side by side in Michael's pickup.

"Cheerleading is a lot of work," Lara told Sally, who was stuck in the middle. "But it's mostly fun."

"Sally was in gymnastics," Michael informed her.

"She got a silver medal in the Junior Olympics two years ago."

"Wow! Congratulations. You have the coordination and skill to cheer, then."

"Unless she turns into a klutz," Michael offered jovially.

Lara leaned into Sally's ear. "Men can be so dense sometimes. Even when they are lovable dads." She straightened to address Michael. "Beautiful young girls don't turn into klutzes—they become charming old ladies, like me."

"You're not old," Sally objected. "And you're pretty. I wish I had red hair like you."

Michael chortled. "She's just digging for compliments, Sally. She's still beautiful, too, in addition to being charming."

Lara shot him a glance across Sally's head, her brows arched, her tongue in her cheek. He smiled back, giving her a blue-eyed wink. "Your hair is beautiful, Sally. I'll tell you a secret. I always hated having red hair. I would have given anything to have black or brown or even dirty-blond hair."

"Really? But yours is so bright and...fun."

"Thanks," Lara said. "I always felt that I didn't fit in with everyone else."

They'd arrived at the white-tile-front ice cream parlor with its red-and-white, candy-stripe canvas awning. The inside hadn't changed much in the seventy-five years it had been in existence. Wire-frame chairs surrounded small wobbly wire-frame tables. Round pedestal stools permanently fixed to the floor lined the long counter, where a soda jerk with a white paper fore-and-aft cap proudly dispensed "phosphates," ice cream sodas and something called a New York egg cream.

Michael found a corner table. A gum-chewing waitress in a starched yellow-and-tan uniform came to take their orders. Sally requested a hot fudge sundae. Lara asked for the same with nuts. Michael opted for a pecan-butterscotch banana split.

While they waited, Michael put a quarter in the antique jukebox. A scratchy Hank Williams crooned "Your Cheatin' Heart" over the speaker system. Sally quizzed Lara about the routines she used to do.

"They weren't nearly as complicated or sophisticated as the ones you do nowadays, but they were fun."

Their sundaes arrived. Michael gaped at the mountain of ice cream, whipped topping, chopped pecans, butterscotch syrup and the three cherries smothering a huge split banana. "Who am I supposed to share this with—the football team?" He groaned unconvincingly through a broad grin.

They spread their paper napkins on their laps, took a collective deep breath and dug in.

"A few basic pointers," Lara mused, after sampling her first decadent spoonful of vanilla ice cream awash in thick chocolate fudge. "Be sure to smile. No matter how much your face hurts, smile. You want people to be glad to see you."

"We have to wear makeup," Sally said, clearly pleased at the prospect.

"Of course you do." Lara grinned at her conspiratorially. "Use it to emphasize your eyes and put a bit of color in your cheeks, but don't overdo it. You don't want to look like a circus clown having a bad-hair day." She winked as she took another spoonful of the calorie-packed concoction. There was probably enough stored energy in one mouthful to carry her through Christmas, which was only six months away.

"Also, be sure to mingle," she added. "Don't just hang out with the girls you know and form a clique. Mix with the others, make new friends. You're competing, but teamwork is really important in cheerleading. If one girl doesn't know her routine, she makes you all look bad, so help one another out. The judges will be watching. Believe me, they'll know if you're better than the girl you're helping, and they'll give you extra points for sportsmanship."

"Sally's a very good team player," Michael contributed.

The girl's eyelids fluttered at her father's compliment.

Lara took a sip of water to cleanse her palate before loading up on another sugar-laden bite of her sundae. "Maybe most of all, though, is to have fun. Smiling is important, but really enjoying yourself is contagious, and that's what cheering is all about, getting people psyched up about their team, even when things aren't going well. You might be able to pretend for a while, but eventually it'll show if you're not really with it. When do your tryouts start?"

Sally glowed. "Next Monday after school."

"I hope you call me and let me know how you did."

She agreed eagerly, then squirmed. "How come Dad wasn't allowed to have you with him at the grand jury?"

The question took Lara by surprise. She looked over at Michael, who gave her a nod of encouragement.

"A grand jury doesn't try cases, Sally," she explained. "Their sole function is to make sure there's enough reason to formally accuse a person of having committed a crime. The rules that apply during a regular trial aren't the same for a grand jury. For example, they can listen to hearsay evidence that wouldn't be allowed at trial."

"What's hearsay evidence?"

Lara considered a moment. "If your girlfriend tells you one of the kids in school got caught smoking behind the gym during a basketball game, that's hearsay, because you didn't see it yourself." She paused. "Have you ever played the rumor game? You know, someone tells something to a person who relays it to another person who relays it to a third and so on. At the end of the chain, you ask the last person what he or she was told. It's never what the first person said. Rumors and hearsay are pretty much the same. Not very reliable."

"So why can a grand jury listen to them?" Sally licked fudge sauce off her spoon.

"Because they're interested in appearances, not proofs. That's what the trial is for."

"But I still don't understand why you couldn't be with Dad when they asked him questions."

Lara chuckled softly. "Because lawyers argue cases, and the grand jury doesn't want to hear arguments." She set her spoon down on the table and took another sip of water. "Let's use a different example from your dad's case, okay?"

Sally nodded and kept eating, though she had slowed down.

"Suppose at school you see someone close your locker and run away with a loose-leaf binder just like yours. You recognize the person who ran away was Jane Doe. You check inside your locker and find your new loose-leaf binder is missing. So you go to the principal and tell her Jane Doe stole your loose-leaf binder.''

Sally nodded again.

''You've accused Jane Doe of a crime. Is it true that she stole your binder?''

''I saw her,'' Sally declared.

Lara didn't reply to the statement directly. ''The principal calls in Jane Doe and asks her if she was in your locker. She says she found it open and just closed it. The principal then asks her why she ran away, and she says because she was late for class. Is her explanation feasible?''

Sally thought about it a minute. ''I guess so. But she could have stolen the binder, too.''

''Exactly. But until you get more information, Jane stands accused of stealing. That's what a grand jury does. It listens to evidence and says there's enough reason to accuse a person. Now, if Jane denies she was the girl you saw because she was in class at the time, and the teacher verifies it, the accusation against her will be dropped. Otherwise, there's a trial and the jury can listen to all kinds of arguments. But the grand jury isn't interested in arguments, only facts or the appearance of facts. Does this makes sense?''

Sally agreed that it did, but that only served to open the floodgates for more questions. They sat there for nearly an hour and a half talking about the law and the procedures used to protect people's rights.

''The key, Sally, is to always look at a situation as if the accused person didn't do it. How would you want to be treated under those circumstances? That's why we say a person is innocent until proven guilty.''

Michael smiled with genuine pride at his daughter. Lara remembered something she'd seen in the paper. ''Isn't Bring Your Daughter to Work Day coming up soon?''

''Week after next,'' Michael said with a quirk of his brow.

''If it's all right with your dad, Sally, maybe you could spend the day with me at the office.'' She reached across the metal-rimmed round wooden table and touched the girl's hand. ''I know you're not my daughter, and if you'd rather spend the time with your dad, I understand, but if you'd like to see what a lawyer does and come to the courthouse and observe, I'd be glad to have you.''

Sally's eyes went wide. ''Really?'' She gazed up at her father. ''Can I, Dad, please?''

''I don't know…'' he temporized, ''I was fixing to show you how we muck out stalls and dip sheep for parasites.''

''Da-ad,'' she complained.

He laughed, unable to keep up the act. ''I think it's a great idea. Just promise me you won't torment Mrs. Stovall with too many questions.''

''If you're going to be my partner for a day, I think you should call me Lara.'' She looked at Michael. ''Is that okay, Daddy?''

He smiled and nodded.

''And ask as many questions as you like, Sally. That's how you learn. If you decide you like it, maybe you can spend some time with me during the summer after school's out.''

''Oh, wow!''

"You might get bored, of course—"

"I won't," the girl responded happily.

"Now that that's settled," Michael said gleefully, "are you girls ready for dessert?" He pushed away his empty dish.

Lara groaned.

"You go ahead, Dad," Sally chirped. "We'll just watch."

Lara snickered. "Gotcha, big guy."

"On second thought, maybe we ought to get out of here and let other people make gluttons of themselves."

Laughing, they left the ice cream shop and climbed back into the truck.

MICHAEL PULLED UP in front of Lara's office.

"Sally, why don't you stay here, while I go inside with Lara. I'll just be a minute."

Her head bobbed to a rock tune on the radio. "Okay, Daddy."

"You don't have to do that," Lara insisted.

"My pleasure." He followed her up the walk, stood by her side while she poked in the security access code and unlocked the glass door.

"I can't thank you enough for what you're doing," he said. They entered the darkened building. "If she becomes a problem—"

"She won't," Lara assured him. "We're going to be fine."

Her ability to handle the legal aspects of his case no longer surprised him, but her aptitude for connecting so easily with his preadolescent daughter did. Had Lara always had a maternal instinct? He thought about the miscarriage after losing her husband. What agony she must have endured when she learned she'd never be able to have children. Had she had anyone to talk to, a friend to commiserate with her, or had she been forced to suffer alone, in silence?

She flipped a light switch and proceeded to her office door. Impulsively, he grasped her forearm and turned her to face him. "Thanks for helping." Before he realized what he was doing, he rested his hands on her hips. Leaning forward slowly, he brought his mouth down to hers. The kiss was gentle, a sweet brushing of lips against lips, a delicate tasting of seduction. It lasted only seconds, but it roused a tormenting ache of pleasure and unbearable need to gather her in his arms, to press his body to hers. With a shock of awareness, he realized what he felt went deeper than a desire—to a primal need, a primitive urge.

A storm of guilt rumbled through him. After nearly twenty years, he'd kissed a woman who wasn't his wife, kissed a woman with lust in his heart. He'd crossed a barrier, and it scared the hell out of him.

Instantly he released her and looked away, ashamed of the cravings that overwhelmed him. He'd never been the type of man to yearn for other women. Once he'd made his commitment to Clare, he'd been absolutely faithful to her in mind and body. But Clare was gone, if not spiritually, certainly physically.

Lara didn't pull back, however. When he met her gaze, he found a flood of passion in her depthless green eyes.

He couldn't say who finally broke the spell. Perhaps both of them did it simultaneously, aware they were treading on dangerous ground.

"I'll see you tomorrow," she muttered. "Thanks

for the hot fudge sundae. I can't remember the last one I've had.''

''Bad timing.'' His voice was both strong and weak, aggressive and pleading. He saw confusion shadow her face. Was he referring to the ice cream or the kiss? ''I've probably ruined your appetite.'' For dinner or another kiss?

''It was worth it.''

LARA'S INSOMNIA that night was made worse by constant recollections of Michael's kiss. Actually, it hadn't been much as far as kisses go—little more than a peck on the lips. Except it was more. That brief physical contact had stirred feelings that had lain dormant for so long. It would be foolish to say she'd been waiting two decades for him to kiss her again, but in her more lucid moments she had to admit the idea had hovered in her mind since the day he'd walked into her office with Spooner.

The idea was ridiculous, of course. She'd been infatuated with him in their school days, nothing more. She'd gotten over him. Out of sight, out of mind. She'd fallen in love with Clay Stovall, married him and totally dedicated herself to making him happy.

Or had she? Had her commitment been unconditional, or had a little part of her never quite forgotten Michael? Would it have changed anything if she'd acted differently? Was that why Clay had wandered— because she'd failed to be a complete wife to him? The notion was downright silly. Clay's infidelity was about Clay and his inability to honor his vows, not about her. She'd done her best. He was the one who'd failed.

Besides, that was all in the past, a part of her life that couldn't be changed, that she'd put behind her.

She should never have let Michael kiss her, never have given in to her whims. Indulging in the sensation of his strong hands touching her, of his lips skimming hers, waking that glorious liquid rush that left her pulse skipping…had been a mistake. He admitted as much when he'd turned his head away. She didn't have to see the look in his eyes to know he was ashamed of what he'd done. He was in love with a dead woman, the woman who had long ago replaced her in his affections. Nothing would ever change that. He didn't want Lara Gorley or Lara Stovall. He wanted Clare. Lara wouldn't allow herself to be used.

She didn't dare get involved with Michael for a host of reasons, not the least of which was that she was his attorney. Even if she wasn't, there were other factors to consider. His wife had been dead barely six months. Emotions were still too raw, too tender, for him to fully comprehend what he was doing, what the implications would be for either of them. And his family would undoubtedly object. Family life was difficult enough without the added distraction of a new woman horning in.

JUST BEFORE NOON the next day, Gretchen came by Lara's office.

"I've got good news and bad news." She settled into one of the two client chairs on the other side of the desk and flipped open her notepad. "The good news is that Felicity Sanchez is squeaky clean. She was a straight-A student in high school, got an associate's degree in automotive science from Coyote Community College, is active in her church and a model of virtue." Gretchen closed the notebook. More seriously, she said, "She really is a good kid."

"What's the bad news?" Lara asked.

"I still haven't been able to find Wayne Fischer. We checked his work record and called his former employers. Nobody's seen him or heard from him."

"Is he just lying low?"

"I doubt it. I've checked to see if there are any outstanding warrants on him. Nada, which means he has no reason to go under cover. On the other hand, some ranchers, especially the smaller ones, occasionally hire on a cash-only basis. Saves them both on taxes, but there won't be any public record of employment."

"So he could be working somewhere, and we just don't know it," Lara concluded.

"Bingo."

"Keep looking. Maybe we'll get lucky." Wayne Fischer was still their most promising candidate for murderer. If he had been the person who sabotaged the MG, he'd have a good incentive for keeping a low profile. "I heard you and Brad split up."

The blonde shrugged nonchalantly. "Easy come, easy go. He's not the only fish in the sea. It's better this way. He really loves those kids, and they need him."

"I'm sorry nevertheless," Lara said sympathetically. "Breaking up is always tough, even when it's the best for everyone concerned."

"Yeah, well, life moves on." She jumped from her seat. "And so do investigations." She slipped her pad into her hip pocket and moved toward the door. "I'll let you know when I get a lead on Fischer."

Lara watched her leave. Gretchen was more upset

about Brad leaving her than she let on, but she'd get over it. Gretchen Tanner didn't strike her as a woman who wallowed in being a victim.

CHEER TRYOUTS were held all week, with results posted daily. Sally survived every cut. Michael told her how proud he was of her.

"I wish Mom was here," Sally said Wednesday night, when she came to him in the living room to kiss him good-night before she went to bed.

"I do, too," he replied, struggling to keep his voice from wavering. He put his arm around her and sat her on his knee. He wouldn't be able to do this much longer. She was growing up so fast. "If you try real hard," he said softly, "I bet you can feel her presence. She's never too far away, Sally. You just can't see her."

She wrapped her arms around him then, and they both cried.

A few minutes later, as he was tucking her in, Sally asked, "Dad, if I make the team, would it be all right if I invited Lara to join us at the pizza parlor?"

Leave it to a child to rebound. He'd promised her a pizza bash in town for all the winners and then to let all of them come out to the Number One for a slumber party. Thankfully, Sheila and Elva had volunteered to oversee what he expected to be a very rowdy night.

"I think that would be a very good idea. Why don't you call her tomorrow and see if she'll be available?"

Sally made the team, and the shrieks and squeals of a dozen excited girls dominated the red-decor pizza joint Friday evening. Lara showed up in snug jeans and a light-aqua, sleeveless tee and slid into the booth next to Michael, opposite Adam and Sheila. Even over the sharp aromas of tomato sauce, garlic, pepperoni and Italian spices, he was aware of her feminine scent. They toasted Sally with iced tea.

An hour later, when the crowd was ready to leave and go out to the ranch, Sally approached Lara to thank her for attending.

"Bring Your Daughter to Work is next Wednesday," Sally reminded her. "Can I still come to your office?" The fear that she might have changed her mind or wouldn't be able to honor the promise waffled in the question.

"You bet. I have a case in court that afternoon, so you'll be able to see me in action."

Sally grinned from ear to ear. "Cool."

Lara smiled over at Michael. "Maybe you and the other kids can join us at the end of the day and we can all go somewhere to eat. There's a Japanese steak house that just opened."

He needed to keep his distance. It would be safer that way, he told himself. He'd crossed a barrier with Lara in her office.

The kiss, he assured himself, had been a mere gesture of gratitude, a not-inappropriate show of friendly, innocent affection between a man and a woman. It had to end there. He couldn't let it develop into something more, something he didn't want to admit or deal with. The best way to do that was to keep his distance. Even if he did consider someday having another woman in his life, this was too soon. He wasn't ready. His children weren't ready.

He tried to convince himself that aching loneliness combined with gratitude had led him to start to deepen the kiss. He hadn't been unfaithful to Clare.

So why did he feel so guilty? Because he deserved to. Because he'd kissed Lara Stovall, and he'd liked it. Because he wanted to kiss her again.

"Great," he said. "But my treat."

ON WEDNESDAY MORNING, Michael was crossing a pasture on horseback where prize heifers were grazing. They'd been bred months ago for fall calves.

He muttered when he saw a downed fence. He'd complained to Webster Hood about the declining standard of upkeep on the spread. Hood had scoffed. "You've been wasting money on overmaintenance for years. I'm just stretching out the cycle a bit."

In this case, Michael noted to himself, he'd stretched it to the breaking point.

It was obvious from the hoofprints that cattle had wandered through the gap. He'd have to round up the strays. More time taken from other tasks.

Then he saw it. A shiny bluish-silver blob in the middle of the field. Even before he reached it, he knew what it was. An aborted fetus. As he drew closer, he spied another not too far away. His stomach clenched. His worst nightmare was coming true.

He yanked the cell phone from his saddlebag and hit a quick dial button. His fingers tapped on his thigh as he waited for the call to be answered. Finally, his assistant picked up.

"I'm on the line between B-3 and D-7, two miles east of Triple Wells," he stated without preamble. "I want a crew out here now to mend the fence between the two sectors."

"It isn't scheduled till next month—" Lopez started to say.

"Screw the schedule. I said now and I mean now.

Then I want you to call Doc Hansen and tell him to get out here ASAP. I suspect we have an outbreak of brucellosis.''

Lopez cursed.

''Exactly. Do we have any more stock coming in?''

''There's another hundred head due in this afternoon from the Rusted Rail, down around Uvalde.''

''Cancel it.''

''I'll have to talk to Web.'' Lopez sounded hesitant.

''Don't bother. I will.'' He disconnected and was about to hit Hood's number, when he reconsidered and called his father.

Adam wasn't happy at the news. ''How extensive is it?''

''I'm not sure yet. I see three—no, four fetuses, but there are undoubtedly more. Until I get a count on the crossover between the visitors and the natives, I can't even estimate the extent of the contamination. For now, we have to quarantine our stock in place and hope this is an isolated instance.''

''Need to check our people, too,'' Adam observed.

The human variety of the disease was known as undulant fever. The irony was that only last year brucellosis had been considered eradicated in Texas. But it wasn't in Mexico. Even if the rancher in Uvalde hadn't bought cattle south of the border and commingled them with his stock, his herd might have been contaminated because the disease could be transmitted aerially.

Michael's third call was to his boss. He reported the situation and the steps he was taking.

''Do whatever you have to,'' Hood told him calmly. ''I'll turn back the incoming shipment and notify the appropriate state and federal animal health authorities. Keep me posted.'' He hung up.

Michael shook his head, not sure if he was pleased the man was giving him a free hand or worried that he was.

CHAPTER TEN

CAROL WAS SHOWING Sally how they researched case law in the outer office when Lara received Michael's call. A warm current ran through her on recognizing his deep voice. Strange, she mused, one kiss and the years floated away. The memories of what had transpired during that long interval of separation weren't erased; they merely receded into a silent pool of yesterdays. The pleasure was short-lived, however, when he announced he wouldn't be able to join them this afternoon, that he wouldn't be seeing her for a while—unless a new development in his case demanded his appearance.

He's pushing me away, was her first reaction. *Dismissing me. It was nice,* he was telling her, *but now I have to get on with life, my life.*

"Is something wrong?" What she really meant was, *Have I done something wrong? Have I disappointed you? Again.*

"We have an outbreak of disease among the livestock. It's serious. I'll be tied up for the foreseeable future trying to keep this crisis down to manageable levels." She heard a deep masculine sigh. "I'm sorry."

Relief warred with concern. "No apology needed," she assured him. "Do what you have to do."

The line was quiet for a moment. Finally, he said,

"I was looking forward to seeing you this evening, taking you out to dinner, even if it was with a bunch of kids. I was hoping maybe you'd come out here this weekend and we could go horseback riding like we used to."

She gripped the receiver and closed her eyes, not sure she wanted to remember those days exactly. After all, they'd ended in disaster. And yet...she did want to go riding with him.

"I haven't been on a horse in years." Did her boots still fit?

"It's like riding a bicycle," he assured her. "You never forget."

Even when you think you have, she reminded herself. *No matter how much you try.* "Maybe not, but the muscles do. I bet I'd ache all over the next day."

"A hot soaking bath and a massage help a lot." He had a smile in his voice. She could picture his lips curving up, his blue eyes twinkling.

"I can take care of the bath part," she agreed. "The massage is another matter."

"I can arrange for both," he said.

The sudden mental picture of Michael's large, brawny hands touching her, squeezing her flesh, rubbing her skin, brought on a flash of heat and a strange melting sensation inside her. She shouldn't be talking this way, yet she didn't want to stop, didn't want him to stop.

The murmur of his voice, even more than his words, told her he was conjuring up the same discomforting images. She wanted to purr. "But not in the near future, I gather. How long do you expect to be tied up?"

Another sigh, this one even more discouraging. "At least a month, maybe two."

A waiting game. Like sweating out a jury verdict. "If it takes that long, I may have to ask the court for a continuance."

"Don't drag this out any more than necessary," he said. "Say when, and I'll turn everything over to Lopez and Hood."

"There's nothing new on your case," she finally told him. She could feel his reluctance to talk about his upcoming trial. But, she reminded herself, it was the one sure link between them. "Gretchen still hasn't had any luck finding Fischer."

"He's probably in jail somewhere," Michael commented, almost casually. "The guy was a loser."

"Gretchen is expanding her search. If he's behind bars, she'll find him. If he's simply lying low, it could be tough."

"Don't forget, he had his jaw wired," Michael reminded her. "Surely he had to get medical treatment somewhere."

"She's checking that angle, but if he doesn't have insurance and pays cash, records may not be easy to find. I've spoken to the sheriff. He's agreed to put out a search for him, too."

Lara regretted bringing up the subject. She'd spoiled the mood between them. But then, like it or not, they were still lawyer and client. They were better friends now, but that wasn't important. Except it was.

Another tense silence ensued. "Will you call me once in a while and tell me how things are going?" she asked.

"You bet. It could be late."

"I don't usually go to bed before midnight, so phone anytime."

"I will." From the way he said it, she knew he would. She also knew she'd be waiting for those calls.

THE NEXT MONTH WAS exhausting chaos. Working closely with state and federal animal health officials, Michael implemented a series of precautionary measures. All fence lines were inspected and where necessary reinforced. Separation between herds was increased as much as possible and areas of quarantine were established. Each herd was tested for the bacteria. One infection was sufficient to condemn an entire group. The gruesome task of slaughter and disposal of the carcasses drained everyone physically and emotionally as huge orange flames and gray smoke columns of crematory pyres clouded the air and clogged the nostrils.

Michael made it a point to see his children every day, if only for a few minutes. The one meal he got to eat with them regularly was breakfast, and it became a sort of ritual. Adam and Sheila had become true surrogate parents now, and Michael continued to be enormously grateful for their unstinting dedication. If anything happened to him, he knew his children were in loving hands.

The other ritual that kept him sane was his nightly telephone call to Lara. It started out with simple progress reports about the livestock situation and the kids' activities. But those subjects soon became repetitive. Some things in life are predictable.

What wasn't planned or anticipated was the sense of nostalgia and intimacy that grew between them. Their conversations sometimes lasted an hour, after which he couldn't have said what they'd talked about, except that he'd never gotten bored. He thought sometimes of Jim Reeves's country song about putting her sweet lips closer to the phone and pretended they were together, all alone. They were alone. Two people who shared memories, pains and tragedies. And a loneliness, when he finally turned out the light, that was almost unbearable.

He wanted more of Lara Stovall than a voice on a telephone, and the shame of it tormented him. But as the song continued to play in his mind, Michael could hear Lara's refrain: *and you can tell the ghost there with you, she'll have to go.*

AMID A PILE of junk mail and bills, the letter from the Homestead Bank and Trust arrived in early September, six weeks after the outbreak of the disease. Almost immediately, the words in the second paragraph jumped out at him: "You are hereby relieved of your duties as livestock manager for the Number One Ranch, effective immediately. This action is taken regretfully but in the best interests of this institution and its shareholders..." The paper floated from his fingers to the top of the desk. He dropped into his chair, as weak and breathless as if he'd been kneed in the groin.

He was fired. He'd lived his entire life on the Number One. He'd dedicated himself to making it the best ranch it could be. This land was in his blood, and now he was being told he wasn't needed anymore. He wanted to think this was a mistake, a mix-up, someone's idea of a sick joke. But he knew it wasn't.

Nedra Cummings, the vice president for investment and management, had signed this dismissal notice, but

Michael had no doubt who was behind it. Webster Hood. Michael hadn't liked the hard-drinking womanizer from their initial meeting, but he might have overcome his personal animus if the two of them had been able to see eye to eye on the matter that really counted—the ranch.

Hood was focused exclusively on the immediate profits to be made in programs that would ultimately be disastrous. Like bringing in outside stock to graze on Number One pastureland. Because of the outbreak of brucellosis, they'd had to destroy five hundred cattle. Five hundred prime stock.

The heat of anger that had invaded his bones a few minutes earlier nearly collapsed to cold despair, but Michael had never been a quitter. He wasn't about to give up now. Not without a fight. Folding the letter, he strode to the door, climbed into his pickup and kicked up gravel as he peeled out of his driveway.

Covering the distance from the house to Hood's place didn't take long. He arrived in the shallow valley to find it crowded with vehicles and people milling around, as if they were waiting for some sort of meeting.

He pulled his truck up next to Brad's Ford diesel, jumped down and slammed the door. The expressions on the faces of the vaqueros and the silence that greeted him told him the word was already out.

Hood wasn't in sight, so Michael stomped up the wooden steps of the wide front porch and entered the air-conditioned bachelor pad. The boss was sitting at his desk on the other side of the room, whiskey glass in hand. Brad occupied Michael's usual seat, with a notebook balanced on his knee. He started to rise and say something, but Michael ignored the embarrassed greeting and stood directly in front of his tormentor. He held out the letter. "Are you behind this?"

"I won't pretend I don't know what you're talking about," Hood replied dryly. "I was consulted, asked for my honest evaluation of your performance, so I gave it."

"You recommended I be fired as livestock manager."

"Look—" Hood's tone was suddenly placating "—you've had some rotten breaks this year—" Michael nearly laughed at the understatement "—but you've become a liability to this ranch."

Quietly, Brad slunk down into his seat, while Hood leaned back, hands folded in front of him. "Because of your negligence, we've lost one-third of the cattle on this spread."

The allegation was preposterous. "You can't possibly lay that disaster on my doorstep," Michael shot back. "I warned you."

"You were the livestock manager. The welfare of the herds was your sole duty. You screwed up." Hood arched forward. "Do you think I don't know Brad here has been picking up the slack? That every time you forget something, or don't have time for it, he's been the one filling in and covering your butt?"

Michael understood now why Hood had given him a free rein during the recent outbreak of brucellosis. He glanced over at Brad Lopez, who clearly wanted to melt into the leather upholstery. Had he known this was coming and not told him? All those times he'd thought his assistant was doing him a favor by volunteering to give Hood the rundown on what was happening so Michael wouldn't have to deal with him…had he been stabbing him in the back? No telling what those reports had contained, what distortions or even outright lies they might have contained. There was a reason his old pal wouldn't make eye contact with him.

"We don't need to pay two people to do what one person can obviously do alone," Hood pointed out. "Now, if you'll excuse us, I'm busy with your successor. I suggest you leave."

Michael looked down at Brad, who stared zombie-like at the edge of the desk. "I'm sorry I ever called you my friend."

With a heavy heart, he redirected his attention to Hood. "I've worked on this ranch all my life. This is where I was born, where I was raised. I know more about this spread than you ever will."

"You're probably right," Hood conceded, "but it doesn't matter. You're finished here."

"Don't be so sure." Michael's chest was pounding, his pulse rapid, but he refused to allow the emotions roiling inside him to gain control. "I'm still a stockholder."

"A minority stockholder. You've been outvoted."

Michael fought to keep his voice level. "I've done my best to get along with you, Hood. I've given you the benefit of the doubt, even against my better judgment. But no more. I won't let you systematically destroy this ranch."

Hood's face suddenly turned bright red. "I don't know what you're talking about, but you start making slanderous statements and I'll slap you with a lawsuit quicker than a rattler can bite. I suggest you save yourself the time, money and pain."

"I haven't even begun." Michael shook his head,

his tone deceptively calm. "Fair warning, Hood, which is more than you gave me."

Hood jumped out of his chair, his knuckles pressed to the desktop as he arched over it. "Be very careful about making threats, First. You can't prove a thing. Now, get the hell out of here."

"Fair warning, Hood," Michael repeated quietly, and had the satisfaction of seeing the general manager's face pale.

Keeping a death grip on his urge to violence, Michael rotated on his heel and strode to the door. Out on the front porch, he realized Hood had followed him. Michael was determined not to let the situation deteriorate further. He reached ground level, aware of all the vaqueros staring at him.

"I was planning on waiting till later to inform you, First," Hood snarled, "in private. But under the circumstances, I reckon this is as good a time as any." He stood at the edge of the top step and spoke directly to Michael, his words loud enough for everyone to hear. "Since you are no longer employed by the Homestead Bank and Trust, Mr. First, you're not entitled to housing on this ranch. On behalf of the bank, I'm giving you thirty days to vacate the house you're occupying."

Michael froze in his tracks. Then he whirled to face the man standing above him. "Leave the ranch house? That's my family's home."

An unpleasant grumble passed among the men standing around.

"Not anymore," Hood informed him. In the new silence, he continued. "It's the property of the Number One Ranch. You are hereby given notice to remove yourself, your family and your private property from it. If you haven't complied at the end of thirty days, formal eviction proceedings will be taken against you. You'll lose, First, so I recommend you start packing now.''

A GLANCE AND Lara knew Michael was upset. He'd been in town only twice in the past six weeks—to review depositions she'd taken from auto supply merchants and a body shop owner. There was nothing controversial in their statements, but Lara didn't want to discuss them on the phone. He'd looked exhausted on those two occasions. Now he appeared to be steaming mad.

"What's the matter?" she asked. "Sally hasn't—''

"It's not Sally," he enunciated as he stomped across the carpet. "Hood and the bank have finally gone too far.''

She was standing at her desk, having risen to her feet the moment she'd heard the fire in Michael's voice outside her office. Carol had insisted he couldn't just barge in, but he had anyway. Thankfully, another client wasn't with her.

"How about taking a deep breath, calming down and telling me what's going on?''

He halted, glowered at her. "Don't patronize me, Lara.''

She felt her hackles rise. "And don't you dare ever barge into my office uninvited again." Her voice tight, she glared back.

He shook his head. "You're right." He dropped into the client chair across from her. "I'm sorry.''

She settled gingerly into her chair, blinked slowly. "Now, what's the problem?''

"I've been fired." His tone was less strident, but it didn't minimize the shock value. "And they're evicting me from my house, my family's home."

He passed the crumpled letter across the desk. She perused it while she listened to him recount the events that had led to words with Webster Hood.

"Did you threaten any specific action? Violence, for example?"

He sucked in his breath and let it out again. "I simply put him on notice that I didn't intend to take this sitting down." He realized he was in a chair and burst out laughing. "Well, I won't sit down for him."

Lara emitted a sigh of relief and flashed him a crooked smile as she picked up her phone and hit a button. "Nelson, Michael First is here. Are you free to join us for a few minutes? Thanks."

"There must be something I can do," Michael insisted. The misery on his face tore at her heart. She had an urge to soothe, to hug. If she hadn't expected her law partner to walk in at any moment, she might have. "I don't care how much it costs. I want that son of a bitch's head on a platter."

"Well, I can't promise you that," she responded, indulging him with a mercurial grin. "But we might be able to make his life uncomfortable." She looked across the room to the opening door. "Thanks for joining us."

"What's up?" Spooner closed the door behind him. Quickly assessing the mood, he soberly approached the desk.

Rising, Lara handed him the letter, then removed a fresh legal tablet from her desk drawer. She journeyed over to the conference table and motioned the two men to take seats.

"I believe we may have cause for civil action. But I'll let Michael explain what's happened."

It didn't take long.

Spooner worried his lip. "Do you have your place homesteaded?"

Michael shook his head. "Never thought it'd be necessary."

The civil lawyer stroked his chin. "Hood gave you verbal notice that in thirty days the bank will initiate eviction proceedings. Is that right?"

Michael nodded.

"Nothing in writing," the attorney muttered, gazing at the ceiling. "We'll take that as a notice of intent. I doubt he has the legal authority to evict, anyway. Okay, here's what you do." He steepled his fingers. "You have until the end of December to declare homestead for the entire calendar year. Go over to the courthouse today and file a claim. It'll be automatically retroactive to January 1."

"Which means they can't evict me?"

"Not necessarily," Spooner warned. "Homestead protects your primary domicile against liens. The bank will claim you don't own it, therefore, you are not entitled to it to begin with, but this will put them in a position of having to prove they do. We can make a variety of other charges, as well. I'm not sure they'll stand up to scrutiny, but then that's what a trial is for. We've already gotten a restraining order preventing them from selling Number One breeding stock. Since your being evicted is based on your not being employed any longer by the Number One, we'll hit them with a suit for wrongful termination and anything else we can conjure up. We'll file the actions separately, request severance so they can't be combined into a single cause of action and demand a jury trial for each count. That ought to delay things if nothing else. It'll also cost the bank plenty in billable hours."

"Hit them in the pocketbook." Michael sounded hopeful. "I can't imagine a more sensitive spot. I can talk to the vaquero families, recommend they file for homestead exemptions, as well."

"That'll certainly muddy the waters, slow things down," Spooner agreed.

Lara frowned before she spoke to Michael. "You want to regain possession of the ranch. If the vaqueros succeed in their petitions, your claim to their land will also be diminished. Are you sure you want to do that?"

He paused to consider the question. "Those families are part of the Number One," he responded decisively. "They deserve security, too."

SINCE MICHAEL WOULDN'T BE functioning on the Number One in any official capacity until the matter was finally adjudicated, he had to decide what to do with his time. He soon found working with his father on the Home Place so relaxing and satisfying that he seriously considered staying there. Except the Number One was *his* home, the place where he and Clare had shared their married life. It was also the only home his children had ever known. What would happen to it now? Would the courts decide it belonged to him and his family? Would his children look back on it as a happy place, one where they had been a family? Or would it represent their father's failure?

On September 16, considerably short of the thirty days Hood had indicated, the Homestead Bank and Trust served Michael with official eviction papers. He wouldn't fight being fired, but he would fight this. Through Nelson Spooner, Michael notified the bank that their action was illegal and that he would not comply. Two days later, the Houston-based corporation was served with a restraining order, blocking the eviction. To Michael's surprise, he heard nothing more from the bank or from Webster Hood. On Spooner's advice, Michael continued to live in the house.

There was only one tense moment two weeks later, when Hood changed the combination to the gate. Anticipating the tactic, Michael had coordinated with the Corderas to get the new code. Using it, he gained entry, then drove directly to Hood's Hideaway, walked in and reminded the general manager that as a stockholder of the Number One he was entitled to free access. He then informed the silent man behind the desk that if he changed the code again without notifying him, Michael would sue him personally and by name for wrongful detention, since the code was needed to get off the ranch as well as on. Hood could have the system changed, of course, but Michael was confident he wouldn't. Bullies, as his son had observed, backed down quickly when they met determined opposition.

Trial date was approaching, though, and Michael knew he had to make several important decisions. One of them concerned Clare's grandmother, Brigitte.

He approached her early the following Monday morning when she appeared to be having a lucid moment. She was finishing a dish of chocolate pudding, her recent favorite.

"How's your hip?"

"Fine, if I don't try to use it." Her pale watery blue eyes twinkled. "It's not getting better."

"The doctor warned it would take time."

"More like eternity." Acceptance rather than bitterness and maybe a hint of the old humor accented her words.

"Do you think you might be more comfortable somewhere else, where there's a staff to take care of you all the time?"

The old woman smiled, a canny expression on her thin lips. "Like a nursing home?" When her mind was clear, it was very clear.

Guilt riddled him. "I want what's best for you." He was sure he was doing the right thing, but...

"You have a family to think about." She paused a moment. "What would Clare say?"

Did she know Clare was dead? She never asked for her granddaughter in clearheaded moments.

"Her concern would be your comfort and welfare." He paused. "You know she's gone, don't you?"

Brigitte looked at him strangely, then said, "Do they have meat loaf? That's one of Gus's favorites. Of course it won't be as good as—"

Was she about to say Clare's? Brigitte was one of the world's worst cooks—except when it came to baking cookies. It was Clare's meat loaf that her grandfather had always raved about.

"Homemade," Brigitte concluded, making Michael wonder if she was playing a mind game with him.

"I bet it's a regular item on the menu."

"When can I move? Never did like being stuck out here."

"How about tomorrow morning?"

"I like to nap in the afternoon, after I finish watering the flowers." Another non sequitur.

Brigitte was far from lucid Tuesday morning when the ambulance came to take her to the Golden Years Nursing Home. Among other things, she carried on about Clare's picture. Michael put the nostalgic rendition of Brigitte's Spokane house in his pickup and followed the ambulance into town. He made sure Brigitte was comfortably settled, saw to it the painting was prominently displayed across from her bed, then drove to Lara's office. It was past noon.

"How about dinner?" he asked. Her blouse was the color of daffodils and brought out the jade greenness of her eyes.

"You mean lunch?" Her red lips curved upward.

Distracted, he said, "I mean going to a restaurant to get something to eat. Now."

She chuckled. "The Dock suit you?"

They decided to take her car rather than his truck. She offered to let him drive. He liked fine cars, and the butter-soft leather of her BMW was luxurious. For a fleeting second he thought of the firm leather upholstery of the MG. He was glad the two vehicles didn't resemble each other.

The air-conditioning vent brought him a whiff of Lara's perfume—a delicate, feminine scent. It intoxicated him, made him vaguely impatient, eager, anxious. He wanted to kiss her but convinced himself this wasn't the time or place. They had important matters to discuss. He told her about Brigitte.

"You did the right thing," was her only comment.

The regular lunch crowd had thinned out. He found a parking space in front of the entrance, got out and came around to her side of the car. She'd already opened her door, but that didn't stop him from holding out his hand to her.

He wondered if she felt the spike of awareness, the surge of energy that was dancing in him. He caught her eye as she straightened, long enough to know she'd felt something.

The pin lights in the maritime-motif dining room burnished her hair with a coppery sheen.

"I talked to Dad over the weekend. We agreed the best thing will be for all of us—the kids, Elva and me—to move into the guest house at the Home Place before the trial."

Lara had a pretty good idea why. She didn't disagree with his decision, but she wanted to hear his reasoning. "Why?"

"First of all, once the trial starts, I don't know how much time I'll be able to spend with them. They need to feel secure, not abandoned. Elva's like a member of the family. She'll do everything she can, but it isn't fair to put this burden on her."

Lara took a sip of her Chardonnay.

"I've also asked Dad and Sheila to take care of the kids if...if anything happens to me. If I get convicted—"

Lara reached across the table and covered his fingers with her palm. She'd sometimes had the feeling he didn't fully appreciate the gravity of the situation he was in, but Sheila had been right. The First men were very good at hiding their negative emotions. Michael accepted that this crisis might not come out the way he wanted. He was preparing.

He sandwiched her hand between his. "If I am convicted," he resumed, "I don't want them dislocated again. I think it'll be better if they're already with their grandparents.''

"Your kids are very fortunate to have you for a dad," she said softly. She wished she had more to offer him than a good defense, but for now that would have to be enough.

"Thank you for being here, Lara. You've come to mean a lot to me."

The words should please her, and at some level, they did, but they also frightened her. He wanted her here now, but would he in the future? She shouldn't even be thinking along those lines. They'd renewed their friendship. Nothing more. It had never been more than that to him to begin with. She was fooling herself to think that now it could be anything else.

CHAPTER ELEVEN

"WE'RE STILL several weeks from the trial, but we need to start developing our strategy," Lara announced after the waiter had delivered their food. Soft-shell crab for her, prime rib of beef for him.

"I figured we'd just tell the truth." He was baiting her.

She refused to bite. "The D.A. has to prove motive, means and opportunity."

He squeezed open his baked potato, added a pat of butter, sour cream. "I'm good for two out of three." His tone was breezy, but with an edge to it. "I didn't have a motive to kill my wife, though."

She sampled her rice pilaf. "The D.A. can present a very convincing case that you did."

He sipped his Merlot. "That I was so angry with her because her grandmother came to live with us that I killed her?" He shook his head. "Pretty weak. I already told you I completely supported her decision. Besides, it doesn't make sense. Being ticked off about Brigitte would give me a motive for killing her, not Clare."

"Malvery has an even better motive to present."

He grunted, filled his fork with another piece of tender beef and brought it up to his mouth. "What's that?"

"Felicity Sanchez." She wasn't surprised when he

rolled his eyes. "Don't forget, the D.A. has a witness who'll testify you held her in your arms—"

"Hood." He snorted and cut off another piece of medium-rare beef. "The man is a lush and a lecher, and he has a grudge against me. He should be easy to discredit."

She set her knife on the rim of her plate. "If this were simply a matter of he said, she said, I would agree with you. But Felicity admits it happened. So do you, for that matter."

"And we both agree it wasn't what Hood's trying to make it appear."

"Doesn't matter. We still have to be prepared in case the D.A. plays that card."

He couldn't deny the point. "So what do you propose?"

Lara speared a piece of lightly battered crab. "If Malvery plays the illicit love card, we trump him. Felicity Sanchez had means, motive and opportunity."

Michael pulled back. "You're kidding, right?"

"She certainly had means." Lara scooped up rice. "As a mechanic, whom you admit you consulted about the car, she was familiar with the MG and had the know-how to sabotage it."

He stopped eating. She went on. "Living on the ranch, not far from your house, she also had opportunity."

Lara watched Michael's face darken as his mind processed the scenario.

"It won't work." He stabbed a piece of meat. "Even if Felicity was hot for my bod and wanted to get rid of my wife so she could have me all to herself—" he snorted at the absurdity of the notion

"—she had no way of knowing Clare would be driving the MG. I told you it was a spur-of-the-moment decision." He bit into the beef, chewed, swallowed. "Besides, we've already decided the killer was after me, not Clare."

Lara nodded. "Which means she wanted to kill you."

"Whoa." He chuckled this time, though his eyes betrayed no amusement. "That's a real stretch. Felicity loved me so much she wanted to kill me. Man, that's sick."

"Stranger things have happened," she reminded him. "We're not dealing with logic here, but emotions, passions."

He sat up, scowled, his eating halted. "You're reading an awful lot into an innocent embrace."

Lara remembered how it felt when he'd taken her in his arms. A table separated them, but even now his closeness whipped up reactions she didn't want to acknowledge—or relinquish.

He put down his knife and fork. "Lara, you can't be serious. You want to accuse Felicity of attempting to kill me because I wouldn't make love to her?"

"It's an approach." She was trying to sound reasonable. "We don't have to accuse her. That doesn't mean I can't raise a question or two along that line. She'll deny it, of course, but the jurors will have an alternative theory to consider."

"You've met Felicity," he countered. "Do you seriously believe she's responsible for what happened to Clare?"

"I don't know." She hated anemic responses. "And neither do you."

He shook his head. "But you're willing to make the jury and the world think she did?"

"Do I have to remind you, Michael, that Texas has the highest capital punishment rate in the country? My job's to establish reasonable doubt in the minds of the jurors."

He settled against the back of the booth, putting more distance between them. "I don't for a moment suspect her of tampering with my MG in an effort to kill Clare or me."

"But you can't tell me who did." She tried to skewer a floret of broccoli and missed. It skittered off the plate. "You have to admit a case can be made against her."

He crossed his arms, the tug of his knit shirt against his shoulders and biceps ridiculously distracting. "Lara, I appreciate that you're willing to pull out all the stops to save my sorry neck. But ruining the reputation of a decent twenty-three-year-old woman engaged to a serviceman who's overseas defending his country, on a mere conjecture—"

"Even if it means making orphans of your children?"

His big hands flexed, and his jaw dropped. "You have some bedside manner, Doctor."

"Don't make it a graveside manner."

His eyes widened with shock this time. Finally, he huffed out a breath of abdication. "I know for a certainty that nothing was going on between Felicity and me. I know beyond a reasonable doubt that she's not in love with me, infatuated with me or interested in me as anyone other than a trusted friend. Please don't ask me to betray that trust or that friendship." He twirled the stem of his wineglass and peered into its blood-red contents before meeting her gaze. "Think about what you're proposing. If you imply she killed Clare, some people will believe it, even if the D.A. doesn't follow up on the lead. She'll never be able to live it down. There'll forever be doubts about whether she had anything to do with Clare's death, always suspicion she was unfaithful to her fiancé. It's just not fair."

He reached across the table and took her hand. His fingers were rough and gentle, warm, yet they sent a shiver of delight through her. "Believe me, I want to be exonerated. But I want it to be honorably, not at the expense of another person's innocence. You understand that, don't you?"

"Of course I do, but I'd be remiss if I didn't consider all the angles, all the possibilities."

"I respect that."

Tension flowed between them. Finally, she extricated her hand and picked up her wineglass. "You were about to tell me what defense you would be happy with," she reminded him, unable to suppress a note of sarcasm.

"Hood." Michael raised his wine to his lips and swallowed a mouthful. "He's the logical choice. We've already agreed Clare wasn't the real target. I was. Hood had no reason to kill her, but he hates me."

"His motive might be hard to prove. He was in the catbird seat. You worked for him. You didn't pose a threat to him."

Michael's eyes mellowed. "I thought we didn't have to prove who else is the culprit, just establish a reasonable doubt."

She nearly giggled. "You're catching on, Cowboy."

He couldn't help but laugh. She liked the sound. Even in the circumstances, there was warmth in it, a hint of intimacy.

Cutting off a piece of delicate crab, she went on. "It shouldn't be difficult to establish means and opportunity for Hood. He had the run of the place. He could go anywhere he wanted. We have his statement that he was at your house the day of the accident."

Michael nodded. "Means shouldn't be a problem, either. As I explained, the MG wasn't a complicated automobile. Hood has enough rudimentary knowledge of mechanics that it wouldn't have been difficult for him to locate the brake line. Besides, I let him examine the car when I finally put it on the road."

Lara's head shot up. "You never told me that."

He paused. "When I got it running I let a lot of people inspect it. Hood among them. I removed the bonnet—the hood," he added with a crooked grin, "and let people check out the engine."

"Did you point out the brake line?"

He reflected a moment. "Not specifically. The younger people, who've grown up with fuel injection and electronic ignition, were fascinated by the old mechanical components like distributor, carburetor, generator. I remember pointing out that the brakes were all drum. No disk brakes on that baby."

She snared a piece of sautéed zucchini. "Who else did you show the car to? And when?"

"Anybody and everybody who expressed interest. All the ranch hands." He held up a finger for emphasis. "Including Wayne Fischer, by the way. Any information on him yet?"

Lara shook her head. "Gretchen's checking other states. He seems to have vanished."

"I'm not sure, but I think he said he was originally from Wyoming. Gretchen might look there." He sipped more wine. "She was with Brad the day I showed it to Fischer. I remember she was excited because her dad had one like it when she was a kid. Brad worked in a body shop in high school and really admired the work I'd done on straightening out the fenders."

"Was Hood interested?"

Michael chuckled. "Sure. It was one of the few occasions we talked like friends instead of adversaries. It's a man thing, I guess, a mutual fascination for machines and gadgets."

Lara lined up the knife and fork in the middle of the plate, then patted her lips with her cloth napkin. "Did Hood ever demonstrate any interest in Clare?"

"Interest?" It took a moment for the question to sink in. "You mean sexual interest?"

Sitting perfectly still, Michael studied her. She watched anger and doubt, then anger, again mar the serene blue of his incredible eyes.

"Are you suggesting," he inquired cautiously, "there was something going on between Clare and Webster Hood?" He waved the notion away with a sweeping motion, almost knocking over his wineglass. "That's ridiculous, Lara. Don't even go there."

"Please hear me out before you jump to any conclusions." She ignored the food before her and stared at him.

"Okay. Go on."

She paused until the waiter had replenished their water and left. "Elva made it very clear his embrace was nothing more than a friendly act of concern. Clare was embarrassed by it and immediately pulled away. My question for you is, could Hood have misinterpreted her distraught impulse as attraction. Could he have been interested in her?''

Michael slouched into the corner of the booth. ''At our first meeting, he commented that she was real nice. It didn't seem like anything more than a neighborly compliment. We hadn't locked horns over running the ranch yet.'' His mind wandered. ''At the Labor Day weekend bash a few weeks later he remarked that she was obviously well organized. He liked women with heads on their shoulders who weren't afraid to take charge.''

''The remark didn't ring any alarms?''

He shook his head. ''Why should it? It's true she had her stuff together. She could organize a picnic for several hundred people, and everything ran together like clockwork.'' He smiled to himself. ''She claimed the secret was delegating the real work.''

''Smart lady.'' Lara tried to grin.

''Yeah, she was,'' he agreed sadly.

This conversation was taking a detour Lara didn't want to pursue. ''Is there any chance he was more infatuated with Clare than you realized?''

Michael pursed his lips. ''His tastes run toward the younger set, to twenty-year-old blondes. Besides, Clare would never have encouraged him or tolerated a come-on.''

''Suppose the show of affection meant more to him than just a friendly shoulder to cry on. Suppose he was interested in taking it further.''

Michael breathed in and let the air out.

''We have no proof of this, Michael. I'm just posing a what-if.'' She continued. ''I see two possible scenarios. Hood went to your house that morning, supposedly to inform you he was taking a steer to market for the food bank—''

''That's always struck me as odd,'' Michael interrupted. ''He could have coordinated the transfer with me in advance. Besides, we'd already given a whole beef to the food bank two months earlier. Why give another one so soon?''

''What did he say when you asked him?''

''That it seemed like a good time. That it was a spur-of-the-moment decision.''

''You believed him?''

''No, but I didn't pursue it. I figured it was another way of him reminding me he was the boss and could do anything he damn well pleased.''

''So why bother coming to the house that morning?''

Michael quirked an eyebrow. ''What are you implying?''

''His actions, clearly out of the ordinary, suggest he had an ulterior motive. It could have been to proposition Clare, but that doesn't appear likely. He must have known she wouldn't be receptive and would tell you if he'd behaved inappropriately. So there is only one other possibility.''

''To sabotage the MG.''

Lara nodded. ''He'd lurked around your house once before. He could easily have been doing it again and saw you leave in the Suburban.''

''He would never have had a chance with her,'' Michael said, after a brief pause. ''Trust me, he wasn't her type.''

Maybe not then, but lonely widows sometimes

gravitated to men who didn't resemble the husbands they'd lost. One of the things Hood and Clare would have had in common was the ranch. If he'd played the solicitous friend carefully enough, he might even have been able to win over Adam and the rest of the family.

"According to Gretchen, Hood's family lost a spread in East Texas years ago. You'd already shattered his hopes of purchasing a piece of the ranch. Maybe his goal was to own the Number One by marrying into it."

Michael looked skeptical. "I don't buy it."

She dabbed her mouth with the white cloth napkin. "It doesn't matter. It's what the jury buys. They may not be sold on it completely, either, but it will give them the doubt they need to come up with a not guilty verdict."

Michael had to admire her. He was adamantly opposed to using Felicity as a scapegoat, but he wasn't balking at using Hood. There was a difference, however. He was convinced Felicity had nothing to do with his wife's death. He couldn't be nearly as sure about Hood. Maybe Lara's scenario wasn't completely on the mark. Maybe Clare hadn't been part of the equation at all, just an innocent victim. Maybe Hood simply hated him enough to kill him.

"You're right," he agreed.

AFTER NINE MONTHS of preparation, depositions, checking alibis and examining evidence, Michael's trial began on a cool Thursday in late October. Predictably, the courtroom was packed.

His father and stepmother were there, as well as his brother, two sisters and their spouses. They had discussed letting the kids attend—well-mannered children could have a positive impact on a jury—but decided against it. Lara didn't contest their decision, but she did ask them to keep the option available for closing arguments.

For this opening scene of what she saw as the main act of a play, Lara selected a conservative suit in dark green that complemented her hair and eyes. She didn't want to draw attention to herself, but she was smart enough to understand she was an attractive woman in a profession still dominated by men. The secret was to acknowledge her position without emphasizing it.

Jury selection took till late afternoon on Friday. It came out evenly balanced: six men and six women. Since their attitudes toward family values were important, Lara had been careful to make sure they basically subscribed to what the First family stood for. The judge was a fifty-eight-year-old mother of two and grandmother of six. Margaret Smith had a reputation for honesty, evenhandedness and no nonsense.

The prosecution presented its case first. Burk Malvery established in his opening statement the reason the state had brought this action. The evidence, he contended, proved beyond the shadow of a doubt that the defendant, Michael First, had exclusive means and opportunity, as well as a powerful motive to kill his wife.

Lara noted he didn't overplay his hand. He simply whetted the jury's appetite for the details that were to follow. She reserved her opening remarks until later. Let the jury see the prosecution's case. Then she'd know where to focus her rebuttal, where to cast doubt.

Opening day of arguments was taken up with experts. They explained the nature of the accident and the conclusions they'd drawn from the evidence. Lara didn't challenge their facts. They were essentially incontrovertible. What she did contest was their interpretation of them.

"Mr. Maris, you have testified that you found hydraulic brake fluid on the ground where Mr. First indicated he'd parked his MG on Tarnished Mountain. Is that correct?"

"Yes, that is so." The forensics expert was a skinny fifty-year-old man who wore a cheap, ill-fitting tan suit.

"Was there much?"

He shook his head. "Not more than a few drops, but it was sufficient to establish it was the same type of hydraulic fluid used in the braking system of the MG."

Lara paced in front of the stand, her fingers interlaced, head down in thought. She glanced up at the witness.

"Having been to the top of Tarnished Mountain, Mr. Maris, would you say the spot Mr. First pointed out was the only logical place where the sportster could have been parked?"

"There are no roads up there. The automobile could have been parked anywhere."

"Yet Mr. First took you to the exact location where you were able to recover the brake fluid. Tell me, if he had not, do you believe, in your expert opinion, that you would have found it on your own?"

"It's very unlikely."

"So rather than hide anything, which he could have done easily by pointing you in another direction, he gave you the evidence you are presenting today. Is that correct?''

Maris stroked his chin. "I guess that's right."

"Doesn't sound like the actions of a man who has something to hide, does it?''

"Objection." The prosecutor stood up. "Calls for a conclusion.''

"Question withdrawn," Lara said. "Mr. Maris, you testified that the hole in the brake line was very small. Would hydraulic fluid have necessarily leaked out when the hole was made?''

An experienced witness, Maris turned to the jury and addressed them. "The hole in the brake line was tiny enough that the fluid would not readily leak out—not like a dripping faucet. It would have to be forced out under pressure.''

"Like when a person steps on the pedal."

"Exactly."

"In your expert opinion, could the brake line have been cut at another time and place without losing hydraulic fluid, if the brake pedal had not been depressed there?''

"Yes, that is quite possible."

"Thank you." Lara walked to her chair next to Michael. "No further questions for this witness."

"I FOUND Wayne Fischer," Gretchen announced, as she came into Lara's office later that day. Michael had sent his family home after court was adjourned with a promise to be there by suppertime. He craved a cold beer, but because he would be driving accepted the offer of coffee, instead.

"Where is he?" Lara asked.

"Dead." Gretchen flopped into the chair across from Michael at the conference table.

He murmured a curse.

"Two days after he was released from the hospital here, Fischer struck out for Wyoming. Got as far as Pueblo, Colorado, where he collided with an eighteen-wheeler. Blood-alcohol content was 2.1."

"Dear Lord." Michael closed his eyes. "Was anyone else hurt?"

"The rig driver. He was in serious condition for a while but survived."

Gretchen brushed a lock of blond hair from her face. "So he's not your man. He was fired a week before the accident, got out of the hospital two days later and left town two days after that. He was already dead when—"

"Damn." Michael was disappointed. He hadn't had much use for Fischer except as a murder suspect. Now the guy was dead, and they were no closer to knowing who had killed Clare.

CHAPTER TWELVE

LATER THAT NIGHT, after Michael had finished helping Beth Ann with her homework and sent her off with her grandmother to the guest house for her bath, he had a visitor. He and Chase Norman, who ran the agricultural side of the ranch, had never quite hit it off as pals, but they were friendly enough. Chase was good at his job, and Michael respected that. In his midfifties, he had three grown children, several grandchildren, had been divorced more than ten years and now lived alone in the modest cabin E. J. Hoffman had previously occupied.

Michael welcomed him into his father's living room, shook his hand and offered him a beer. The two men went out to the kitchen. After twisting off the tops on a couple of long necks, they settled down at the kitchen table.

"I'm a little embarrassed about this." Chase studied his beer bottle. "I should have remembered it earlier." He crossed one knee over the other. "You know Web has an open invitation for people to stop by his place on Saturdays after work."

Michael had never taken him up on the offer. He wasn't interested in drinking parties, and he certainly had no burning desire to spend time with Webster Hood. "Yes," he said dryly.

Chase gave him an understanding smile. "I only

dropped by twice myself. It's not my scene. I'll leave the loud music and fast women to the younger set. But today, when I was thinking over what the D.A. would be asking me on the stand, I remembered a remark I overheard the last time I went to Web's place. Brad Lopez was there—''

Something Lopez had never mentioned, but it explained a few things, like calling Hood by his first name and following his lead about bringing outside cattle onto the ranch. Michael was convinced the two had discussed Brad's ''compromise'' proposal in advanced. It wasn't something the ranch hand would have come up with on his own.

''I heard Web tell Brad in a joking way he'd gladly give him your job if he could find a way to get rid of you.''

Michael went still for a moment. ''When exactly was this?''

Chase huffed uncomfortably. ''The Saturday before Clare died.''

An ugly knot formed in the pit of Michael's stomach. ''What was Brad's response?''

''Nothing at first. Fischer was there. He made a smart comment about Brad not being able to tell a sheep from a goat. Brad laughed and pointed out he was a cattleman.''

They tended to look down on sheep and goats. ''What happened after that?''

''Everybody had a good chuckle, including Brad, and the party went on.''

''Do you think Hood was serious?''

''I didn't at the time. From what I could see, he was just venting his frustration about you getting that restraining order preventing him from selling any more breeding stock.'' Chase drank. ''He's even more furious with you now that the vaqueros have filed homestead applications.''

He looked across the table at Michael. ''I reckon you're aware things haven't been going well on the ranch since you...left. Web threatened to evict the Corderas. Their son reminded him there's a boot hill on the Number One. Ruben Garcia and several others echoed the sentiment.''

Michael raked his fingers through his hair. The state of affairs was worse than he imagined.

''Web's running scared. Brad...well, Brad isn't exactly the brightest bulb on the porch. Everyone realizes that. They help him only because they care about the ranch.''

Chase climbed to his feet. ''What I've just told you probably doesn't mean anything, but I figured you had a right to know. I'm real sorry about what's happened. Clare was a fine woman, and you're as good a rancher as I've ever met. If there's anything I can do—''

''Are you willing to testify to this?'' Michael wasn't sure if Chase would be allowed to. It might be thrown out as hearsay, but he'd let Lara decide that.

''You bet. And thanks for the beer.''

THE D.A. CALLED Brad Lopez to the stand. The new livestock manager was uneasy as he took the oath and sat down. Many people were uncomfortable when they had to face large groups; most of them relaxed after a while. Brad Lopez didn't.

Over the next half hour, Malvery drew a varied picture from his witness. Michael First, the nice guy.

Michael First, the good rancher, family man, father. Then came a crucial question.

"Mr. Lopez, would you say the defendant has a temper?"

Brad ran his finger under the collar of his new dress shirt. "He doesn't get mad often, but when he does, he gets real mad."

"Does he become violent?"

Brad lowered his head. "Sometimes."

"Can you give us an example?"

Clearly uncomfortable, Brad began. "When he was still the livestock manager, he hired a temporary ranch hand. This guy, Fischer, left a gate open and a bunch of young horses got out. One really nice colt broke his leg and had to be put down. Michael was pretty upset."

"What did he do?" Malvery prompted.

"He caught up with Fischer that evening at the bunkhouse. Gave him a royal chewing out, I can tell you."

"How did the confrontation end?"

"Michael knocked his lights out. Did it with a single punch. Broke the guy's jaw."

"No further questions." Malvery returned to his seat.

Lara rose and approached the witness stand. "Mr. Lopez, this incident you just recounted—who threw the first punch?"

"Well, Wayne Fischer did."

"So Mr. First was simply defending himself. Funny you didn't mention that. How would you describe your relationship with Mr. First?"

"We're friends." But Brad didn't look at him.

She raised her eyebrows. "Just friends? Didn't you

work for him as assistant livestock manager until he was fired by the Homestead Bank and Trust?''

He lowered his gaze. ''Yes.'' The word was very soft.

''Mr. Lopez, please speak up. The jury didn't hear you.''

''Yes, I was,'' he blurted out, almost defiantly this time.

''Before Mr. First was relieved of his duties, did you visit Webster Hood socially at his house on the Number One?''

''Sometimes,'' he admitted reluctantly.

''In fact, you visited Hood's Hideaway regularly to drink with him, didn't you?''

Lopez shrugged. ''I guess.''

''On one of those occasions, before the death of Clare First, did Mr. Hood tell you he would gladly give you the livestock manager's job if he could find a way to *get rid* of Mr. First?''

''I don't…uh.''

''Yes or no, Mr. Lopez.''

''Yeah, but—''

Lara took a pace toward the jury, then spun around to pin the man on the stand with a piercing stare. ''When you learned that Hood was trying to find an excuse to *get rid* of your *friend* as livestock manager, did you inform him? Warn him?''

Brad's chin practically rested on his chest. ''No.''

''I didn't hear you.''

He raised his head. ''No, I didn't.''

''Because you wanted your friend's job and the substantial pay raise that went with it.'' It wasn't a question and didn't require a response. ''Some friend.'' She spread her hands on the rail of the jury box, peered into the faces of the people there and spoke over her shoulder. "You were the one who discovered the MG and Clare First's body. Is that correct?"

He nodded. "Yes," he vocalized in a rusty voice.

"It was in a narrow ravine alongside Tarnished Mountain, a rather remote area of the ranch. No cattle, sheep or goats were kept in that area, were they?"

"Since our herds had been reduced, we didn't need to use that section," Lopez answered.

"So what were you doing there?"

His eyes went wide. His Adam's apple bobbed as he swallowed hard. He looked suddenly scared. "I was just passing through."

"Going from where to where?"

"From Triple Wells on my way to—"

"To Hood's place? To have a few drinks with him?"

"It was Saturday afternoon."

"But why drive by way of Tarnished Mountain? Why take that route? It's not the most direct way, is it?"

"Sometimes I take different roads. To check fences, gates, things like that."

"Did you know on that particular day that Michael and Clare were meeting there?"

"No."

"You just happened to be passing Tarnished Mountain a little while after Clare First plunged to her horrible death. Interesting." She moved toward her place at the defense table. "No more questions."

Michael sat, remarkably calm on the outside. When Brad Lopez descended from the stand, their eyes locked for what seemed a very long interval. Brad quickly left the room.

"PLEASE STATE your name and occupation for the record," Burk Malvery directed in his well-modulated baritone.

Wearing an expensively tailored western-cut, powder-blue suit and string tie with a large silver-and-turquoise bola, the witness epitomized the successful rancher. "Webster Hood. I'm the general manager of the Number One."

"You were, at the time of Clare First's death, the defendant's superior?"

"That's right. He was the livestock manager. I also have a manager for the agricultural part of the ranch."

"Would you characterize him as a good livestock manager?"

Hood hesitated enough to convey reservations. "He's real good with animals, but I wouldn't say the same about his management skills."

The D.A. spun around, feigning astonishment. "Why is that?"

"In recent months he'd also become neglectful of his duties."

"Neglectful of his duties." The D.A.'s brown eyes played over the jury. "Would you please elaborate?"

"I authorized an expensive inoculations program for our livestock, but he failed to administer the vaccines. The cattle got their shots only because his assistant, Brad Lopez, took the initiative and did it."

"Is that the only instance in which the defendant failed to properly and conscientiously discharge his duties?"

Hood shook his head in a way that suggested he

wished he didn't have to tattle. "Because of his negligence, one of our beef herds became infected with a bacterial disease. We had to destroy five hundred head of cattle, about a third of our stock."

"Must have been costly. What action did you take as a result of the defendant's negligence?"

"I reported the matter to Nedra Cummings, the vice president for investment and management. She relieved him of his duties."

Malvery spun around. "She fired him. How did he respond?"

"He threatened me."

"With bodily harm?"

"He didn't specify."

"In prior testimony, we learned that the defendant can be violent. Did you ever personally see this kind of violent behavior manifested in his relations with his wife?"

"I know they fought. I inadvertently walked in on a shouting match between them. He left the poor woman in tears."

"What was the fight about?" Malvery asked.

"Their son was picked up for smoking pot. Michael blamed her for the boy's behavior, said she wasn't a fit mother."

Murmurs rippled through the courtroom. Michael closed his eyes, but it didn't shut out the pain or slow the thumping of his heart or the anger poised behind the humiliation.

"Did you intercede in any way?" Malvery asked.

Hood shook his head. "I gave her a hug." He shrugged. "It was the best I could do."

"How about the other extreme?"

"I don't understand what you mean," Hood said, but the statement came across as disingenuous.

Malvery prowled the middle of the well. "About a week before Clare First was killed, didn't you walk in on an intimate embrace between her husband and a young woman who works on the ranch—"

"Your Honor—" Lara rose to object "—the district attorney is leading the witness."

Judge Smith nodded agreement and addressed the D.A. "Rephrase the question."

Lara knew the objection wouldn't prevent the information from coming out, but it disrupted the rhythm of the interrogation and dissipated some of its shock value.

Burk Malvery rolled with the punch. After a series of similar questions, he established that Hood had caught Michael holding Felicity Sanchez in what he characterized as an intimate embrace. "No more questions. Your witness."

Lara rose and stepped into the middle of the courtroom. "Mr. Hood, you've stated under oath that you saw Michael First and Felicity Sanchez in an embrace. Were they kissing?"

"Not exactly," Hood admitted.

"Not exactly?" She pulled back. "What does that mean? Either they were kissing or they weren't. Did you see them kissing? Yes or no."

"No."

"You saw them merely holding each other. Yes or no."

"Yes."

"How?"

"What do you mean how?"

"Where were their arms?"

He treated the question as a joke. "Around each other."

Lara spread her arms. "Show me."

"What?" Hood boggled. So did half the people in the room. A woman giggled.

"Hold me the way you saw the defendant holding Ms. Sanchez."

"Your Honor—" Malvery climbed to his feet "—defense counsel is turning this into a circus."

"Ms. Stovall, what are you doing?"

"Your Honor, the witness says he saw Michael First and Ms. Sanchez in an embrace. I want the jury to know exactly what the nature of that embrace was. Mr. Hood maintains it didn't involve kissing. How were they touching—"

"I don't appreciate theatrics in my courtroom."

"I apologize, Your Honor. I mean no disrespect, but I'm confronted with a dilemma here. I believe the witness, wittingly or not, may be misrepresenting the facts in this case. A demonstration will take but a second."

Lara could see the ambivalence on the judge's face. Had Malvery objected at that precise moment, he probably would have won, but Lara had been careful to stand between him and Smith.

"Very well," the judge conceded without enthusiasm, "but make it quick."

"Mr. Hood—" Lara followed up immediately, lest she lose the momentum "—would you please step down here?"

Hood was slow to respond, but he had no choice.

"Both Mr. First and Ms. Sanchez were standing, I assume," Lara began.

"Yes."

Lara placed her hands on Hood's arms and rotated him toward the gallery but facing away from the jury. She didn't want to give him an opportunity to undermine her by his expression.

"Assume I'm Ms. Sanchez." Lara moved up as close to him as she could without actually touching him. "Where are my hands?"

"Uh, around my waist."

Lara circled him, her hands not quite meeting in back, just above his belt. "Like this?"

"Um…yeah."

"And where are your hands—that is, Mr. First's hands?"

"Across your…her…shoulders."

"Go ahead," she prompted.

She adjusted the angle of her head so she was facing the jurors and barely touching Hood's chest. "This way?"

"Yes."

"Everyone, please note this position," she instructed the jury, then dropped her arms and pulled away from the man so abruptly he nearly staggered. "Thank you. You may return to the stand now."

Hood sat behind the chest-high barrier, clearly shaken. Before he could regain his balance, she posed the next question.

"You have sold off quite a large proportion of Number One livestock, have you not?"

"Yes."

"And leased the excess pasture for grazing by herds of cattle from outside the Number One?"

She saw Hood tightening up now, which was the way she wanted him. She'd had enough experience with juries to know they could sense discomfort in a witness, the kind that went beyond the stress of simply testifying, the kind associated with shame, guilt or fear.

"Did Mr. First object to your program?"

"He opposed most of my decisions on principle."

"On principle. You mean simply because you were the person who made the decision?"

"The spread had been in his family a long time. He couldn't accept that he wasn't still in charge."

"In this case, did he warn you that bringing outside animals onto the Number One would be dangerous, that it would introduce sources of contamination foreign to the native stock?"

"He expressed that concern, yes."

"So it wasn't solely on principle. He had valid reasons. And he was right, wasn't he?" When the witness failed to respond, she considered forcing a reply but decided to push on. The jury already knew the answer. "Would you tell the jury what brucellosis is?"

"Your Honor—" Malvery stood up in place "—the witness is not a veterinary expert."

"If it please the court, I have here a veterinary manual that is widely regarded as a definitive text on animal diseases, their symptoms, treatment and cures. I offer it as exhibit twenty-eight."

"So ordered."

She handed Hood the heavy tome, already marked to a certain page. "Please read the highlighted passage."

He held it up. "'Brucellosis causes abortions and infertility in cattle, as well as lower milk production. It is transmissible to people as undulant fever. The bacterial infection in humans results in severe flulike symptoms and debility that may persist for months or years. Treatment is not always successful.'''

"Sounds pretty serious for man and beast. Is there any record of brucellosis ever existing on the Number One prior to this outbreak?"

"Not that I'm aware of."

"In fact, until this infestation, wasn't it considered eradicated in Texas?"

"Yes."

"I repeat my question. Was Michael First justified in objecting to your bringing outside cattle onto the ranch?"

"I guess so."

"You guess so? A disease that has never existed on one of the largest spreads in Texas breaks out under your watch, threatens livestock and people, and you guess he was right in objecting?" She shook her head in disbelief.

"It wouldn't have happened if a fence hadn't fallen."

"Ah, the fence. Whose responsibility was it to maintain fences?"

"His." Hood was obviously pleased he could pass the blame.

"But you modified his existing maintenance schedule, didn't you? You delayed repairing the fence that ultimately collapsed. Isn't that right?"

"Yes, but—"

"Didn't Mr. First warn you that that section of fence was in dire need of immediate replacement? Didn't you refuse him the materials to get it done? In spite of the reported weakness of the fences, didn't you still insist on bringing outside animals onto the Number One?"

"Your Honor—" Malvery rose to his feet "—I must object. Not only is defense counsel browbeating the witness, but all this testimony is irrelevant, since it took place months after the death of Clare First."

"It goes to my premise that the witness has a personal animus against Michael First, Your Honor, that he distorts facts for his own benefit."

"Move on, Ms. Stovall," the judge ordered.

With a polite nod, Lara continued. "Where were you on the morning of Saturday, January 19, the day Mrs. First was killed?"

"At my home on the Number One Ranch."

"Did you go to the residence of Michael and Clare First? And if so, at what time?"

"I was there about eleven in the morning."

"For what purpose?"

"To let him know I was taking a steer into town to contribute to the food bank."

"Isn't that normally the job of the livestock manager? Why didn't you tell him to do it?"

"He wasn't around."

Lara raised a finger. "Ah, so you didn't go there to inform him *you* were taking a head of cattle to town, but to instruct him to do it."

"Well, no. I was fixing to do it."

Lara planted a puzzled expression on her face. "Why did you do this personally, when it would have been normal for you to instruct your livestock manager to do it?"

Hood demurred. "It was just something I wanted to do."

"You'd had a staff meeting with Mr. First the previous afternoon. Why didn't you tell him then?"

"I guess I forgot."

"You forgot you were giving away over a thousand pounds of beef on the hoof?" Her raised eyebrows made it very clear she didn't find the witness very credible. "The First family has been donating a head of beef in the name of the Number One for some years. Is that right?"

"It's a tradition we wanted to continue."

"'We.'" She paused to let the word sink in. "But you didn't give it in the name of the Number One, did you? You gave it in the name of the Homestead Bank and Trust."

"The bank is the major shareholder, just like the First family used to be."

"But—" she hesitated as if a little confused "—when the First family was the major shareholder, the beef was contributed in the name of the ranch, wasn't it? Now that the bank is the chief shareholder, the beef is contributed in their name, rather than the ranch's. Is that correct?"

"I don't see what difference it makes."

"Perhaps the jury will," she replied offhandedly. "Did you see Michael First at his house?"

"No."

"But you saw his wife?"

"Yes. I passed the word on to her to relay to her husband."

"What was she doing when you got there?"

"I have no idea. She was in the house. The housekeeper called her for me."

"How long did you have to wait for Clare First to appear?"

"Maybe two or three minutes."

"What did you do during that interval?"

"Nothing, just stood around waiting for her."

Without even asking, Lara had established he was out of his vehicle. "What did you talk about when she arrived?"

He shrugged. "I told her what I was doing. That's all."

"How long did that take?"

"I don't know. A minute?"

"Did she indicate when she expected her husband home?"

"She said he'd taken the kids somewhere. I don't remember her saying anything about when he was due back."

"Where was she when you left?"

"She'd already gone inside. I'd heard a bell ring. She said it was her grandmother calling her."

Lara brows rose, as if this were a new bit of information, a complete surprise. "So she left you alone outside while she went in to attend to her grandmother?"

Again a shrug, but it was more guarded. "Yeah."

"Did you see the MG while you were there?"

"Sure. It was parked in the garage."

"The garage was open?"

"I'm not sure if they ever closed it." Again he'd given her more than she'd asked for, establishing that the vehicle was readily accessible to anyone.

"You'd seen the English sports car before?"

He smirked. "Everyone had. He was always showing it off."

"You had a chance to see it up close and personal when he first put it on the road, didn't you?"

"Like I told you, he showed it to everyone."

"Did he let you drive it?"

"Are you kidding?" Hood sneered. "Nobody ever

got behind the wheel of that toy but him, not even members of his own family.''

Lara examined the intense concentration on the faces of the jurors and was satisfied that they'd understood this validated her earlier assertion, which she would reinforce in her summation, that Michael was the real target of the sabotage that killed his wife. "Did he ever take you for a ride in it?"

"Yeah. It was cool."

"How did the engine run?"

He stroked his chin. "I have to admit he did a good job rebuilding it. Purred like a kitten."

"How about the transmission? I've heard it had a tendency to jump out of gear. Is that true?"

"Well, it did pop out of second once when we were tooling around."

"How did Mr. First handle the situation? Did he cuss, stop the car, kick the tires, perform repairs on the spot?"

Hood snickered. "He clutched it back in and kept going like nothing had happened."

"So he didn't miss a beat. He wasn't surprised or disturbed about it?"

"He just seemed to take it in stride."

Lara paced casually across the front of the judge's raised platform. "You said he never let anyone else drive the MG," she reiterated. "So whoever tampered with the brakes must have expected Michael to be his victim, didn't he?"

The D.A. was on his feet in a flash. "Your Honor, defense counsel is asking the witness to draw a conclusion he has no way of knowing."

"Unless he was the person who tampered with the brakes."

The judge banged her gavel. "Objection sustained." She turned to the jury. "You will disregard Ms. Stovall's last comment." She peered at Lara. "And defense is again advised not to make prejudicial statements."

"Yes, Your Honor. Sorry." She addressed the witness. "Was anyone else around when you had your meeting with Clare First that Saturday morning?"

"Not that I could see."

"So there are no witnesses to how long you were there?"

He cocked his head. "No. I guess not." The response was wary.

"You had time to go over to the garage and inspect the MG, before and after she arrived, didn't you?"

"But I didn't."

"You could have checked under the hood, even tampered with the brakes before you drove off again, couldn't you?"

"I didn't touch the brakes."

"But you have no witnesses to verify that, either, do you?"

"Why would I fiddle with the MG?"

Lara gave him a feral smile. "Good question." She let the moment linger. "By your own admission, you and Mr. First didn't get along very well. How about his wife? How did you get along with her?"

"She was a nice woman."

"Nice enough to take in your arms when she seemed distraught?"

"I was trying to comfort her," he replied haughtily, but it came out like a whiny excuse. "She looked like she needed a friend."

"Isn't it curious? When Mr. First consoled a worried young woman, you conclude it's somehow lascivious, but when you take his wife in your arms, it's perfectly innocent. Or maybe your interest was more than just friendly.'' She leaned against the rail of the jury box. ''Maybe your snap decision to deliver a steer to town was made as an excuse to see Clare First when you realized Michael First wouldn't be around.''

''That's not true.''

''You were waiting in the wings to comfort her once. Did you hope to console her again?''

''It was nothing like that,'' he insisted in a raised voice.

''Then how was it?'' she persisted.

''You're making it sound like there was something going on between Clare and me, when there wasn't.''

''Certainly not on her part, Mr. Hood. She was a loving and faithful wife and mother. But you had another agenda, didn't you?''

''I don't know what you're talking about.''

Lara arched her brows in the classic expression of disbelief. ''Your family used to own a good-size spread in East Texas, isn't that right?''

He waved the comment away. ''That was a long time ago.''

''And your family lost it due to mismanagement?''

His jaw tightened. ''It was a bad economy. My old man was sick.''

''So instead of owning a family ranch now, you're an employee, a hired hand?''

''I'm more than a ranch hand.'' He poked his chest. ''I run the place.''

''But you don't own it. Now, if you could get Michael First out of the way, you'd have had a chance with Clare First. And if you were able to marry her, you'd be an owner again, not merely hired help. Is that what you had in mind?''

''That's not true.''

''We've heard testimony that it wouldn't have been difficult to sabotage the MG, that it would only take a few seconds. Michael First had been generous enough to show you his antique automobile, and the tools were right there in the garage. Clare First went into the house to attend to her grandmother, giving you plenty of opportunity to stroll over to the MG. Enough time for you to use the hacksaw hanging over the workbench. It only took a couple of strokes across the brake line, didn't it? Another second to snip the emergency brake cable. Then you got back into your truck and drove away, confident that the next time Michael First got behind the wheel of his little sportster, he'd die.''

''Your Honor,'' the prosecutor objected, ''defense counsel is bullying the witness. Is there a question here or is she testifying?''

The judge nodded her gray head in agreement. ''Counselor, ask your question.''

''Yes, Your Honor.'' Lara peered at the man on the stand. ''Mr. Hood, when you sabotaged Michael First's sports car, did you intend to kill *him* or the woman who'd rejected you?''

''Your Honor.'' The prosecutor again sprang from his chair.

''None of that's true,'' Hood shouted, his face red.

Mutterings rustled through the gallery.

The judge banged her gavel. ''Ms. Stovall, you're trying my patience.'' She addressed the people in the box. "Ladies and gentlemen of the jury, you will disregard defense counsel's last question."

"I have nothing further for this witness," Lara announced, and sat down next to Michael.

CHAPTER THIRTEEN

THE WITNESS was excused and the prosecution rested. Mercifully, the judge called a recess for lunch. Everyone, including Michael's family, traipsed out into the hall. Lara mechanically gathered the papers she'd strewn across her table and stuffed them carelessly into her briefcase. Michael studied her. She was good. Awareness of her ruthless determination not only reassured him but made him unexpectedly proud.

"What was your point in having Hood put his arms around you?" He'd almost laughed at Hood's reaction, but there'd also been a stab of jealousy. "I don't like the thought of that sleazebag touching you."

She chuckled. "Apparently, he wasn't too eager, either. That was the point. I figured he'd be reluctant to embrace me tightly or provocatively. I wanted the jury to go away with the image of you holding Felicity in a merely friendly, big-brother sort of way."

"And if he'd wrapped you in his arms and kissed you wildly, passionately?" He made light of it, though the notion brought a sickening knot to his stomach.

Lara laughed. "That might have been better." At his startled expression, she added, "He'd already stated under oath there hadn't been a kiss. If he'd kissed me, he would have undermined his own credibility."

"Why didn't you have him demonstrate how he held Clare?"

She shook her head. "The shock effect was gone. Besides, if he showed more body contact or affection in that demonstration, it would have reflected unfavorably on Clare, and I don't want to put the victim on trial. No," she said conclusively, "the jury will go away with the image of Hood consoling Clare the way you consoled Felicity—purely platonic."

He almost reached out and touched her, then remembered where he was. "Thank you for respecting Clare's memory."

"I do respect her." Lara took out her cell phone and flipped it open. "I need to check in with Carol."

"I'll wait for you outside."

While she nodded and poked in numbers one-handed, he passed through the swinging gate and walked down the aisle to the double doors of the courtroom. Webster Hood and Brad Lopez were outside, a few feet away. Michael started past them.

"Real slick lawyer you got yourself. I like the perfume she wears. Fell in love with it the first time she came to see me."

First time? Lara had only mentioned visiting him once. This must be another of Hood's word games.

"A real fox, too."

Michael refused to be goaded and kept moving.

Hood laughed. "Bet she's worth every cent you pay her."

The press of the crowd made it impossible to get by his antagonist without inching closer to him. As he did, Hood muttered in a stage whisper, "Your highly paid mouthpiece came on to me, buddy-boy. I didn't have to do a thing."

Involuntarily, Michael clenched his hands and drew himself up. He heard cameras clicking behind him.

Hood smirked. "She wanted a real man, Mikey-boy, not some cowboy who smells of cattle dung and sheep dip. She initiated—"

Michael's vision narrowed and his scalp tingled as rage possessed him. He resolved to avoid an open confrontation, but his muscles seemed to tense of their own accord. Brad slipped up beside him and clasped his wrist in an iron grip, pinning Michael's arm to his side. It was this confinement, more than the taunting words, that made him want to lash out physically. Gideon, who'd sidled closer when he heard Hood's baiting remarks, grabbed his brother's other arm.

Claustrophobia smothered him. As blood pounded through his head, Michael leaned into Hood's face. "Stay clear of me and my family," he hissed, in what he thought was an undertone, "or I swear to God, I'll kill you." On a racking exhale, he shrugged and shook off his restrainers.

A security guard stepped between the two men, but he spoke to Michael's companions. "Better take him outside and let him cool off."

"He's fine," Brad assured him, sounding like an old pal.

Michael did an about-face and bumped into a man shooting a videocam. Behind him, standing next to Adam, Lara was staring at him with as hard an expression as he'd ever encountered.

The guard shooed everyone away. "Move along, folks. There's nothing to see."

"We're meeting Gretchen at the office in twenty minutes." Lara's tone was stiff and formal. "She's picking up sandwiches. Leave your truck here and come with me.'' She marched to the door of the court-house.

''Better get out of here,'' Adam said anxiously.

The revived clamor of voices echoing off the marble walls surrounded Michael, momentarily disorienting him. The look in Lara's eyes, guarded, angry, yet strangely vulnerable, filled his mind.

Outside, he climbed into the BMW. She drove in silence to the office. In the side parking lot, she stopped, killed the engine but made no move to get out. Even with her hands still clutching the steering wheel, he could see she was shaking.

''Would you mind telling me what the hell that was all about?'' She wasn't shouting, but there was unmistakable rage in her tightly controlled voice.

''He suckered me.''

''Too bad you were so slow to figure that out.'' She lowered her hands and swiveled to face him. ''I've been trying to establish that you're not a violent man, that when you hit Fischer, it was in self-defense.''

''It was. We have witnesses that he threw the first punch.''

''And their testimony won't make a damn bit of difference now because half the courthouse saw you about to attack Hood.''

''I never raised a finger to him,'' Michael pointed out.

''No,'' she snapped, ''you threatened to kill him. If Lopez and your brother hadn't been there, you'd be cooling your heels right now in jail on charges of assault and battery, and your bail would probably be revoked. That show of temper, Michael, totally undermined your credibility—and mine.''

Feeling like a schoolboy called to the principal's office for breaking a window when all he wanted to do was hit a homerun, he said, ''I'm sorry.''

''Save it for the sentencing phase.'' She opened her door, got out, slammed it behind her and strode into the building.

THE AFTERNOON SESSION was frustrating. Michael listened as character witnesses swore his praises. Instead of bolstering his morale, their accolades made him feel like a charlatan. He watched the jury, made eye contact when he could, searched for sympathetic faces. Most of them were blank.

His mind kept sneaking back to Lara, the way she'd looked at him in the lobby of the courthouse. Despair had lurked behind the shock and anger. Her grimace had conveyed another emotion, too, one that made his chest ache. She was scared.

Around five o'clock, Judge Smith recessed for the day.

''I bet you could use an adult beverage,'' Michael told her, as she gathered up her notes and stuffed them into her attaché.

She sighed.

He relieved her of the briefcase when she closed it, gently put his hand on the small of her back and escorted her down the aisle to the double doors. His father was waiting for them on the other side.

''I'm off to Dave's soccer practice,'' Adam told him. ''Sheila's already there.''

''It'd be great to be outdoors for a change with

nothing more demanding than yelling and cheering,"
Lara said. "Why don't we go, too?"

Relieved that she seemed to be over her pique at
him, Michael trailed her through the front door.

"Follow me to my place, Michael, so I can change
clothes? I'll leave my car and go to the game with
you, if that's all right."

"No use taking two vehicles," he agreed.

At her house, just inside the door, he grasped her
shoulder and coaxed her around to face him. "I'm
sorry I'm making your job so tough."

She bit her lip, an uncharacteristically shy gesture,
a crack in the armored persona she'd put on display
ever since the trial began.

"I promise to do better." With the side of his index
finger, he lifted her chin so he could see her eyes. She
met his, but with a kind of guilty hunger. He knew
exactly what she was feeling at that moment.

Slowly, he brought his mouth down to hers,
skimmed her lips, reestablished separation, paused.
The second time their lips met, he deepened the kiss,
and she responded. Tentatively at first, unsure. Then
her arms wound around his back and tightened their
grip. For one terrible, wonderful moment, he thought
he was going to lose it.

Her body quivered in his embrace, his hardened
with pent-up need and hunger. The sensations of her
pressed against him, breasts, hips, the smell of woman
beneath her delicate perfume, sent his blood pounding. He couldn't have opened his eyes if he tried. His
anatomy responded on its own. He could barely keep
from ravaging her.

Her arms moved from behind his back to the front
of his chest. She firmly pushed him away. They were

both panting hard. Neither of them was willing to make eye contact.

On a breathless sigh, she said, "I need to change clothes."

He nodded. When their gazes finally met, he managed a smile. After a heartbeat, she smiled back.

"I won't be long." She spun on her heel and retreated into her bedroom.

His pulse still racing, his manhood still on alert, he wandered from the living room to the dining room and examined the crystal and china that had so impressed Sheila. His mind wasn't on heirlooms, though. He was disconcertingly preoccupied with the image of Lara in the next room slipping out of her gray suit and teal silk blouse. He pictured her long legs rising to her panties, her flat tummy tapering up to her bra.

In the first months after Clare's death, he'd felt no interest in other women. Grief had suppressed all passion. But as his life adapted to new patterns, old needs and desires had begun to flare up. Never more than when he was with Lara. His libido made him feel disloyal to Clare's memory, but instincts couldn't be denied. He was on trial for his life, yet his body and his mind were focusing on the woman in charge of saving it.

He grimaced. His wife had been dead ten months. He was a grown man, trapped between today's problems and yesterday's mistakes.

Lara emerged from her bedroom in a plaid cotton shirt and bleached-out jeans. She'd pulled her fiery-red hair back and tied it into a ponytail with a kelly-green ribbon. Michael saw before him the girl of twenty years earlier. Fresh. Vibrant. Eager, yet shy. "Ready?"

Exhaling, he grabbed his jacket.

Soccer practice was already under way when they got there. Dave was good. He had the agility and speed the game required, but if he kept growing at the rate he was now, in another year, two at the most, his height would make him more suited to basketball—or football, if he ever put on weight.

"How's the trial going?" Dave asked warily, when practice was over.

"We're doing fine," Lara assured him. "Your dad will testify tomorrow."

"Can I be there?"

"Grandpa's already cleared it with the principal," Michael said, "for you and Sally to attend."

"Really?" Dave was obviously excited about going to court, but there was also apprehension in his keen blue eyes.

"Right now," Adam said, "we have to get home. You're excused from class tomorrow, but not from homework."

"If I don't see you later tonight, I will in the morning, son." Michael put his arms around the boy. Dave gave Lara a hug, as well, then ran after his grandfather.

"You've made another friend." Michael was inordinately pleased that the two were getting along so well.

"I told you he's a smart kid."

She was being flippant, but Michael could see by the color rising to her cheeks and the tantalizing prominence of her freckles that she was touched by the teenager's show of affection.

"You deserve a big, juicy steak," he said, as he escorted her to his truck.

"I need brain food tonight. Let's pick up catfish

and take it to my place? I even have a bottle of wine in the fridge.''

This time when they entered her house, there was no pausing in the hallway, no body contact. She slipped into attorney mode—for the time being, at least. ''Make yourself at home,'' she told him as she got out dishes and silverware for their carryout meal. ''You'll be here awhile. We have a lot to cover.

''Are you absolutely sure you want to do this, Michael?'' She got paper plates out of the pantry and replenished the paper napkin holder. ''You don't have to take the stand in your own defense, and by doing so, you leave yourself wide open to cross-examination.''

''I know,'' he said with a huff of frustration. ''You've explained it to me several times. I have no new information or unique perspective to add to the evidence, and you're afraid Malvery will make mincemeat out of me.''

''After that episode in the courthouse today, I'm doubly worried. He's good at what he does,'' she reminded him. He'd already painted Leon Cordera, the most prominent of the senior vaqueros, a bootlicker, willing to say anything on behalf of the First family.

Michael slumped in his chair for a moment, then straightened. ''You've done a good job of defending me, Lara. I couldn't ask for a better attorney, but ultimately I have to defend myself. I have to let the jury see and hear me, not other people talking about me. As for my confrontation with Hood…I'm not a hothead, and by taking the stand, I can show them I'm not. I can prove it.''

''Pride,'' she said, not sure if she meant it in praise or reproach.

His gaze met hers. "I wouldn't be much of a man without it."

The softness of his voice contrasted with the hardness of his words and the determination in his blue eyes. The combination had her blood racing, her chest warming. "Let's get started."

They spent nearly two hours reviewing his testimony—what she would ask, what he could volunteer, as well as the tone he should use—then another two hours trying to anticipate the prosecution's questions. Lara wasn't surprised when he chafed at the spin she put on some of her questions.

"That's exactly the response Malvery is hoping for. If you get impatient, you're in serious danger of spouting something stupid, maybe even untrue, because you're being defensive."

"What am I suppose to do—be an automaton?" he retorted. It was after ten. He was tired, wound up, frustrated.

"It'll be better than losing your temper," she argued almost as heatedly. "I'm not saying you can't show any emotion, Michael, but it better be the kind the jury can admire. Love, compassion, sadness, even offense at a few of his questions. But hot temper will make the jury fearful and turn them off in a heartbeat."

He nodded. She was right.

"Take a deep breath before answering each question. Think about what you're going to say and how it will be heard by the jury. You're not there to duel with the district attorney. Your sole mission is to demonstrate to the jurors that you're an innocent man caught up in a tragic nightmare."

They went over his testimony again.

Finally Michael rose from the couch and stretched his arms over his head. "Can we take a break?"

"Yeah, I'm ready, too."

"You mentioned a bottle of wine earlier." They'd had soft drinks with their catfish and hush puppies.

"In the fridge," she said. "Why don't you pour it while I freshen up?"

He found the Chardonnay on the bottom shelf, located a corkscrew in a drawer and removed wineglasses from an overhead cabinet. After pulling the cork, he discovered his energy was back and took the bottle and glasses into the living room.

He was walking a fine line, a tightrope. He'd loved...still loved...Clare. He owed it to his children to honor her memory. Yet he wanted Lara. A man could control his urges, the passions that drove him, but he couldn't ignore them. He needed a woman in his life. No, that wasn't fair. It assumed that any woman would do, and that certainly wasn't true. He needed a woman he could trust, someone he could share his deepest secrets with, someone who knew and accepted him for who and what he was. He needed Lara. She'd been a part of his life once. She'd become a part of his life again.

But he wasn't thinking in terms of mere companionship now. His mind and his body were focused on intimacy, when he needed to concentrate on the key to the rest of his life—getting acquitted of murdering his wife. With that hurdle behind him, maybe he could put things in perspective. Guilt, fierce and shame-filled, gnawed at his insides because, at the moment, all he could think about was making love to Lara.

IN THE BATHROOM, Lara splashed water on her face to wipe away the cobwebs formed by the tedium of legal maneuvering. She loved the law, but she had to admit she'd been having difficulty concentrating on it this evening. Riding next to Michael in his truck, standing beside him at the soccer field, then sitting across from him in her kitchen had been pure distraction. Even as her words centered on testimony and rules of evidence, her mind kept wandering to Michael's kiss earlier in the evening. No benign affection this time, but the beginning of something erotic, strong and demanding. The taste and texture of his lips and the feel of his body pressed against hers had been like a cup of water in the desert, necessary to life. All evening, she'd tried to reel back the thirst, but it only tormented her more.

Her experience with men since Clay's death had been limited, but not so restrained that she didn't recognize a man's desire when he touched her. Desire in both of them. She wanted Michael to kiss her again. She wanted more than a kiss. These past few hours, seeing him reclining on her couch, his toes wiggling in his socks after he'd pulled off his boots, the top of his shirt parted, so that she constantly caught glimpses of the curls of black hair peeking above the buttons…distraction wasn't a strong enough word. Tomorrow would be a crucial day in his trial, and here she was fantasizing about her client's body. Real smart, Counselor, she upbraided herself.

He was waiting for her in the living room. Tall, broad shouldered, narrow-hipped. His black hair tousled from dragging his fingers through it. His blue eyes danced, as if he saw what was running through her mind.

He handed her a glass of the white wine, then clinked his glass against it.

"Here's to a short trial and a favorable verdict," she offered.

"And to us. Let old acquaintance not be forgot."

Acquaintance. Such a bland word. Too bland for what she felt back then, when she was a teenager full of hopes and dreams. Is that what she was now, a convenient old acquaintance? Someone with no future?

They sipped, their glances meeting over the rims of their wineglasses. She'd never forgotten those beautiful eyes, not completely.

"I'm glad to have you in my life, Lara." He coaxed her onto the couch beside him and draped his arm over her shoulders. When she didn't say anything, he asked, "Are you glad to be back?"

"Hmm." As if it were the most natural thing in the world, she rested her head against his chest. The solid warmth of his body had her blood racing. "I'm glad."

He stroked her arm, making her breath catch. She could hear his heartbeat. Slow, steady, dependable. She shut out vision, concentrated on touch and spread her hand on his chest. His nipple peaked against her palm. Her own nipples hardened. "Life throws us curves sometimes."

"Unkind curves," he murmured sadly. She felt his pulse pick up a beat. "But I like your curves. Have I told you that?"

She couldn't help but lift her head at the playful intimacy in his voice. She smiled up into his laughing eyes. "As a matter of fact, you haven't."

Her respiration was labored as she rubbed the thick, firm ridge of pectoral muscle. "Your curves aren't so bad, either."

He lowered his head and captured her mouth with

his. For a fleeting moment panic bolted through her. Was she worried he'd hurt her again? Or was she just afraid he would stop doing what he was doing? She unlocked her lips, invited him in, the man she'd wanted so many years ago, the man she wanted still. She'd been a kid then, young and naive. Not anymore. Wherever this was leading, she was following him with her eyes wide open. No excuses this time.

He moaned softly when they parted, his body grown rigid with pent-up need. A tiny voice in her subconscious told her this was all wrong. She was his lawyer; he was her client. But she shut the notion out. She knew she was acting on emotion, not common sense, that emotions were untrustworthy, not permanent. What she needed at this stage in her life was something more solid than the rush of hormones. But she'd take the rush and every fleeting moment of pleasure it promised. She just wouldn't depend on it to last, or on him to stay.

"We'll be more comfortable in the other room," she murmured. "I have a bed in there."

MICHAEL PROMISED HIMSELF he'd go slowly, that he'd savor each second with her, prolong the rapture. He didn't, of course. More than ten months of abstinence made patience impossible. Even as his mind urged endurance, his body raced toward the precipice. They tore at each other's clothes, touched each other with a desperation that was uncontrollable. His fingers fumbled. His mouth ravaged. He was molten steel. She was liquid fire. They fused in an instant explosion that left them both breathless. She took the leap with him, shuddered in the headlong vault over the edge in a single euphoric release.

Then she laughed. It wasn't what a man expected

when he made love to a woman. He started to pull away, but she locked her wrists behind his neck and held him captive. She grinned up at him, eyes wide and searching, while laughter bubbled through her body—and his.

"You're wonderful," she said happily. He was still inside her when she began to wiggle.

"Dear God," he muttered. He sucked air in between his teeth as his vision blurred.

"I've only just begun."

He covered her mouth with his. Their tongues darted, danced, then settled into a rhythmic tango. The slow cadence deepened, became more intense. Heat spiraled through him. He slipped his arms under her back, rolled across the king-size bed. Her knees settled beside his hips. He watched her take him until all his senses, save feeling, deserted him.

LARA LAY BESIDE HIM, her head nestled in the crook of his shoulder, her hand draped across his flat belly. He was slipping into the twilight of relaxed contentment when she spoke.

"Why did you threaten Hood at the courthouse?" Her soft voice rippled along his skin. "You must have known you were being snookered." She raised her head and gazed at him, the clear green depths of her eyes seeking for understanding. "Why didn't you just walk away?"

He drew a finger along the line of her jaw. "He said some things about you I didn't like."

She pressed her palm against his chest and rearranged her body against him, her breast brushing his side, searing his skin with velvet warmth.

"Sticks and stones, Michael. I'm a lawyer. I'm used to being called names."

But names can hurt, with a pain that lasts far longer than sticks and stones.

"He wasn't talking about my lawyer. He was talking about you." He angled himself so their eyes met. "You can change being a lawyer, Lara, but you can't change who you are."

"And who I am needs defending. Is that what you're saying?"

He stroked the side of her face with his knuckles, cupped his hand behind her head and brought her lips down to his. "Who you are—" he kissed her mouth tenderly "—deserves to be defended from the likes of Webster Hood."

She wasn't appeased. "I can take care of myself." She would have pulled away if he'd given her a chance.

He didn't. He combed his fingers into the luxuriant brilliance of her hair and held it. "I don't doubt that for a minute, sweetheart. But wouldn't you like company, someone at your side?"

She slipped out of his grasp, settled on the pillow next to him and drew the sheet up to cover her nakedness.

"I don't need protection, Michael."

He wondered if she could hear the loneliness that tainted her words. She'd spent her entire life guarding herself from people who should have offered her sanctuary. Her parents, her grandmother, her husband. And now from him—again.

"I didn't think I did, either." He buttressed himself on his elbow to view her and propped his head with his fist. "The big, strong, eldest son of Adam First was always in control." She turned at his self-mockery to study his face. "Except that now I need you to save my life. Figuratively and literally."

He scanned the swell of her breasts under the sheet. Unable to resist, he slipped his hand beneath the cotton percale and sought the smooth contours. She blinked slowly and her breathing went shallow as his fingers stroked her warm flesh. He wanted her again. He couldn't get enough of her. "Why did you go into the practice of law, Lara?"

Confusion clouded her expression. She exhaled. "I already told you. It's interesting."

"Hmm." Her skin was like velvet. "I reckon it was more than that." He trailed a finger across her belly. He couldn't stop himself. "I suspect you went into law because you want to see people live by rules, not simply by impulse or selfish convenience. Like your parents."

She chuckled, making her flesh ripple beneath his palm, shooting darts of stimulation through him. "You're talking psychobabble, Michael." But even in his preoccupied state, he noticed she was listening.

His fingers wandered lower. "I figure you became a defense attorney because you wanted to protect people from intimidation and arbitrary power. Like your grandmother."

She brushed his hand away. He'd gone too far. "That's nonsense." There was annoyance, even anger, in her words. But he could see her mind was also working.

"You're probably right," he agreed lightly. Unwilling to be completely diverted, he leaned over and kissed her on the cheek. When she didn't immediately respond, he planted a big sloppy one on her mouth. She wanted to resist him. He could tell. But he knew how to be very persuasive.

CHAPTER FOURTEEN

MICHAEL STARED UP AT the reflection of moonbeams dancing on the ceiling. Lara was curled beside him, her respiration an undulating murmur. Clare had slept like that.

The echo of her presence brought a lump to his throat. Clare hadn't been gone a year and already he was in another woman's bed. Guilt growled like an avenging lion.

Lara's chest rose with each leisurely breath. She'd given herself to him, and he'd taken. In a few hours, he'd have to meet her eyes from the witness stand, answer her questions about the woman he'd loved. He'd have to face his family, his children and swear he'd loved no other.

In all their years together, he'd never been unfaithful to Clare. He'd never had a desire to be. But now, while he stood before the world accused of murdering her, he'd had sex with another woman. Not just sex. What he'd experienced was more than the union of flesh. It went deeper. And that in an odd way only made it worse.

He'd been unfair to Lara years ago. He was being unfair to her now.

Carefully, he disengaged himself from her and slipped out of the bed. In the thin gray moonlight, he located his far-flung pieces of clothing, tiptoed out of the room and closed the door. The latch clicked. He padded down the hall to the living room which was still ablaze with light. Self-consciously, he dressed, noting the nearly full wineglasses on the coffee table. He shook his head. This night had been a mistake.

A SOUND AWAKENED LARA. Her initial reaction was confusion, followed by the recognition that she was in her bed. Her next response was fear that someone was in the house. Then came the realization that indeed she wasn't alone. Michael was with her. But beside her the bed was empty.

She climbed out and snagged her robe from the back of the bathroom door and stepped into the hallway. She found him in the living room, pulling on his boots.

"You're leaving?" She'd known from the beginning he would.

"I should go." He got to his feet. "Your neighbors—"

She laughed. "It's a little late for that."

God, what had she done? She'd violated one of the sacred tenets of professional ethics—not to become intimately involved with a client. She'd compromised herself with the one man she'd sworn to remain aloof from. He was on trial for his life. Her mission was to save him, not make love with him. Knowing how much she wanted him, how much pleasure she took in being in his company, how safe and secure she'd felt in his arms—tormented her.

She'd sworn she wouldn't make herself vulnerable to him again, but then he'd kissed her and she'd begun to waver. He'd touched her and she'd melted like a schoolgirl. But she wasn't a schoolgirl anymore.

She'd known exactly where his caresses were leading. She'd been complicit in his advances, even leading him to her bedroom. She was a double fool, for she would do it all again, given the opportunity, knowing it would never go any further. He'd gotten up from her bed in the dark, and now he was leaving. As he'd left her before, except this time she had an even better idea of what might have been—if she'd been worthy.

She waited until he'd retrieved his hat from the table in the hall. "Last night was a mistake, Michael."

Instead of arguing, instead of telling her how much it had meant to be with her, he nodded. "Wrong time. Wrong place."

His averted eyes spoke of guilt and shame. At least he hadn't called her Clare when they were making love. But of course it was her he'd been thinking about. Lara couldn't blame him. He'd loved his wife. Clare was the woman he'd always wanted. For him there could be no other.

"I won't let it happen again," she muttered.

"I understand," he replied quietly, without a protest. "I'm sorry I jeopardized your position. It was all my fault. I shouldn't..." He let the words dwindle off. "When this is over—"

"Maybe we can remain friends," she said coolly.

He raised his head and met her gaze. "Friends?" The word harbored a plea. "You're very special to me, Lara."

She forced a smile. "An old acquaintance." Tightening one arm across her belly, she used her other fist to close the cleavage of her robe at the base of her neck. "Court starts at nine, only a few hours from now. Remember what we talked about. Stay cool on the stand.''

''I promise.'' He paused at the door observing her. His finger reached for his hat and stopped. In three swift steps, he stood before her and placed his big, warm hands on her shoulders. ''Thank you,'' he said softly, and kissed her sweetly on the lips.

She resisted the urge to close her eyes. She needed to see things clearly from now on, not let her judgment be clouded by his presence. Hadn't she promised herself to take what pleasure she could, without regrets, then move on?

After the door was closed and locked, and the sound of his pickup had receded into the night, she returned to her bedroom. Tomorrow would be a crucial day in court. Being at the top of her game was paramount. She needed some sleep, but all she could think of was the man who had shared her bed.

Yes. It had been a major mistake.

MICHAEL ROSE to take the stand in his own defense. The front page of the morning paper showed him scowling at Webster Hood with malignant hatred. Witness Threatened, read the headline.

Lara had prepared him as best she could for the ordeal he would have to endure. Then she'd made love to him. The memory both warmed and frightened her.

For the occasion, he was wearing a conservative western-cut gray suit with darker gray piping, white shirt and an understated blue tie. His dark hair, freshly trimmed, was neatly combed. He was an imposing figure in the dock. A healthy, prosperous rancher whose large hands suggested he'd achieved his success by dint of hard work. Lara tried not to dwell on what those hands had accomplished the night before—or the wedding ring he still wore.

Many of the jurors heard his rich baritone for the first time when he answered Lara's preliminary questions—name, address, age. A virile voice of confidence and self-assurance.

After reviewing the family history, his education and ranching experience, she got to the crux of the matter.

"Please tell us what happened on January 19 of this year."

Carefully, she led him through that day's sequence of events. His feeding his own horses showed a man who wasn't afraid to get dirty. Having breakfast with his children demonstrated his close family involvement, as did taking his daughters to a friend's house for the weekend and letting his son go off with a buddy to tour the local fort and stay overnight with him.

Lara reviewed Brigitte's condition and let him explain that a nurse had been hired to look after her for the afternoon and night in question, so he and Clare could get a respite.

Several jurors nodded approvingly when he explained how beholden Clare felt to the grandmother who had taken her in when her parents were killed in a car accident. Two women in the jury blinked slowly when Michael recounted how difficult and demanding it was to care for a bedridden Alzheimer's patient. "What was Clare's frame of mind when you left her on the top of Tarnished Mountain?"

Here Michael paused and let emotion show. This wasn't staged. If he'd had his way, he would have

been placid and unruffled—grown men didn't cry—
but recollection of that day and of the woman he had
pledged his life to cherish and protect unsettled him.

"We were both in a jubilant mood," he said, a
noticeable huskiness in his voice. "We'd been
through a difficult period, and now we were getting
on with our lives, with our marriage."

Lara waited a moment. Her pulse jumped in antic-
ipation of the next question. "Michael, did you love
Clare?"

He avoided meeting with her and faced the jury. It
was what she'd instructed him to do, but she felt be-
reft, dismissed, when his gaze avoided her. "With all
my heart."

She paused once more. "Did you kill her?"

"No."

She nodded to him, a quiet, professional bow of
approval. Turning away, she announced, "Your witness."

BURK MALVERY ROSE slowly from his chair, moved
into the middle of the well and faced the defendant.
Lara had warned Michael, he would probably start off
quietly, almost sympathetically.

"You say, Mr. First, that you loved your wife. Did
she love you?"

"Yes. Without a doubt."

"How, then, do you explain her falling into the
arms of Webster Hood after having a fight with you?"

Following Lara's advice, Michael picked out the
key word to quibble over. "It wasn't a fight, Mr. Malvery. We had a disagreement. She was understanda-
bly upset."

Malvery clasped his hands behind his back and

paced in front of the dock. "What did you disagree about?"

Michael paused, as if searching for the right words, though he and Lara had gone over this subject repeatedly. "I was concerned she was wearing herself out, spending too much time with her grandmother at the expense of herself and the rest of the family."

"You mean neglecting you, don't you? She wasn't performing her wifely duty." There was a man-to-man sneer in his tone.

Michael laughed, which immediately dissipated his own tension. "If you're referring to sex, Mr. Malvery, I assure you, there was nothing wrong with our sex life." He didn't dare look at Lara, because he didn't trust himself. Last night had been special. It had also been a violation of vows—for both of them.

Yet, he felt something for Lara that went far beyond the need for physical release. He wanted to share every aspect of his life with her. Did that mean he loved her? It was too soon, his fate too uncertain. But something enormous was happening, and she was at the center of it.

"You claim you loved your wife, Mr. First. Yet you held another woman in your arms."

"Mr. Malvery, I was always absolutely faithful to Clare. I'm equally sure she was completely faithful to me."

"What about Felicity Sanchez? Do you seriously expect these good people to believe you hugged that pretty young woman and it did nothing for you?"

Michael refused to be rattled. "If you're asking whether there was affection in letting her cry on my shoulder, the answer is yes—the affection of a big brother for a kid sister. If you're suggesting there was any sexual involvement, you're wrong.''

"Come, come, Mr. First. You're a strong, healthy male. Surely you must have strayed from time to time. Men do.''

"Is that a confession on your part, Mr. Malvery?''

The courtroom rippled with snickers and chuckles. The prosecutor's face reddened. ''Your Honor, will you please direct the defendant that he's here to answer questions.''

"Mr. First,'' the judge intoned very seriously, "please limit your comments to responses to direct questions.''

"Yes, Your Honor, except I didn't hear a question—I only heard an innuendo.'' He gazed at the prosecutor, whose disposition had not improved. "What was the question?''

"Were you ever unfaithful to your wife?'' Malvery snarled.

"No,'' Michael stated flatly, categorically.

"You and your attorney, Ms. Stovall, dated in high school and college, didn't you?''

"Yes,'' Michael admitted, uncertain now where this was going, uncomfortable with the prospects of where it might lead.

"You were practically engaged, I understand.'' When Michael made no response since there had been no question, Malvery added, "Is that right?''

"No, it isn't. We hung out together, but there was never an offer of marriage or even a discussion of it.'' He glanced immediately at Lara and saw the stoic expression on her face. Unwilling to explore what emotions might be smoldering behind the professional facade, he quickly turned his attention to the prosecutor.

"Ms. Stovall moved back to Coyote Springs only a couple of months before your wife's death. Did you reestablish your relationship with her at that time?"

"No," Michael insisted a little too loudly. It came out sounding defensive and untruthful. He vowed to rein in his reactions.

Malvery quirked an eyebrow. "It's just coincidence that a few months after your old girlfriend comes back to town, your wife gets killed in a staged automobile accident."

Lara jumped to her feet. "Your Honor, where is this going?"

Before the judge could respond, the prosecutor spun to face Michael, his voice heated and hostile. "Tell us, Mr. First, where did you spend last night?"

Lara was around the side of the table in a flash. "Objection, Your Honor. This line of questioning is completely irrelevant, immaterial and highly prejudicial. May we approach?"

The judge motioned for them to come up to the podium. "What's going on here?" She placed her hand over the microphone used for recording.

In a hushed tone Lara declared, "Where Mr. First spent last night is of absolutely no relevance to this trial, Your Honor."

"It goes to the defendant's credibility," Malvery insisted in the same intense whisper.

"In what way?" Judge Smith inquired.

"Mr. First spent last night with Ms. Stovall," said Malvery.

Smith shifted her gaze to Lara, who made no attempt to deny it.

"In my chambers. Now," she ordered.

Lara's chest was thumping as she followed the judge and opposing counsel through the doorway to the left. She'd told Michael to be prepared for the unexpected, but this went even beyond her darkest fears. If the prosecution brought out her relationship with Michael in court, it would almost certainly make her defense of him suspect. She'd have to ask for a mistrial and this horror would begin all over again with another attorney. She had to do what she'd advised her client: take a deep breath and consider what impact her statements would have on her audience.

"Now, will one of you tell me what's going on here?" Margaret Smith demanded, after they were in her office, the door closed.

"I have it on good authority—" Malvery jumped in before Lara had a chance to speak "—that defense counsel and her client spent the night together. It goes to the credibility of the defense, that he's a faithful family man. It certainly puts into question the conduct of my esteemed colleague. In fact, I shall be recommending legal sanctions against Ms. Stovall for ethics violations—"

"Before you accuse me of anything—" Lara had recovered from her initial shock and was fully prepared to do battle "—you better have proof of more than two people spending time in the same house, a house with four bedrooms and a sofa bed. Or you'll be the one finding yourself in front of an ethics committee. Actually, you probably will anyway." She addressed the judge. "Since when is the prosecutor's office allowed to spy on defense counsel?" She glared sideways at her opponent. "Who is the source of this information?"

"I don't have to tell you—"

"The hell you don't," she shot back.

Smith raised her hands to calm the rhetoric. "Who told you they were together last night?" she asked the D.A.

Malvery huffed. "A police patrol saw her client's truck parked behind her house last night."

"Using the police to invade my privacy is an abuse of power that could be a big stain on your political résumé," Lara retorted.

"That's enough," Smith declared. She'd settled into her brown-leather chair, the black sleeves of her robe billowing. "What about it, Malvery? Did you use the police to monitor the activities of opposing counsel?"

"It was a routine patrol, Your Honor."

"Then how did they know what to look for in my rear driveway?" Lara asked. "And why did they report it to you if you hadn't given them instructions to do so?"

"This is a high-profile case," Malvery responded. "It's not unreasonable that they would recognize your client's vehicle or be aware of where you live."

"Bull," Lara snapped. "That doesn't explain why they reported it to you. Your Honor," she appealed to the judge, "for the record, I will stipulate that Mr. First spent part of the night in my home. We were going over the testimony he would be giving today. The man is on trial for his life."

"I suspect you compared more than notes," Malvery mocked.

"Your Honor," Lara pleaded, "even if the district attorney were to have incontrovertible proof of an unethical relationship between my client and me and not merely innuendo gleaned from illegally obtained circumstantial evidence, his statement is prejudicial on the face of it. Where my client was last night has nothing to do with the events that took place on January 19. As for my alleged unethical behavior, Mr. Malvery doesn't have proof. And even if he did,'' she blustered on, "it would still be inadmissible. Unless, of course, he can produce a court order allowing him to violate my privacy and that of Mr. First, who, I remind the court, is innocent until proven guilty and is, therefore, still entitled to fourth amendment protections against unreasonable search and seizure.'' She was nearly breathless. "If Mr. Malvery does have such a court order, I demand he produce it now.''

The judge looked askance at the district attorney.

"I don't, Your Honor, but—''

"Your Honor,'' Lara persisted, "if this line of questioning continues I will have no choice but to immediately move for a mistrial. Further, I will request an inquiry into a possible ethics violation by the district attorney's office in this case, with a recommendation that it include a review for possible violations of fourth amendment rights in other trials conducted by Mr. Malvery's office.''

"Counselor?'' Judge Smith stared at the prosecutor.

Malvery steamed, but he was cornered. "Under the circumstances, Your Honor, I withdraw the question.''

Smith nodded. "I'll instruct the jury to disregard it.''

"Thank you, Your Honor.''

"Don't thank me yet, Ms. Stovall. When this is all

over, there may still be an ethics inquiry into your
conduct in this matter.''

UPON RETURNING to the courtroom, Lara gave Michael a nod, which he understood to mean she'd gotten the matter of their spending the night together
suppressed. He breathed a quiet sigh of relief. The
last thing he wanted bandied about was that he was
sleeping with another woman. Making love to her had
felt so perfect, but Lara was right, it had been a mistake. The woman he'd spent most of his life with, to
whom he'd vowed his eternal love, had been dead
less than a year. He'd sullied his grief, betrayed her
memory and been unfaithful. Not only that, he'd put
Lara's reputation and professional career in danger.
He certainly wouldn't be a role model for his teenage
son or his maturing daughters, if his sexual activities
were made public.

During the interruption, Adam had risen from his
seat in the gallery behind the defendant's table and
stepped outside, taking out his cell phone as he went,
apparently in response to a silent ring. Two minutes
later, he reappeared and confided something to Sheila,
who then left the courtroom.

Being shot down in his attempt at intimidation
clearly stuck in the district attorney's craw, because
his tone now became markedly hostile—an attitude
that had a strangely calming effect on Michael. He
gave concise, no-frills answers to most of the remain-
ing questions.

After more than two hours of grilling, he was excused. Since there were no requests to recall witnesses, the judge adjourned for the day. Tomorrow
closing arguments would begin, then the jury would

be given instructions and the task of deciding if Michael First was a murderer.

Adam, Dave and Sally met Michael and Lara outside the double doors. The rest of the family was gathered a little way off. "You did fine, son," Adam said, though he didn't seem particularly pleased. Michael wondered if his father had grasped the significance of the prosecutor's aborted question and was disappointed in him.

"I'm afraid I have bad news," Adam told both of them.

Michael put his arm around the shoulders of his son and daughter. "What is it?"

"Brad Lopez was found dead a few hours ago. Apparently, he committed suicide."

Michael was stunned. It didn't seem possible.

Lara grasped Adam's arm. "When? How?"

"Why?" Michael asked.

They moved to the side of the lobby as people streamed by.

"Last night," Adam told them.

Michael closed his eyes briefly as the news sank in. "How's Selma?"

"Mighty upset. After hearing Brad's testimony the other day she told him she wasn't taking him back. She couldn't believe he'd betrayed you the way he did."

"I'm so sorry." Lara reached out and clasped both the men's hands. Michael's was cold. She gazed at him. "In spite of everything, I think you would have forgiven him."

Michael pictured Brad's face when he'd told him he was sorry he'd ever called him his friend. Still, Brad had stepped in to protect him from doing something stupid. He swallowed the bitter remorse that rose from his stomach. "Does Gretchen know?"

Adam nodded. "She was the one who relayed the information to me."

"Suicide," Michael muttered. "I can't believe he'd do that."

They advanced to the door.

"The police are investigating, of course," Adam said. "But right now that's what it looks like. A single shot to the head."

CHAPTER FIFTEEN

THE COURTROOM WAS absolutely silent as Lara rose from her seat and stepped into the middle of the well. She turned to the jurors and scanned their faces before commencing her summation.

"Ladies and gentlemen of the jury, a loving and much-loved mother was killed in an accident that could only have been designed to happen. The evidence isn't in dispute.

"Did Michael First have means and opportunity to kill his wife? Without a doubt. But why would he use his antique car, an automobile he devoted a year to restoring, to kill her when there were plenty of other vehicles available for him to sabotage? Why would he do it under circumstances that were sure to point the finger at him?

"And of course, we come back to motive. All of you have had experience with marriage. All of you know that not every minute and every hour of marriage is connubial bliss. Yet the prosecution hasn't been able to come up with a single witness or direct you to a single fact that even remotely suggests there was a serious crisis in Michael and Clare's marriage. To the contrary, everyone agrees they loved each other deeply and were ardently devoted to their family."

Lara paused to let the image sink in.

"Michael First had no motive to kill the mother of his children, but there were those who had reason to eliminate him. We've heard testimony that Webster Hood wanted—in his own words—to get rid of Michael, so he could give the animal manager position to Brad Lopez, a man he knew he could manipulate and control, something he definitely couldn't do with Michael First.

"Let's examine *his* means and opportunity.

"We know he was at the First home the day Clare was killed. We know his showing up was completely out of the ordinary, that his reason for being there was calculated, that he was alone, unobserved for long enough intervals for him to tamper with the MG, a vehicle he had previously been allowed to inspect.

"Webster Hood, in short, had means, motive and opportunity."

Lara studied the somber jury before her. She had their sympathy—at the moment. But it was easy to convince people with one-sided arguments. The challenge was to keep their allegiance when they heard the rebuttal.

"Now let's look at Brad Lopez, a man Michael trusted. He also had means and opportunity." She paced the shiny rail, her voice low, intimate, a confidante speaking to trusted friends. "Did he have a motive to kill his boss? Let's examine the evidence.

"We have testimony that Webster Hood told Lopez he'd give him the livestock manager job if they could find a way to get rid of Michael. We know Brad Lopez coveted Michael's job, because he never told him of Hood's offer. Lopez also undermined Michael, siding with Hood when the general manager wanted to bring outside cattle onto the ranch. A disaster followed, Michael was fired, and Hood made good on his offer to give the job to Lopez.

"But, ladies and gentlemen of the jury, we cannot call Brad Lopez to account for his actions. We cannot question a man who had every reason to harbor a guilty conscience—" she paused for emphasis "—because the night before last Brad Lopez committed suicide."

Two hours later, Judge Margaret Smith instructed the jurors on their options and their duties in the case of the state versus Michael First. They filed out. Court stood adjourned pending their verdict.

"THEY'RE TAKING their sweet time," Michael groused. He was sitting on the patio at Gideon's house, watching the kids play an impromptu game of soccer. Lara was lounging in another chair, paging through a legal journal, trying to catch up on her reading. Because they were expected back in the courtroom within an hour of a verdict being announced, Michael had rented several suites in the refurbished Coyote Hotel, so they could stay in town, but they spent most of their time at his brother's house. The place was big, but not big enough for anyone to get any real privacy. Everybody was working conscientiously to be polite and considerate, which added to the already strained atmosphere. Only the younger kids seemed oblivious to the tension.

The jury had been charged early Friday morning. Now Sunday was already more than half over.

"Slam-dunk decisions usually go against the defendant," Lara told him, as she flipped pages without looking up. "They're weighing all the evidence thoroughly because they have doubts."

"Of my innocence or guilt?"

She was tempted to remind him there was no such verdict as innocent. Only not guilty. But she didn't figure this was the occasion to preach the nuances of the law.

"Malvery gave them a lot to think about," she said. He'd belabored Michael's capacity for violence, alluded to the outraged confrontation with Hood in the courthouse without actually mentioning it.

Michael got up, took a step to the side, seemed to forget why and sat down again. "Do you think he convinced them?"

She recognized the apprehension in his question. "I think they're trying to weigh the easy answer against the right one."

He was more restless than she'd ever seen him. But then, she was scared, too. In capital crime cases, the verdict, whether guilty or not guilty, had to be unanimous. Long deliberations often meant the jurors were trying to convince one last holdout in order to avoid a hung jury.

She worried, too, on another, deeper level. They'd kissed. They'd touched. They'd made love. There was no reprieve for her transgressions, no appeal, no pardon. The verdict on what she'd done was in, and it terrified her. She was in love with Michael First. She had no right to his love. She never had. He didn't love her. They were *friends*.

"How can you be so calm?" he grumbled. He was on his feet again, looking down at her.

"What makes you think I'm calm?" She flashed him a taut smile.

He snorted, unimpressed by her sangfroid, then relented and smiled back. "Is it always like this?" He collapsed into the chair, his long legs extended. "How do you stand it?"

"Comes with the territory." Except she'd never before had this kind of personal investment in a decision twelve other people had to make.

Her cell phone didn't ring until after four. Lara and Michael stared at each other during the first harsh gurgle, then she flipped it open and listened. The jury had reached a verdict. She hung up, her heart pounding. No judgment had ever been this important to her, or so filled with personal implications. She gazed at Michael. His face was dark, the vein in his neck throbbing wildly. The adults in the house magically appeared and silently gathered around him.

Within the hour, everyone was packed into the courtroom, waiting for the judge to appear.

"All rise," the bailiff cried out as Her Honor Judge Margaret Smith came out of her chambers and strode to the bench. She bade everyone be seated. The clatter of feet and the rustle of clothing was all that could be heard. The side door opened and the room fell deathly silent. Michael's breathing became shallow. The jurors trooped in. These twelve people held his fate in their hands. What would happen to his kids if he was found guilty? He knew his father and Sheila would do their best to guide and protect them, but how do children live with the knowledge that their father has been convicted of killing their mother? How does one cope with being the offspring of a murderer?

He sat stiff and straight on the hard wooden seat, peering at the faces of the men and women lining up in two neat rows. Their expressions were serious, pensive. A woman—the retired schoolteacher, if he recalled correctly—made brief eye contact with him. Her glance said something, but what?

The man behind her stared at him, then moved with ramrod precision—a soldier doing his duty. They all filed neatly into their places, their shoulders rounded with fatigue, their heads up with a kind of resigned relief.

Michael's palms were damp. Sweat trickled down his spine. The minutes dragged on for what seemed hours. He heard the shuffling of feet, the muted coughs. The tension in the room was like a viscous liquid drowning him. As if from afar, the judge's words floated toward him like an incoming wave.

"Has the jury reached a verdict?"

"We have, Your Honor." The forewoman handed the bailiff a folded paper to take to the judge. Smith opened it, then slowly read words written there.

"Will the defendant please rise."

He climbed to his feet, his limbs heavy. Lara stood beside him. He wanted desperately to touch her but didn't dare.

"In the case of the People of the State of Texas versus Michael First on the single count of murder in the first degree, we the members of the jury find the defendant—" there was an anticipatory pause "—not guilty."

The room exploded with hoots and applause. The judge rapped her gavel, demanded order. Michael held up his head, closed his eyes and sucked in his cheeks in a silent prayer of thanksgiving. This nightmare was over.

He barely heard the rest of the proceedings, the judge dismissing the jury with the thanks of the court, the words telling him he was free to go. His mind was numb until he felt the slap on his back and his brother's arm slipping over his shoulder. He glanced at Lara. She was smiling. There were tears in her eyes.

He reached out to her and landed a soft kiss on her cheek. He wanted more, but this wasn't the time or place. Besides, too many people were closing in on them, separating them, patting him, shaking his hand.

"Dinner is definitely on me," Adam declared. "The biggest steaks this town has to offer."

"Can I have a cheeseburger?" Sally asked.

Adam laughed a little too hard. "Sweetheart, you can have whatever you want."

Michael saw Lara's face break into a confused smile as she backed out of the circle crowding around him.

He grabbed her wrist. Even in the tumult and jubilation around him, he could feel her trembling. "Come with us," he said, putting his arm across her shoulders and snuggling her up against him. "I want to toast you tonight."

The hesitation of a few seconds earlier slid away. Cupping her elbow, he propelled her through the double doors into the lobby. He wanted to take her to a quiet corner and kiss her. Not a chance. A blitz of flashes and TV cameras surged toward them. He should have had a statement prepared, though he doubted in the excitement he would have remembered a word.

"Keep it short," she muttered as the mob surrounded them.

He thanked family and friends for their support, especially his outstanding attorney, and expressed relief that the ordeal was over.

"But it really isn't," he said later to his family outside the hearing of the children. He turned to Lara. "I know you had to point the finger at Brad in your closing argument. He betrayed me, but I don't believe he sabotaged my car. I don't think he committed suicide, either. There's still a killer out there, except now he's murdered two people."

ADAM HAD CALLED ahead and reserved a room at the Remington Steak House. Dinner was a loud and noisy affair, and far from private. People kept popping in to congratulate Michael on his acquittal and to praise Lara for her defense.

"Of course, you had an advantage," said Flora Crystal, who'd been on the cheerleading squad with Lara. Flora now had six kids and weighed close to two hundred pounds. "You knew he was innocent. Anyone who's had contact with Michael realizes he couldn't kill anyone, much less a woman."

He was aware not everyone would agree. Already he'd seen strangers stare at him, then turn away. He hadn't heard the words yet, but he knew he would: he got away with murder.

As friends from years past stopped by, they inevitably discussed the experiences they'd had in common.

"Remember the junior rodeo," Buck Buchanan said, "when Rocky Danners put the burr under Michael's saddle?" His thick blond hair was gone now, except for a sparse fringe above the ears.

"Dang near killed him," Gideon piped up. "Michael, of course, just laughed it off."

Lara grinned at the recollection. "He retaliated, as I recall."

"Not Michael," Gideon countered. "He was too much a gentleman and a sport."

An uneasy feeling crept down her spine. "But he cut Rocky's girth."

Gideon let out a guffaw. "He would never do a thing like that. I cut it. With my trusty Boy Scout knife."

Lara remembered her earlier remark to him that he was always trailing his big brother around. Gideon had idolized Michael. She had the impression he still did.

"Rocky ended up breaking his foot," Michael responded with a shake of his head. "It was a damn fool thing to do."

Lara's mouth fell open. "You—" She stared at Gideon. "But...I thought...Michael—"

"So did everybody else." Gideon grinned, apparently unrepentant.

She turned to Michael. "You knew about this all the time. Why didn't you say anything?"

He cocked his head, his blink merry. "I did. I told everybody I hadn't cut the cinch. If people didn't believe me, it was their problem. You didn't expect me to turn in my own kid brother, did you?"

Lara was aghast. She, too, had assumed he'd done it.

"You should have realized he wouldn't do anything like that," Kerry observed, across from her. "Not his style. If my big brother wanted to even the score, he would have challenged Rocky to a fight there and then."

"Since he didn't," Gideon pointed out, "I figured I had to take matters into my own hands."

Michael looked at Lara, mirth dancing in his blue

eyes. "You really thought I did it, even after I denied it?"

"I—" She was mortified. The freckles on her nose probably stood out like warts. "I misjudged you. I'm sorry."

He grinned. "You weren't alone."

His easy acceptance of her unfairness irked her. She'd blamed him for being blind to the feelings she kept so tightly reined in, and the whole time she hadn't seen his essential honesty. She'd assumed he was lying, when experience should have taught her differently.

Lara Stovall wasn't given to snap decisions. The practice of law required deliberation. She had made it a hallmark of her personal life, as well. But she made a snap decision now. Coming back here had been a mistake. Deep down inside she'd probably known all along it would be. This "homecoming" had been a fool's journey. It was time to end it, to put this town and Michael First behind her, once and for all. No more illusions. No more fantasies.

It wasn't until the meal was over and they were outside that they got a chance to talk again. Michael took her hands in his. "Lara, you've given me back my life."

"I'm pleased I was able to win your case, Michael. Happy we've been able to bring this ordeal to a successful conclusion."

He swung their arms and snickered. "You sound like a press release." He tugged her toward him, nearly unbalancing her, and kissed her hard on the lips.

She pulled back, extricated her fingers from his, dipped into her purse and extracted her car keys. "Go home with your family, Michael,'' she said with a weary chuckle. ''Enjoy your freedom.''

''I'll see you tomorrow,'' he promised.

''Take some time for yourself.'' She opened the BMW door and crawled inside. ''Your kids need you. The rest can wait.''

''Rest?'' He was perplexed.

''The suits against the bank.'' She started the engine. ''Good night.''

She turned on her lights, checked her rearview mirror and drove out of the parking lot into the street.

Michael stood there, stunned. Was she saying goodbye?

MICHAEL AND HIS FATHER SAT in rockers on the front porch of the restored Home Place, sipping from long-neck bottles of beer. The evening air was cool and comfortable, the gentle breeze refreshing. It was the kind of evening ranchers and farmers savored, a satisfying reward to a busy day. In spite of his acquittal, too much sadness, too much uncertainty filled his life for the night to bring contentment, rest.

''I was about your age when your mother died,'' Adam said, jolting him out of his reverie. His father occasionally mentioned Helen, but he never talked about her death. ''She'd been sick for over a year. During those last six months we both knew she was dying. I had plenty of time to prepare myself.'' He rotated the bottle on his knee. ''But it didn't make any difference. Nothing can prepare us for the shock of death. A part of me died with her.''

Michael was sixteen when his mother had succumbed to cancer. His world, too, had changed. He remembered his father carrying on with brave determination, but Michael had been old enough to see it for what it was—a front. In their own private ways, they'd mourned. Adam had delved into running the ranch. Michael had immersed himself in schoolwork and sports. He'd become the star quarterback on the high school football team. Lara had been by his side then, consoling him in the quiet moments when he'd had to fight his grief, then cheering him on to further conquests, new victories.

"It's not an easy period in a man's life to be without a woman," Adam said.

Michael was disconcerted by this shift in the conversation. His father had discussed the facts of life with him when he was an adolescent. Not in terms of the mechanics of intercourse—the First children had grown up on a ranch, where animals were frequently and openly bred, so the physical aspect of sex wasn't unknown or mysterious. Self-control and respect for women had been his father's message. And because Michael had seen the love and devotion of his parents, he had accepted the lesson. He hadn't gone into his marriage with Clare totally inexperienced, but he hadn't been the football team's prime stud, either.

"I've made a pile of mistakes," his father went on. "I wallowed in my loneliness. Regarded my misery as the price for survival."

A night bird chirped in the darkness beyond the porch rail.

"I always figured there was only one woman for a man," Adam continued. "I certainly believed it when your mother was alive. I never looked at anyone else from the moment we fell in love. Like you and Clare. After Helen died...I wasn't unaware of opportunities, but I rejected them because I didn't feel I had a right to another chance at happiness.''

He placed his right boot on his left knee.

''Then, after more than fifteen years, I met Sheila.'' His voice softened. ''Not many men find two women they can truly love in a lifetime. She filled the void in me. It wasn't that I loved your mother less. In a way, it was because I'd loved her so much that I was able to understand what I felt for Sheila.''

Adam pensively sipped his beer.

''I have to ask myself, though, if there might not have been other Sheilas out there for me in the meantime.'' He chuckled mildly. ''Don't get me wrong. The wait was worth it, but there were an awful lot of empty nights in between.'' He massaged the back of his neck. ''What I'm trying to say, son, is don't reject an opportunity for love because you foolishly think you don't deserve it.''

Lara.

Around eleven-thirty Michael wished his father good-night and went to his room in the guest house. He couldn't sleep. He'd been exonerated in Clare's death, but he'd lost so much. His wife, his work, maybe his home. Restless, he got up, dressed in the clothes he'd taken off and went out to his truck. A moonlight drive might clear his head, help him plan the future.

He wanted to crawl into Lara's bed and hold her close. He needed to feel her body spooned against his, to feel her respond to his touch. To respond to hers. But it was after midnight now. She'd be asleep. She wouldn't appreciate being woken up at almost two o'clock in the morning. She'd made that clear.

It was impossible not to remember the night they'd

spent together. Impossible not to ache for more nights with her.

He drove aimlessly, but he wasn't surprised when he arrived at the house where he and Clare had shared fifteen wonderful years together. They'd created four beautiful children, dreamed dreams for them and for themselves. He'd expected to end his days here—with her. To while away quiet afternoons in the sun, watching grandchildren pull the same silly stunts on their parents their kids had pulled on them.

Life wasn't fair. People learned that as children, yet they kept hoping it would be different for them. Michael understood now that no one escaped injustice. Clare hadn't. He hadn't. His children hadn't.

Lara hadn't.

He wanted her in his life. The question was if she would have him. He'd come so close to saying he loved her, but she'd stopped him, backed away.

He'd hurt her all those years ago. Hurt her without even realizing it. She'd let him go without a tear, without a whimper. None, at least, that he could see or hear. She'd hoarded the pain inside. He should have known she would. Growing up in the house she had, she found it dangerous to let her feelings show. Feelings were used against her, and she'd learned too well how to hide them. Even from him.

She'd tried hiding them from him this time, too, but he'd seen the soul in her eyes, felt the longing, tasted the hunger. Yet there were doubts. On her part and his. Unanswered questions. Suspicions.

She hadn't been convinced at the beginning that he was innocent of Clare's death. He hadn't been sure she wanted to get him off. What did that say about a future relationship?

He parked in front of the darkened house and got out. He could barely discern the garden on the side that Clare had planted and tended with such diligence and devotion. At least the darkness of night cloaked the weeds that had invaded it in the months since she'd died.

He climbed into the truck and backed away from the building and the memories it held. He drove a little-used road that wandered across a prairie. The sky was huge here, crowned with twinkling pinpoints of starlight. The moon, nearly full, bathed the land in pewter tones. A night for dreaming, for cuddling, for making love. It wasn't a night to be alone, but he was.

He stood once more at the foot of Clare's grave. The unweathered granite tombstone glowed in the silvery rays of the crisp autumn night.

He sat on the cold bench and stared at the stone slab. *Clare Levine First, 1967-2002. Beloved Wife and Mother.*

"The jury decided I didn't murder you," he announced. "Isn't that nice? It's not over, though. I still don't know who killed you. Do you? I wish you could tell me. But I'll find out. I'm not sure how, but I won't give up."

He shifted on the hard seat.

"I don't know how to tell you this. You remember Lara Gorley, the girl I was going with when I met you. She's Lara Stovall now. Her husband was killed in the Gulf War. She was my defense attorney."

He paused and tried to swallow the lump forming in his throat. "Clare, you know I loved you. I always will, but..."

He brushed away the tears that dripped down his face.

"Lara and I...we've sort of taken up where we left off before I met you. I don't love you any less, sweetheart, but I think I love her, too. I need her."

CHAPTER SIXTEEN

LARA TOSSED AND TURNED in her bed. She was used to sleeping alone, used to the quiet solitude. Liked it, in fact. But how does one ever get used to loneliness?

She'd kept her distance from Michael in the parking lot that evening, even though she wanted more than anything for him to take her in his arms and hold her. Just hold her. That would have been reward enough. He said she gave him back his life. For a brief while, he'd given her back hers, too. Given back what she'd never had.

She hadn't planned on falling in love with Michael First—again. When she'd returned to Coyote Springs her intent had been to stay away from him, not only because he was married, but because he represented the final episode in her unhappy life in this town.

Which raised the question of why she had come here at all. This place didn't represent a pageant of joyful events, Christmas carols and homemade sweets. Her parents' house had never rung with song and laughter. The only time she felt whole, felt wanted and carefree, was when she'd been with Michael.

Her parents were dead. The grandmother, who had been such a malevolent presence for so long, had gone to her eternal reward. So why had Lara moved back to Coyote Springs, a place of unfulfilled expectations and bitter disappointments?

Because she was tired of the pace in big cities, she told herself. Because she could never feel completely comfortable in an apartment tucked stylishly between never-sleeping on-and-off ramps, where the lights below blocked out the stars above. A partnership in a prestigious legal firm in the big city was the dream of every law student. She'd achieved that, and it had left her sullen, indefinably discontented and unbearably lonely. Which still didn't explain why she'd returned to Coyote Springs.

To crow at the ghosts? To banish them once and for all? To let them see she lived here now on her terms? Or was it to show Michael First she didn't need him, she'd never needed him?

If that had been her secret goal, she'd failed.

She lay in the dark and let tears wet her pillow. She wanted Michael more than ever.

THE SUN WAS STREAMING into the bedroom when Michael opened his eyes. Almost eight o'clock. He hadn't slept that late in years. He raised his fists into the air and stretched, luxuriating in the invigorating sensation of muscles contracting and releasing. He'd been sitting on his butt too long; he craved hard physical labor, a day in the saddle, the sun overhead, the wind in his face. He laced his fingers behind his head and smiled. Free for the first time in months. No more court appearances. No more threats of death or life in prison stalking him. He could come and go now at will, a man unfettered. He could pursue whatever or whomever he chose. He rolled out from under the covers, showered, shaved and made his way to the main house. The children had already left for school. He must have really zonked out not to be roused by their noisy morning routine. He wanted to give them all a big hug.

Elva greeted him as he entered the kitchen and poured him a cup of hot, strong coffee.

"Where is everybody?"

"Your dad's out in the barn, tending the horses. Sheila's gone shopping for fabric to make the girls new dresses for Christmas." Hard to believe it was less than six weeks away.

"She's made each of them three outfits already."

Elva laughed. "She's having fun. I have pancake batter all made up."

"I'm still full from last night." He saw the crest-fallen expression on her face. "But I've got room for a short stack."

"Bacon or sausage?"

"Neither, thanks. Just your light, fluffy flapjacks and more of this delicious coffee."

Twenty minutes later, he joined his father in the horse barn. Adam was inspecting a yearling's fetlock. The sleek black warmblood colt had cut himself a week earlier when being loaded into a van.

"The staples will be ready to come out in a few days," Adam commented from his crouched position.

The telephone on the wall a few stalls down rang.

"Would you get that?" Adam laughed. "Probably Sheila wanting to know if I like stripes or plaids for the girls' dresses."

Chuckling, Michael lifted the receiver.

"A man from the sheriff's office is here," Elva said anxiously. "He wants to see you right away."

The lightness in his mood instantly vanished. "What about?"

"Won't say, but he insists it's important."

"I'll be right there." Michael hung up and told his father about the visitor.

"I'll come with you." He patted the colt and made sure the gate was securely closed when he left the stall. "Maybe they have new information on Brad's death."

Father and son trudged to the house.

"I'd like to hear it wasn't suicide," said Michael. "I wonder why they'd come all the way out here to tell us, though. The phone would have been a lot cheaper in gas and time."

He tried not to feel a stab of panic when he found Deputy Wesley Janick waiting for him in the kitchen of his father's house.

"Mr. First—" he addressed Michael "—can you tell me where you were last night?"

"What's this about?" Adam asked.

"I need to know where your son was last night between midnight and 5:00 a.m."

"Why?"

Janick ignored the older man and spoke to Michael. "Will you answer my question, sir? Where were you last night between midnight and 5:00 a.m.?"

"Here on the ranch. What's going on, Deputy?"

"Where? At your house?"

"I'm staying over in the guest house with my kids."

"Were you there all night?"

"I went out to drive around for a while. It had been an emotional day. I couldn't sleep."

"Alone?"

"Yes. Everyone else was in bed."

"Where did you go?"

"I drove around. Stopped by my house. Why these questions?"

"Do you own a handgun?"

Adam gripped Michael's shoulder, a signal to shut up.

"Deputy," Michael said, "I'm not answering any more of your questions until you tell me what this is about."

Janick studied him a minute. "Webster Hood was found this morning outside your residence on the Number One. Shot to death."

"Oh, my God," Elva exclaimed, and covered her mouth with both hands. Her dark eyes were wide with fear.

"And you think I might have killed him? That's ridiculous."

"We have your public threat on camera."

"I didn't kill him. I never even saw him last night."

"I'll have to ask you to come with me, Mr. First."

The nightmare was starting all over again.

LARA DIDN'T LOOK any better than Michael felt when she showed up at the county jail just after ten o'clock. He'd been placed in a different interrogation room this time, but it was no better. It, too, reeked of unwashed bodies and fear.

"Are you all right?" There was panic in the question.

"Just get me out of here. Fast."

She sat on the edge of the seat across from him, her red hair a burst of color in this drab world. He stifled the urge to reach across the table. Besides, she kept her hands primly in her lap, as if she didn't want to be contaminated by the surroundings. By him. Or perhaps it was just that people could be watching through the one-way glass.

Michael massaged his temples. "Lara, what the hell's going on? First Clare, then Brad, now Hood. We've got a serial killer running loose."

"We don't know Brad was murdered," she said weakly. At least her eyes didn't ask if he was guilty.

"I had doubts about his so-called suicide before. Now I'm sure he didn't kill himself."

"Maybe" was all she said, but he could see the worry tightening her features. "Did they read you your Miranda rights?"

He shook his head. "But I refused to answer any more questions."

A ray of hope flashed across her face. "So you didn't tell them anything?"

Michael wanted to kick himself. He should have learned from his first experience with the lawman. It hadn't been that long ago. "Janek wanted to know where I was last night." He should have shut up right then and there. Not that it would make any difference. Eventually he'd have to furnish an alibi. "I told him I couldn't sleep." He gazed at Lara, at the subtle shadows of fatigue. She apparently hadn't slept much, either. He had to force the image of her tossing in her bed out of his mind. "I admitted driving over to my house during the night. As soon as he asked me if I owned a handgun, though, I refused to say another word. That's when he told me Hood had been shot to death and insisted I come down here for questioning."

Lara showed no emotion as she rose and tapped on the glass. "Let me do the talking."

"I think I'm getting the routine down pat," Michael responded sarcastically.

Burk Malvery and the sheriff entered the room, followed by the deputy.

"What have you got?" she asked the D.A. bluntly after he was seated. The word sparring she usually enjoyed held no appeal this go-round. Too much had happened. Too much she didn't understand.

"Your client admits being in the place where the decedent's body was found during the period the medical examiner has determined was the approximate time of death."

"His statement is inadmissible. He wasn't read his rights."

"Is he planning to take the fifth?" Malvery lifted his left brow in shock. "Doesn't matter. The statement was voluntarily given to the police." He showed his teeth in a caricature of a smile. "Or has he found an alibi to say he was home in bed with her?"

Michael stiffened, a scowl hardening his features.

"Careful, Burk," Lara said. "You've already admitted to a judge that you abused your office once. Don't push it."

"Prickly this morning, aren't we?" He grinned.

"What else do you have?" she pressed impatiently.

"We obtained a warrant to search his residence. Recovered a .38 caliber revolver that appeared to have been recently fired. Ran a ballistics test. Guess what? It's the murder weapon."

Michael took a deep breath and let it out.

"My, haven't you been busy little beavers?" Lara

commented. This information was utterly devastating. "Find any prints on it?"

"We did, Counselor. His."

"Since it's his gun, that seems natural enough. But it hardly proves anything. Any prints on the handle and trigger?"

"Partials. Inconclusive," Malvery admitted.

"He hasn't been living in that house since before the trial began. Anyone could have broken in and gotten the gun, then returned it to frame him."

"No sign of a break-in. Whoever went in had a key." The D.A. leaned back in his chair, very pleased with himself. "We also have a videotape of your client threatening to kill the decedent in the lobby of the courthouse."

"A statement made in the heat of the moment," Lara countered, but the knot in her stomach was getting tighter. "If you arrested everyone who ever said 'I swear I'll kill you,' we'd have to incarcerate half the population."

"You're probably right," Malvery agreed casually. "But I believe there's enough evidence here to establish probable cause." Then he added, "And win a conviction."

"Is Mr. First under arrest?" she asked.

He paused to consider, looked at Michael, then at Lara. "Not right now, though I have enough to hold him. I want to check out a few more things first." He rose confidently to his feet. "Perhaps in the meantime, he'll be able to come up with something better than 'I was sleepwalking.'"

MICHAEL STOOD on the jailhouse steps, closed his eyes and inhaled deeply, not that it relaxed him. He was free, but for how long? And who else was going to be killed?

"Was your wife having an affair with Webster Hood, Mr. First?"

He spun around and faced a reporter with a microphone. A man stood behind her with a shoulder-mounted TV camera.

Lara stepped in front of him and covered the lens with her hand. "We have no comment. Save your film."

The reporter measured her, hesitated, then signaled the cameraman to shut down. As they retreated, Michael felt someone clamp on to his shoulder. He spun around, ready to do battle, and found it was his father. Sheila was at his side. They both looked somber and frightened.

"We're driving back to the ranch so we'll be there when the kids get home from school." Adam handed his truck keys to his son.

"Dad—" He'd made a decision. "I want you to call Kerry in Dallas and have her find a place for you and the kids to stay for a while. And take Elva. Today, if possible." The urgency in his request was unmistakable.

Sheila compressed her lips between her teeth, her face marred by fear.

"You're that worried?" Adam asked.

"Not worried, Dad. Terrified. I've lost my wife and a guy I believed to be my friend. Now the man I thought was responsible for their deaths has been murdered at my house, and it looks like I'm being framed for it. I can't take a chance on losing anyone else."

"Come with us," Sheila pleaded.

He shook his head. "I can't. Running away will only make me look more guilty. Besides, if someone is determined to get me, they'll only follow. I can't put anyone else in jeopardy. I'll be home this afternoon to tell the kids I love them, but I want you to get them out of here. Please. I'm counting on you."

Sheila was glassy-eyed as she clenched his wrist. "Do what you have to do, Michael. The children will be fine."

"I know they will." He bent and kissed her softly on the cheek, then shook his father's hand.

He went with Lara to her office. Neither had had anything to eat all day. She asked Carol to send out for sandwiches and led Michael into her office. He closed the door.

Desperately, he took her into his arms, reassured and tormented by the feel and smell of her. He wanted to rip her clothes off, bury himself in her, confirm they were both alive. He brought his mouth down, pressed his lips to hers and nudged them open with his tongue. He was beginning to probe—

"No." She tried to wrench herself away from him. "We shouldn't be doing this." But he refused to set her completely free.

With a finger curled under her chin, he raised her head. "Is that my attorney speaking or the woman I made love to a few nights ago?" he murmured.

"Both." Her spine was rigid.

He released her, then leaned against the desk, feet crossed. "I don't believe you."

He'd had time to think the past few hours. He wasn't fully reconciled to Clare's death. Maybe he never would be. But he was alive. He wasn't completely sure what he felt for Lara. At some level, he loved her. Not the way he'd loved Clare, but the emotions that whirled within him went much deeper than friendship. He was being absolutely honest, though, when he said he was glad to have her back in his life. An offer of marriage right now would be premature, but he wanted to explore the possibility. Surely she could see they owed it to themselves to find out how compatible they truly were.

Her heart hammering, Lara swung around to face him. It startled her to realize how shaken she was by this man who always told the truth. Even when it hurt. She blazed at him. "I don't care what you believe."

"Another lie." His voice was gentle but compelling. He crossed his arms, his biceps bulging against his dark-blue knit shirt. She didn't want to consider how his strength made her feel, how his touch melted her. Then she saw it—the white band of skin where his wedding ring had been. He'd removed it.

Her breathing faltered. She turned away, moved toward the conference table, though his image followed her, the sensations of his touch still percolating within her.

"If the lawyer doesn't want to have anything to do with me, I guess I can hire another." He might have added that he didn't want another woman, that he wanted her in his life permanently. But she didn't give him a chance.

"I can recommend several good criminal attorneys."

"But not one who cares as you do."

She sighed. "That's precisely the problem, Michael. I am your attorney. Yes, that can be changed easily enough. But it would solve only half the problem."

''What are you talking about?'' he asked in a fierce retort.

''Do you love me, Michael?''

His jaw fell, and he stammered. ''Yes.''

Was the hesitation because of the shock of the question, because he didn't honestly know or because he didn't want to make a commitment? She couldn't tell. It didn't matter.

''No, Michael,'' she said. ''You only think you do.''

The room fell silent for several heartbeats. His gaze never left hers. ''That's pretty damn arrogant, isn't it?'' His slow-to-rise anger seemed to be building. ''You telling me what I feel.''

Her legs suddenly turned watery. She slid sideways onto a conference chair. ''I'm not doubting your sincerity. I'm simply questioning the validity of your emotion.'' How could she make him understand? ''Patients fall in love with their doctors all the time. It's not unheard of for lawyers and clients to develop an affection for each other.''

''Affection.'' He pushed away from the front of the desk. ''Is that what you call it?'' He took a long stride toward the window, then spun around to confront her. ''This is more than affection.''

He was silhouetted against the afternoon light, an inviting tower of pure masculine power. She remembered the warmth of his embrace, the comforting smell of his skin close to hers. ''We're still talking about emotions,'' she reminded him.

''And you don't trust them. Is that it?''

She combed her fingers through her hair in a fit of frustration. ''They lack permanence.''

''Love doesn't,'' he insisted. ''Not true love.''

Uncontrollably, her voice rose. "And how can we be certain it's true love?"

The question jolted him and defused his mounting temper. "Now you're being cynical," he chided.

"Maybe," she admitted, none too happily. "But I've got history on my side." A cold, clammy ache lodged itself inside her. "I thought you might have loved me twenty years ago. I saw you as my knight in shining armor, come to save me from the wicked witch."

He folded his arms across his chest. "I think you're mixing metaphors," he offered, in a vain attempt to lighten the pall that had settled over them.

"You gave me hope and courage."

She'd worked so hard at doing everything right. She hadn't slept with him because he hadn't declared a commitment to her. She hadn't smothered him, been too forward or too distant. She'd played by the rules the grown-ups had given her. Still she'd lost.

"If I'd known how deeply you felt—"

"You would have left Clare?"

He looked away. She hugged her middle against the chill that shivered through her.

"You loved her, Michael. I don't doubt that for a moment, and I'm thoroughly convinced she loved you."

He shook his head, frustrated by his inability to understand. "So where does this leave us now? Why can't you get past what happened twenty years ago?"

She almost laughed...or cried. She wasn't sure which. "You see me as your savior, not just in the courtroom, but in your bed."

He didn't deny it, because he knew it was true. Michael First didn't lie. Damn him.

"I need you, Lara," he entreated.

She would always be a substitute for Clare, his one, true love.

"Because you're lonely," she said.

The confusion on his face confirmed her worst fears. "Is that wrong?"

"No," she acknowledged. Hadn't she taken him to her bed for the pure gratification of it, with full awareness that it was temporary? "It's just not enough."

She needed someone to value her for herself, not for what she could give him. A companion she could trust beyond all imagination. A man with whom she could relax, share pleasures and vulnerabilities. She wanted with all her heart for Michael to be that man, but she wasn't sure he could ever be.

"I'll be glad to help you find another lawyer. I recommend Dexter Thorndyke, if he's available. Then I'll be leaving Coyote Springs."

His face went blank, and his jaw sagged as he looked at her, wide-eyed. "Leaving? Why?"

The phone rang.

"My place isn't here," she said. "It's better this way."

The phone rang again.

"Please reconsider," he begged. "Whatever our differences—"

The phone rang a third time. She walked behind her desk, picked up the receiver, listened, thanked the caller and hung up.

"The sheriff's people are at the Home Place now with a search warrant," she announced.

"Great." He threw himself into the chair across from her. "Just what the folks need—the cops ransacking their place. Elva's blood pressure must be through the roof. What are they looking for?''

"Gloves, clothes, anything that might have blood-stains or powder marks on it.'' She picked up her pencil and held it over her legal pad. "Where did you keep your handguns?''

So the interrogation was beginning. "Will you promise me one thing?''

"If I can.''

"Will you hang around until this business is resolved?''

Their eyes met, and the air between them seemed to pulse. Finally she nodded. He sighed. At least she wasn't bailing out on him in his hour of need.

"Now, how many handguns do you have and where do you keep them?'' she asked.

He rested his head against the back of the chair. A strange lethargy stole over him as exhaustion swept through him. "I have a .22, a .38 and a .44, and they're all kept in the gun case at my house. Along with the shotguns and rifles.''

"Locked up?''

"Of course.'' Restless, discouraged, he jumped to his feet and strode to the window. The thought of her leaving rattled him. "The key is on a ring in a box in the laundry room. Out of the reach of small children.''

He roved the carpet, came to the bookcases and spun around. Her posture was very professional, but wrinkles marred her brow. She was as unsettled as he was. "Did they tell you where Hood's body was found?''

"Around the side of the house. In the garden.''

A cold shiver wormed its way down Michael's backbone. "When?"

"A little after ten this morning by a farm worker who'd gone there to see if any pecan tree limbs needed supporting. The medical examiner puts the time of death anywhere from midnight to around three a.m."

Michael closed his eyes. "Which means his body could have been there when I was."

"Did you get out of your truck?"

"For a few minutes." He paced in a circle, remembering the night.

"Did you go into the garden?"

He nodded. "Close enough to notice the weeds were getting high."

"So your footprints will be there."

He exhaled loudly through his nose. "Probably."

"Did you see anything unusual?"

"Like a dead body, you mean?"

Lara's expression hardened in annoyance. "Like someone having been there before you. Plants broken. Marks that suggested somebody or something had been dragged."

He shook his head. "I doubt he could have been there then. You're right. I would have noticed if the area was disturbed."

"What time did you leave?"

"I got to bed around three, so I'd say I left there around one-thirty."

"Where were you in the meanwhile?"

He hesitated, unsure how she would interpret the answer. "At the family cemetery."

Her face closed up. She jotted down more notes.

He went behind the desk, pulled her to her feet and

settled his hands on her shoulders. "I went to tell Clare…about us."

Lara looked embarrassed. He'd thought she'd be pleased. Apparently, he was wrong. But then, he'd been wrong about her so often he shouldn't be surprised.

She sat down again, and he returned to the window and faced out. "I was at the cemetery from roughly one-thirty to nearly three," he recited. "Sorry, no living witnesses. Does that help?"

"It means Hood was killed after one-thirty, assuming your garden is where he was killed." Her tone was very detached, very professional.

"Lara, what the hell's going on?"

She raised her head. From the way she studied him he knew she understood he was asking about them, not about murder. He started toward her, determined now to hold her in his arms until she melted, when there was a knock on the door. A split second later Carol barged in to deliver their food and drinks.

Like puppets dancing on invisible strings, they silently separated, then came together again at the long conference table. They unwrapped their sandwiches and sat opposite each other. Michael bit into a ham-and-cheese on rye.

"Who do you think killed Hood?" she asked.

"Someone who hated him." He munched on a pickle. "Or feared him."

She pulled out the tasseled toothpick from her turkey-and-bacon club, removed the middle layer of toasted wheat bread and reassembled the sandwich.

"Suppose Hood had an accomplice, somebody other than Brad," Michael posited. "Hood could have threatened to expose him, it came to a show-down and Hood lost.''

Lara shook her head. ''He couldn't very well expose the other guy without exposing himself.''

Michael scowled. She was right. ''We have to assume whoever killed Hood also killed Clare and Brad. Suppose Hood was bumped off because of what he knew.''

''Like the identity of the murderer,'' she concluded with cautious enthusiasm. But then her expression darkened. ''That doesn't compute, either. Why wait until now to eliminate him? Wouldn't it have made more sense to do it before Hood went on the stand?''

''Unless he just figured out who the murderer was.''

''Why not take the information to the police?'' Lara asked.

Michael pushed away from the table. ''Maybe he didn't get a chance. Or he tried to blackmail him. Or—'' he spread his hands ''—he might not even have realized he held the key.''

Lara's face brightened as she warmed to the logic. ''Those are three possibilities.''

''Where do we go from here?'' He glanced up from his contemplation of the carpet. ''Was his truck found there? It certainly wasn't at the house when I was.''

Lara's brows went up. ''Good question. I'll check. If it wasn't, that means he came with the murderer.''

The phone rang. It was Adam calling to tell Michael that Kerry's husband, Craig, was flying in at seven the next morning to pick everyone up. Michael glanced at the clock. Not even three yet. The children wouldn't be home till four-thirty.

"I'll be there in time for supper. At least we can all be together tonight."

"Go home," Lara said, after he hung up. Gently, she nudged him toward the door.

"Come with me."

She shook her head. "I have things to do here, and you need to be with your family. Your kids don't deserve what's happening to them." She kissed him gently on the mouth but pulled away when he tried to deepen it. "I'll see you tomorrow."

He left, grateful for her support, disappointed she was so willing to let him go. The seesaw of their relationship was driving him crazy. One moment they were in each other's arms, as intimate as two people could be with their clothes still on; the next, she was the professionally detached attorney. And sometimes, she was somewhere in between.

CHAPTER SEVENTEEN

As HE DROVE ALONG Travis Boulevard, trying not to think about how empty this life would be without his children and his parents around, he noticed a billboard for the Golden Years Nursing Home and felt a pang of conscience. Sheila and Elva had visited Brigitte periodically since she'd been transferred there five months ago, but on the few occasions when Michael had, she'd been asleep, and he hadn't bothered to waken her.

He followed Coyote Avenue over the river to the sprawling, single-story nursing home. The woman at the reception desk greeted him by name.

"Is Mrs. Levine still in room 143?"

"Yes, sir. You can go right on down."

He made his way along the corridor, past a man asleep in a wheelchair and an old woman using a walker with the aid of an attendant, found the room, paused, then tapped on the half-closed door. The room he entered smelled of potpourri, disinfectant and medicine. A hospital smell. Brigitte lay in her bed, dozing. The TV on the wall had the volume set at an incomprehensible murmur.

"Brigitte?"

Her eyes fluttered. "Hello, Michael." She smiled. "How nice of you to come visit me."

Her voice was thin and reedy, as if she didn't get

to use it much, but it was her recognizing him that surprised him. He stepped forward, took her fragile hand in his and gave her a soft kiss on the cheek. She was even thinner than when she'd arrived, her skin as delicate as rice paper. "How have you been?"

"Take me out into the sunroom. I want to see the garden."

"Not many flowers this time of year." An early November frost had killed off most of the summer's stragglers.

"Then I'll look at the weeds." She cackled. "They always grow." She pressed her call button.

He was at a loss what to talk about.

"How are the children doing in school?" she asked, apparently sensing his discomfort.

"Real well. Dave is on the soccer team, and the girls are busy with their dancing and singing clubs. Sally made the cheerleader squad."

A nurse appeared in the doorway. "Yes, dear, what can I do for you?"

"Help me up. My grandson is going to take me out into the garden."

The woman hesitated, glanced at Michael, who nodded, left the room and seconds later brought in a wheelchair. With practiced dexterity, she had Brigitte out of the bed and into the chair, a plaid blanket tucked around her tiny waist.

"She tires easily," the nurse whispered in his ear when he started wheeling the old woman out. "There's a bell button by the door if you need any help."

He pushed her slowly down the wide corridor, past the nurses' station, and followed a sign that pointed to the right. At the intersection, a bulletin board announced a variety of civic events, from rock concerts to meetings of the philatelic society. He wondered how many of the residents ever attended any of them—or wanted to. Brigitte pointed to a poster for the food bank.

"That's Clare's," she informed him.

He recognized the artwork she'd been working on the day she died, the last thing she'd done—a holiday table surrounded by eight people. Three generations. An older couple, a younger set and four children, one of them a toddler. The turkey on a chipped platter wasn't very large, and the vegetables in mismatched bowls weren't particularly generous. But the expressions on the faces of the people sharing it said it was a feast, that for a little while they had enough to eat and were thankful for it.

"She had a Norman Rockwell gift for capturing a mood," Brigitte mused out loud. For the moment at least, she seemed perfectly lucid. Then she added, "I must tell her when I see her how much I like the petunias."

Petunias? The small vase in the middle of the table held scraggly wildflowers, not petunias.

"She'll like that." He pushed on to the garden.

Her comments rambled after that. He sat with her for about fifteen minutes, until she quietly dozed off. Without waking her, he maneuvered her chair back to her room and called the nurse.

"How aware of things is she?" he asked.

The woman in a white uniform replied, "There are moments when her mind is perfectly clear, but they fade quickly, and there are fewer and fewer of them. She may not have much time left. We'll do everything we can to make her comfortable."

He thanked the nurse, left the room, then stopped to examine the poster again.

"Well, I'll be damned." The flowers painted *on* the vase were petunias. She'd said *when I see her,* meaning Clare. Did Brigitte know her days were short, as the nurse had indicated? The premonition brought a chill to his spine and a lump to his throat.

Suddenly another thought presented itself. When had the artwork for this poster been delivered to the food bank? He remembered Clare's panic that Saturday morning because she wasn't sure she could get it finished in time. If it wasn't turned in that day, she'd explained, it wouldn't make the holiday schedule.

Had she dropped it off when she'd driven into town to pick up her grandmother's emergency resupply of medications? He tried to remember but couldn't recall her having anything with her except her handbag.

A few minutes before Michael had come back from the lake, Webster Hood had stopped off to announce he was taking the steer into town for the food bank. Maybe Clare had asked him to drop the artwork off. A little strange, though, that he'd never mentioned it.

Suddenly, this poster seemed very important, and there was only one way to find out. The food bank was just a few blocks away. He'd stop over there and inquire.

LARA STARED at her desk, at the appeal for a client who had been sentenced to five years in prison for possession of a controlled substance with intent to sell. She shoved the papers aside. The appeal could wait. Michael couldn't. She picked up the phone.

"I heard," Gretchen told her after saying hello.

"This is really terrible. My contacts tell me it was Michael's gun and that Hood was shot in the back of the head, execution-style."

"You have well-placed sources," Lara replied. She hadn't heard that last bit. She hadn't asked Malvery anything about the gunshot, whether it was at close range or if there had been any signs of a struggle. She needed to get her act together. Stop daydreaming about Michael as a man and start concentrating on him as a client.

"I need to see you. We have to put our heads together, figure out what the hell's going on." Lara was getting shrill. She softened her voice. "And work out a strategy. Can you come over here, to the office, now?"

There was a slight pause. "How about I drop by your house at six? That'll give me time to check out a few things."

Lara had hoped to get this meeting out of the way, go home and crash, maybe seek inspiration with a glass of wine and a hot soaking bath.

"Okay," she said dully. "I'll see you then."

THE FOOD BANK WAS a large tin warehouse, the metal shelves lining its walls crowded with packaged goods, crackers, cake mixes and paper products. The open center was taken up with pallets of canned fruits, vegetables and potted meats, as well as sacks of flour, beans and rice. A small no-frills office had been constructed of unpainted plywood in the corner to the left of the sliding metal doors.

Michael had known Lois Jansen since high school. She'd run the concession stand at the ballpark in those days and had worked for the food bank the past five years.

"Hello, Michael." Her greeting was friendly, but he got the impression she was uncomfortable. As connected as she was in the town's grapevine, she'd probably heard the news of his most recent interview with the authorities.

"I was visiting Clare's grandmother and saw the poster on the wall for the holiday food drive."

"A real classic, isn't it? Your wife did such lovely work."

"I was wondering when she brought it in. I remember her racing to meet the deadline."

Lois shook her head. "Oh, Clare didn't bring it in personally. She called, said she'd finished it but didn't have time to deliver it. Something about having an appointment."

Their date on Tarnished Mountain. Maybe Elva dropped it off on her way to San Antonio. He asked.

"No, Clare said Elva was leaving for a shopping spree in San Antonio. She wondered if we had anybody here who could come out to your place and pick it up."

"Did you?"

"As a matter of fact, that friend of yours had just stopped in. She offered to go out, so I sent her."

"THANKS FOR COMING." Lara closed the door. "We'll have to work really fast. The D.A. has enough to arrest Michael if he wants to. The fact that he hasn't means he must have reservations. I need something to convince him whoever killed Hood also killed Clare and Brad."

"So you think Brad was murdered, too." Gretchen

rested her hip on the arm of an overstuffed easy chair. "I wondered if you would. Where do you want to start?"

Lara had been wrestling with that very dilemma. The deck was really stacked against Michael. His gun. His house. And he admitted being there at the time of the murder.

"See what else you can get out of your sources, any scrap of information that might exonerate Michael. Check alibis. We need to know where everybody was between midnight and six-thirty a.m. the night before last."

"You're not asking for much." Gretchen snorted. "They'll all say they were home sleeping. Anyone in particular you have in mind?"

Lara was too wired to sit. "I wish I did." She dragged shaky fingers through her hair. "Start with the people who are least likely to have alibis, I guess."

"The guys who are sleeping alone, you mean."

Lara almost laughed. "Yeah, I suppose I do."

"What are we aiming for as far as motive?"

"Hood posed a threat to someone." She sat on the edge of the couch, her shoulders stiff. "Or somebody hated him enough to kill him. Who might that be?"

Gretchen bowed her head in thought. "Most of the hands and all the vaqueros detested him. I think the bigger question is who hates Michael enough to frame him by using his .44?"

Lara sighed. "Who could possibly hate him that much?"

Gretchen shook her head and shrugged. "The guy's a straight arrow."

Lara's composure was beginning to fray. "Did you

say .44? I thought…'' She was sure Malvery had said Hood was shot with a .38. Maybe he misspoke or had been misinformed. No, the police wouldn't make a mistake like that.

"What?"

"Nothing. I must have misunderstood."

Gretchen cocked her head and narrowed her eyes. "What did you misunderstand?"

"It's not important."

"Maybe it is." Gretchen's voice hardened. "What are you holding back?"

Lara realized her hands were shaking, and the pieces were beginning to fall into place. "How do you know Hood was shot execution-style with a .44?"

Gretchen snickered, but warily. "I told you, I have well-placed sources in the department."

"Excuse me a minute." Lara started toward her bedroom. She'd call the sheriff rather than the D.A. Kraus would give her straight answers.

"Where are you going?" Gretchen asked.

"Too much coffee. I've been living on it for days." She walked toward her bedroom. She wanted to close the door but was afraid it would draw attention. Fortunately, the telephone was on the bedside table out of view from the hallway. She picked up the instrument.

"You don't have to call anybody," Gretchen said from the doorway.

Lara spun around. The private detective had a gun pointing at her.

"WAS GRETCHEN by herself when she brought it in?" Michael asked Lois. He was practically bouncing from one foot to the other. It didn't make sense, yet it did. Gretchen and Brad. Lovers. Until Selma took him back. What about Hood?

"Yep. Went out to your ranch and came right back. Webster Hood was leaving when she came in the door carrying the poster—"

"Webster Hood was here?" Michael felt as if he'd been sucker-punched.

Lois nodded. "Stopped by to tell me the packing plant would be calling—"

Michael was already out the door. He jumped into his truck, his thumb tapping out a number on his cell phone. No response. He dialed another number but got the answering service.

"If this is important, I can page Ms. Stovall, sir," the slightly bored voice on the other end said.

"This is an emergency," he nearly shouted into the tiny instrument.

"I'll see if I can locate her," the woman replied with the urgency of a turtle crossing a road. "What number can she reach you at?"

He gave her his cell phone number and clicked off. He'd stop by her office. Maybe she was still there and just not picking up.

"LET'S GO BACK to the living room." Gretchen moved to the side of the door and waved the gun. "You first. And please don't try anything. I have very good reflexes and several trophies for marksmanship."

Lara moved on rubbery legs. She didn't doubt the athletic blonde's claims. At the end of the hall, she turned right into the main living area. The phone rang again. Instinctively, she started toward it.

"Hold it right there," Gretchen ordered. "Turn around."

Lara complied. The phone rang two more times, then stopped. Gretchen sidestepped to the couch and, with the sweep of her arm, knocked the lamp off the end table.

Eyes wide, Lara cried out, "What are you doing?"

"You're about to be the victim of a burglary gone bad," Gretchen explained. "Women burglars tend to take what they need and leave. It's the men who like to break things. This'll be a little misdirection."

Lara nearly blurted, "You're crazy," but managed to swallow the words. No sense provoking a woman who'd already murdered three people. "I don't understand," she said, almost as curious as she was terrified. Aware of a strong criminal desire to confess, not in apology but to brag, she said, "Explain it to me."

Gretchen knocked over the other lamp. The bulb imploded with a pop. She backed into the dining area, grabbed the runner from the middle of the table and whipped it away, sending Grandmother's two-hundred-year-old Imari plate to the floor. Lara cringed and held her breath as it bounced once on the carpet, then shattered on the marble tile. A small moan escaped her lips. The only thing of any value she had from her family was gone. Strangely, she felt a jab of relief.

Using the cloth runner, Gretchen braced her hand on the back of the china cabinet and with a mighty shove brought it crashing forward. Lara jumped back as shards of glass and Waterford crystal scattered across the living room rug.

"Hey, this is fun," Gretchen told her, but she still had the gun pointed steadily at Lara.

MICHAEL SWERVED around the corner onto Lara's street, his truck tires squealing on the pavement. Ahead on the right, stood the pseudo-English Tudor house. A car he didn't recognize was parked in front of it. Pulling up behind it, he noted the rental agency decal on the bumper. Gretchen used rental vehicles.

He was running up the sculpted concrete path when he heard the unmistakable sound of glass breaking. He reached the entryway in seconds, twisted the un-yielding doorknob, rang the bell and pounded on the door.

"Lara," he shouted, "let me in."

The door sprang open.

"Run," Lara yelled from inside.

"I'll kill her if you do." Gretchen's voice came from behind the door, deadly calm and menacing. "Come in if you want to see her alive."

He was too late. Dread weighed on him like a sod-den cloak. With no other choice, he crossed the threshold. Twinkling glass lay everywhere. Uphol-stery was ripped open, its stuffing tossed about. A tornado might have gone through the place. Lara stood on the far side of the living room, facing him.

"What the hell's going on here?" he demanded, and hoped he came across as more in control than he felt.

The door behind him closed. He spun around.

"Join your girlfriend, lover boy." Gretchen waved the pistol at him.

"Are you all right?" He stepped over ruined furniture and broken pottery toward Lara. The carpet crunched under his boots.

She nodded. "So far." Her voice was low, angry as well as frightened.

He reached for her, but Gretchen objected. "Not that close."

She had a gun. He wasn't superhuman. He froze six feet from Lara.

"I figured it out too late," she said. "I'm sorry."

Michael surveyed the area for a weapon, a diversion. Found none. "Let me see if I have this right. You sabotaged the car when you picked up the artwork. You were trying to kill me so Brad would get my job."

"I had him wrapped around my little finger, but I wasn't about to be some cowhand's wife." She gave a little chuckle. "I'd made a play for Hood, but he wasn't interested in marriage, and I wasn't interested in being another one of his playthings. No security there."

Michael started to bend down to pick up a brass candlestick.

"Don't touch that."

"Sorry." He straightened. "Force of habit. The kids are always leaving things lying around."

She was smug and proud. "My plan still would have worked after that cattle disease mess—" her tone hardened "—if that peabrained wife of his hadn't decided she wanted him back. I considered getting rid of her, but then Brad would have been stuck with his bratty kids." She chuckled. "I'm not the mothering type."

"Why did you have to kill him?" he asked, relieved that Brad hadn't committed suicide after all.

"Just because he couldn't do trigonometry didn't mean he couldn't add two and two."

Michael stroked his chin contemplatively. He felt like an actor in a play. "He found out you delivered Clare's artwork to the food bank that day—"

"Like I said, he wasn't so dull he couldn't figure things out. He just didn't do it real quick." She laughed. "But then, neither did you."

"Did Clare tell you we were meeting on Tarnished Mountain?" Michael had to keep her talking. Unfortunately, the path to her wasn't clear. He couldn't lunge at her.

"She was real excited about it, too. Said it was a special place." Gretchen smirked at Lara. "After four kids and fifteen years of marriage, she still had the hots for him. Quite a man." She grinned at him. "Then the old lady rang her bell, and Clare ran inside. It hardly took a minute to cut the brake line. I told you my daddy used to have an MG like it. How was I supposed to know you were going to trade cars?"

"Why did you kill Hood?" Lara asked.

Michael listened for sounds outside. The neighborhood was as quiet as a church between services.

"Because he saw her at the food bank that day," Michael supplied. "He knew she'd been to the ranch house after him."

"Why didn't he mention it at the trial?" Lara demanded.

Gretchen giggled. "Nobody asked him."

Lara blanched, her freckles popping out in high relief.

"He agreed to keep his mouth shut and Brad could keep his new job, if I'd join him in a few, shall we say, intimate acts. It was fun for a while after Brad ditched me for his old lady, but when he suggested I take another try at you and do it right, I knew it was only a matter of time before he turned on me.'' She suddenly became bored with their delaying tactics. ''We've talked enough.'' She waved the gun, motioning them toward the hall. ''I was planning to shoot you here, but it might be more interesting if they find you together in the bedroom.''

Lara's heart was pounding. She tripped, sending a silver tray clattering. ''Right,'' she whispered in the din, and hoped he heard her.

''Careful,'' Gretchen cooed. ''Wouldn't want you to get hurt.''

As they entered the narrow passageway, Michael clasped Lara's hand. It felt warm, rough, steady. Her whole being seemed to be swallowed up in his fingers. The master suite was at the end of the hall; doors to smaller bedrooms stood open on both sides. As they approached them, Michael twitched his thumb.

''Now!'' He bolted to the right. Lara flew in the opposite direction, leaped over the bed. Gunshots rang out. She dropped instantly to the floor on the far side.

Had Gretchen shot Michael? Lara's chest ached. She forced herself to breathe. *Make a decision. Quick.*

She grabbed the bedside lamp and threw it at the door. It crashed as another shot rang out, splintering the white enamel-painted door frame.

Was Michael all right? She hadn't heard a body fall, couldn't hear any gasping. Was he already dead?

Sweat pooled between her breasts, under her arms, in her shoes. She had to find out. Would the mattress slow a bullet?

A shadow crossed the doorsill. Gretchen or Michael?

Suddenly, there was a clattering, grunts, curses.

Another shot.

"Let me go," Gretchen screamed.

"Stop fighting," Michael growled. "You'll only hurt yourself more."

Lara jumped up. Just outside the doorway, he had Gretchen's arms pinned to her waist from behind. She was kicking, even as blood spewed from her right ankle.

The gun lay on the floor. Lara kicked it under the bed.

"She shot herself in the foot." He grunted as he fought to restrain the flailing killer. "Must have hit an artery."

Bright-red blood splattered everywhere, on the floor, walls, ceiling.

Lara flung open a closet door, grabbed a belt hanging there.

Adrenaline-crazed, Gretchen was still kicking wildly.

Michael picked her up and slammed her face-down on the bed.

Gretchen huffed, breathless, then let out a screech of agony when Lara quickly made a tourniquet of the belt, twisted tight above the bloody wound. The hemorrhage subsided.

"Call 911." Michael was holding Gretchen's arms at her side, though her fight had literally lost its kick.

Lara was still on the phone in her bedroom when two policemen broke down the front door and barged in, guns drawn and held firmly with both hands.

Michael glanced up. "Her pulse is strong, but she needs medical help fast."

"They're on their way," one of them replied, holstering his weapon.

"How did you get here fast?" Lara asked, shaking, trying to assure herself Michael was safe.

"A neighbor reported a domestic disturbance and shots being fired," the other officer explained.

Lara shook her head. "Domestic disturbance. I like that." She was starting to laugh, when Michael climbed to his feet and gathered her in his arms.

"YOU SET US UP," Michael complained to Rudy Kraus. He and Lara were sitting in the sheriff's office, drinking really bad coffee. They'd answered questions and given their statements.

"That wasn't the intent," Kraus replied. "Malvery was convinced you'd killed Hood. I knew damn well you couldn't have, any more than you could have killed Clare or Lopez. I suggested he use a little misinformation to get a reaction. He told you Hood had been shot with your .38. When you didn't blink an eyelash, Malvery said you were either an Academy Award-caliber actor or you honestly didn't know which gun had been used."

"That's why he didn't have me arrested."

Kraus nodded. "He was afraid he'd come off in the press as vindictive."

Lara grinned, remembering her conversation with him on that very subject. "What about the execution-style killing?"

"It was true, but it was another detail we purposely didn't release. The only way she could have known about it is if she was in some way involved. Another nail in her coffin.''

''Couldn't she have gotten the info from her contact on the force?'' Michael asked.

''Her contact was Wesley Janick. He divulged only what I let him. He never told her about the gun or the style of killing. Gretchen was counting on you not knowing who her source was, so she could get away with saying anything and attributing it to him.''

''I thought of something else—too late,'' Michael admitted. ''By the time Chase Norman came to me with the info about Hood trying to talk Brad into *getting rid* of me, Brad and Gretchen had broken up, but they were still together when Hood made his veiled offer. She would have known—''

''Everything happened so fast after that I didn't get around to asking her about it, either,'' Lara confessed. ''Brad admitted it on the stand, so there seemed no point. Except I should have questioned why she hadn't told us about it in the first place.''

''Maybe two people would be alive if we'd been more on our toes,'' Michael acknowledged, his hand reaching out for hers. She gave it to him easily, greedily.

''Don't count on it,'' Kraus advised him. ''Gretchen Tanner is a killer. If you had challenged her, she probably would have killed you, as well.''

It was two o'clock in the morning when they finally stepped outside. No reporters, but Adam was waiting patiently. He drove them out to the Home Place. After a shot of brandy and warm showers, they slept in separate beds.

At eleven o'clock the following morning, they appeared in the office of the district attorney for Spring County.

"What now?" Michael asked conversationally. Four hours sleep hadn't been enough, yet he felt better than he had in months. He'd driven Lara to her house, where she'd changed clothes and packed others. She wouldn't be living there anymore.

"You're a free man," Malvery assured him.

Michael wondered if he was supposed to thank him for giving him his liberty after ten months of persecution.

"I'm real sorry you had to go through all this, Mr. First. I can only tell you that when I brought charges against you for your wife's murder, I sincerely believed you were guilty."

"Well, that's a consolation."

Lara shot him a warning glance, though her eyes were twinkling. If she started laughing, he'd have to hold her in his arms again.

"All the evidence was against you, you know," he told Michael. "Means, motive and opportunity. An absolutely open-and-shut case. But—" he grinned mischievously "—it was too obvious. A setup. I hope you don't mind me saying this, Mr. First, but even you aren't that clever, because you see, on the circumstantial evidence alone, I can still get you indicted and convicted."

An icy sword of panic rammed its way into Michael's belly. Cold enough to take his breath away. "On the other hand," he replied mildly, "you seem to have a problem with underestimating the intelligence of juries."

The smirk on Malvery's face faded. "Just be grateful Gretchen Tanner has confessed, not only to your wife's murder but to Brad Lopez's as well as Webster Hood's. And pray she doesn't recant. Or that a slick defense lawyer doesn't get her off.''

The self-satisfied grin again in place, Burk Malvery rose from his chair and extended his hand. ''I hope there are no hard feelings, Mr. First. I wish nothing but good fortune for you and your family in the years ahead.''

Michael accepted the hand. ''Thank you.''

''Don't feel bad,'' Lara said, as he drove away from the D.A.'s office. ''I think you're very clever.''

''I'm glad to hear that.'' He wasn't planning on separate beds tonight.

''Where are we going?''

He slid a glance over at her. ''A very good question.''

''You're in the driver's seat,'' she reminded him.

''Am I?'' He turned onto North Travis. ''They installed a spa in the new penthouse suite of the Coyote Hotel. I made reservations so we can check it out.''

''Presumptuous,'' she murmured, then smiled. ''And clever.''

''Yeah, well, I was wondering if you might let me show you just how clever I can be.''

''As I said,'' she replied with a laugh, ''you're in the driver's seat.''

EPILOGUE

THICK OAK LOGS FLAMED brightly in the massive stone fireplace. The room was snug and warm, in spite of the north wind slashing the Home Place. The mouthwatering smells of mulled wine and hot cider blended with the pine scent of the Christmas tree and the rich aroma of baking mince and apple pies.

"Have I told you how beautiful you are?"

Joy bubbling inside her, she lifted her hand and brushed Michael's cheek, then dragged her fingers against the subtle grit of shaven whiskers. Enough to give her beard burn, she mused, if she wasn't careful. "You may have mentioned it once or twice."

"I wouldn't want to leave you in doubt," he murmured close to her ear.

No chance of that. She raised herself on tiptoe and kissed him lightly on the cheek.

Smiling, they wandered over to the buffet, where Sheila was refilling the grog bowl. Carols played quietly on the sound system, melding with the happy noise of children playing.

"Home was never like this," Lara told Sheila. Michael squeezed her hand. "Thank you so much for inviting me."

"We wouldn't be here today in this festive mood if it wasn't for you." Adam poured her a cup of the hot spiced wine.

Lara accepted it. "You're exaggerating."

"I don't think so," Sheila said. "You're a part of this family now."

ALL DAY LONG vaquero families and friends from town had been stopping by the Home Place to share holiday cheer and congratulate Adam First and the rest of the family on regaining title and control of the Number One Ranch. The big celebration would be in the spring, on Adam's birthday, which, until the bank took over the ranch, had been observed as a kind of founder's day.

"The bank caved in awfully fast, didn't it?" Judge Ronnie Mayhew mused. He was sitting on the couch with his wife, across from their hosts.

Kerry, dressed in Christmas red, sat next to her father, holding his hand. She laughed. "They didn't have much choice, what with being hit with lawsuits from individuals and the state over the brucellosis debacle. They were facing major damage claims."

Sheila, on Adam's other side, smiled. "When Michael was granted his request for homestead, it clouded the bank's clear title to the land, especially after he talked the vaqueros into filing their own claims, as well."

"There was also the little matter of nobody to run the outfit," Adam contributed. "They'd fired Michael. His replacement had apparently committed suicide. And the general manager had been murdered." He snorted. "Tough to get applicants for the jobs under those conditions."

Mayhew chuckled. "I'm sure having a standing offer to buy the place from your son-in-law didn't influence the bank's decision to sell in the least."

Craig Robeson, standing behind Kerry, squeezed her shoulders. She gazed up at him, her eyes warm with affection, and patted his hand. "He's a life-saver," she said with a wide grin.

"WHAT'S THE LATEST on Gretchen?" Michael asked Rudy Kraus. They were over by the picture window, watching a storm move in.

"Sang like a bird." The sheriff tipped his beer bottle.

"Why?" Lara had her fingers securely entwined with Michael's. "Why didn't she just keep her mouth shut?"

Kraus shook his head and shrugged. "I don't reckon I'll ever understand the criminal mind. She told us details that have even the D.A. convinced she's the real killer."

"Any chance she'll recant?" Michael prompted. Malvery's comment that he could still get him convicted of Hood's murder on the circumstantial evidence alone might have kept him up at night if Lara hadn't been doing a better job of it. She'd rented a small town house *temporarily*, but she hadn't mentioned anything more about leaving town, and Michael hadn't asked, afraid of what she might say.

"Nope. The D.A. made absolutely sure we did everything exactly by the book. Her confessions are rock solid. She won't be able to slip out of them." Kraus gave Michael a broad grin. "Relax, son. No way Malvery will be coming after you again."

Ronnie Mayhew moved up to join them, a glass of red wine in hand. "Besides, Malvery's moving on."

Lara's brows rose. "Already?"

"Took a job with the attorney general's office in

Austin,'' the judge informed them. ''I expect we'll be seeing his name on a ballot in a few years.''

Michael snorted. ''He'll have to excuse me if I don't vote for him.''

Kraus laughed. ''I don't reckon he's counting on many votes in Coyote Springs.''

MICHAEL AND LARA STOOD on the hill above the Home Place. The wind rippled the dry grass of the prairie before them. The air was heavy; the sky, ominous.

He had his arm cradled around her slender waist. ''Not a very pretty place this time of year.''

She snuggled up to him, comfortable in the shelter of his embrace. ''Places aren't important. It's the people who inhabit them.''

She gazed up at this shadowed face, at the tension around his eyes. ''Do you want me to?''

''Yes,'' he said, without hesitation. There was a ferociousness in his reply that made her smile.

She tightened her hold on him. ''Then I guess I will.''

''I love you,'' he whispered, his lips close to her ear.

''Oh, Michael,'' she murmured against his chest. ''I love you, too.''

''Being with you brings me a peace I never thought I could have again.'' He kissed her softly on the temple.

''Clare was a part of me,'' he acknowledged a minute later, not in apology but explanation.

''And she always will be. I understand that, Michael. She was a good person. I wish I'd gotten to know her.''

"Have you forgiven me for being so self-absorbed and blind?"

She snuggled closer. "More important, I've forgiven myself. I was weak when I should have been strong. I let you go when I should have fought for you."

"You're a fighter now," he assured her, his affection resonating inside her. He stroked her back as the wind swirled around them and the first drops of rain pelted the ground. This would be the third major storm in the past week. The creeks, rivers and lakes were filling fast. The danger now was flooding. The drought had played itself out. The green years were coming.

"Lara, will you—"

She raised a finger to his lips to silence him. "Don't ask me, Michael. Not yet." He looked suddenly sad. "Oh, I want to hear the words, more than you can ever imagine. I guess I've been dreaming of hearing them since the day I met you." She tightened her grip around his waist. "But it's too soon yet. We're friends. That's enough for now. You and your children still have grieving to do before you heal. I can wait."

He lowered his mouth and caught hers. The kiss was long and ardent. "You won't have to wait long."

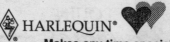

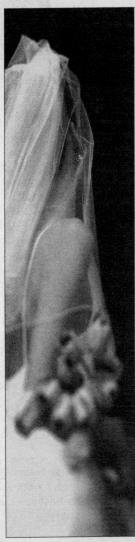